FALLING

BACK

TOGETHER

by

s u s a n   c a i r n s

Visit my website at: www.susancairnsbooks.com

DEDICATION

For Shannon, Michelle, Candi, Natalie, and Caroline.

The five points to my star!

Thank you for always being there when I need you,

for always reassuring me that I'm not alone.

TABLE OF CONTENT

CHAPTER 1

Sara

"Sara? Dr. Rosen will see you now," Jill yells and waves at me through the glass window separating the office from the waiting room.

I don't respond. I never do. She's a judgey, stuck-up, perfect, blond bitch.

With my earbuds in and the music playing very quietly, I get up off the god awful plastic chair, sling my backpack over my shoulder, and walk straight to Jacqui's office. As usual, she's got her back to me as she tries to find my file in the long filing cabinet behind her desk. I would think she'd have that thing on the top by now—it's not as if I don't come here three times a week.

I walk past her butt swinging in the air, pull her payment out of my book bag, a bottle of Moscato, then go lie down on the leather sofa. That's what I see people doing in the movies when they go to their shrink, so why wouldn't I do it? The more I pretend this isn't my life, maybe the better off I'll be.

"Sara? You think you could take the headphones off?" Jacqui stands and steps away from the filing cabinet.

"I was getting there. It's not like I can't hear you. And why don't you have my file in your priority pile yet? I doubt you have other patients who come here more than once a week."

"Actually I do, and your file is with my repeat offenders."

"'Repeat offender?' Are you trying to make a funny?" I cock my head and give her the most overly exaggerated smile I can muster.

"I know, I know. It wasn't funny, and I should stick to my day job. You don't have to remind me."

"Well, it seems you're starting to really know me."

"That's my job. So let's get down to business, shall we?" She takes a seat in the leather wingback chair directly across from the couch.

"I guess we should, considering that's what I'm here for. So what do you want to talk about?" I pull the buds out of my ears, wrap the cord around my phone, then drop it onto my chest. I roll my head against the arm rest so I'm looking at Jacqui.

"I believe that's my question." She gives me a pointed look with both eyebrows raised.

"Maybe it is, but I feel like I'm always the one who decides what we talk about, and that's not really fair to you." I clench my teeth together so I don't laugh at her annoyed expression.

"Okay, smart mouth. Why don't you tell me what happened today that's making you so evasive?"

"Do I have to?" I whine and look back at the ceiling.

"Sara, we go through this three times a week. By now you should know my answer to that question."

Hmm, should I continue to be a smartass? Jacqui's staring at me, almost as if she's trying to steal the answer directly from my brain. Yep, smartass it is!

"Quite honestly, I'm still having some major issues with the chairs in the waiting room. Maybe if you didn't keep me sitting out there so long, I'd be more

10

open when I come through the door." I tip my head toward the closed door behind her.

"Sara," she warns. "I'm here to listen to you. You can tell me anything, not only as your therapist but also as your friend."

"But see, that's the thing, Jacqui. You're not really my friend. I don't have friends, and I kind of want to keep it that way." I'm totally lying. Jacqui is seriously one of my only friends.

"I can respect that. Why don't I start then?" She gives me a once-over. "Why aren't you wearing your work uniform? Don't you have to go in after our session?"

"I'm off today, but even if I did have to work I'd call off, because I have to pack."

"Okay, why do you have to pack? Are you planning on moving? Going on a trip?"

"No, I wasn't planning on moving, but Elaine is moving to some sort of retirement community in Arizona, I think."

"And she's selling the house, so you have find another place? Or are you doing the neighborly thing and helping her pack for her move?"

"No. She's not selling, but her grandson is moving into her apartment and doing some sort of rent-to-own bullshit, so I have to move. I guess he just got a teaching job here or something." I rub my eyes, hard, with the heels of my hands.

"And he wants to rent the upper apartment to someone else?" She taps her stylus against the side of her iPad.

"No. Elaine said her stipulations included that I be able to stay in the apartment."

"I guess I'm not seeing the issue, Sara. Why are you moving?"

"Come on, Jacqui, he's a guy. Not only that, but he's in his twenties—he just finished grad school. I can't do it." I throw my hands out to the side and clench my fists.

"Hmm, okay. Well, we've talked about new and different ways for you to get over your fear. Not every man in their twenties is Trent. You talk to men in that age group on a daily basis at work, so why don't you think you can live above one?"

"Oh my god, do we need to go over this again? Trent, the rat bastard, was a nice guy the first time I met him too, and look what he took from me…" I sweep my hand out, motioning toward everything around me. "He took everything. Everything! So no, I'm not going to give him a chance. I don't have to trust this guy, who I don't even know, and let him get that close to me. Plus, work is different. I see those douches for, what, a half hour? Maybe longer depending on if they loiter after they finish eating."

"I think you should at least meet him before you decide for sure that you want to cause yourself the hassle of trying to find a new apartment, within your budget, that you actually like, without having a guy around your age living near you. You've lived there for five years now? You love that apartment. I think you need to give him a chance. Plus, depending on his hours, you may never have to see him. Teachers work during the day, and you work midnights. You might not even cross paths."

"Ugh, are you not going to let this go? Or, am I going to have to listen to this shit until I give in?"

"Probably, but that's why you come here—to help you get past the things that hold you back in life."

"Whatever. I'll talk to Elaine and see if I can meet him, but only if she's there. And when that doesn't change my mind, I'll start looking for a new place."

She smiles. "It's a start. So I know that you haven't been to a group session in quite some time, but I'm hoping that since you don't have to work tonight, you might be willing to go to one later, say about six thirty?"

"Why? This breakthrough making you think I need more therapy?" I stick my right arm out over the side of the couch as I look at her.

"No, I want you to go because I have a new client attending. She's fifteen, and since you were fifteen when you were attacked, I think if she hears your story, she might start to open up." Jacqui looked hopeful.

"God, you're so annoying."

"So you're going?"

"You know, since I don't have to work, I just might have big plans."

"Really? What do you have planned for later, other than packing, which you've decided not to do?"

"Well, it seems that I'm going to group tonight. Apparently I have to tell my damn horror story again just so it may help someone." I put my arm back over my eyes.

"Thank you, Sara. I know that you get tired of talking about it, but honestly, you may help someone else realize that they're not alone."

"Whatever. Are you done psychoanalyzing me for today?"

13

"Not quite. How's the rubber band therapy going?"

"Subtle." I roll my eyes and breathe out a deep sigh. "It's fine. I still haven't cut in over a year. My skin thanks you." I peek out from around my arm and smirk at her.

"Don't joke about this. I want to know if it's really helping you." Jacqui sets her iPad on the desk next to her and leans toward me.

"It's helping. When I get the urge, I snap one of the bands, and it seems to take the thought of cutting away. For a while, anyway."

"That's good. Are you still writing down how often these urges are happening?"

"Yes, Mom. I have my notebook, and it goes everywhere with me."

"Well, I can see how much you want to talk about this, so let's go back to Elaine and her grandson."

I blow out a harsh breath. "Can we not and say we did?"

"No. I really want you to give meeting him a try. Think of it as an experiment to see how strong you are, to show how far you've come in the past eight years."

"How about we let it go for now and talk about it next time?"

"I'm only agreeing because your time is up and we have to get over to group. Do you need a lift?"

"Nah, I have my rust bucket. And if I drive with you, I can't escape if shit gets too deep."

"Fine, I'll see you in a little while."

"Sounds like a plan. Later, Jacqui," I call over my shoulder as I walk through the door.

14

Thank god Jill isn't staring out the sliding window as I escape. Damn Jacqui. Despite what she thinks, I usually veg after our sessions and think about what we talked about. Now I have to hall ass to the other side of town to tell some poor unsuspecting teenagers my shitty life story. There's one good thing about group though—no men. Well, unless they've changed it to a co-ed group, in which case I'll murder Jacqui.

As I'm standing in the hall and waiting for the elevator, a guy about my age walks out of an office a couple doors down on the right. Even through I've put my earbuds back in, he still smiles and says hi. I just turn away from the elevator doors and head to the stairs. I can't be stuck with a guy in a small windowless room that has no means of escape.

I wasn't always like this. After shit first hit the fan, I used sex as an escape, a way to get all of my pain out. Then I discovered cutting was a much easier way of making myself hurt physically. It didn't involve anyone else, and I didn't have to worry about some guy thinking we'd be together forever. Now Jacqui's trying to cure me of that, so I've moved on to rubber band therapy and tattoos. At least they give me the pain I need to get by.

"God, I'm so fucking broken, it's not even funny," I whisper to myself as I push open the fire door and head down the stairs. When it slams shut, I jump and turn to look behind me. "Thank god no one followed me."

And as usual, I'm talking to myself. If the fact that I just left a shrink's office, I'm wearing all black, and I

15

have a massive amount of body art doesn't scream that I'm a psycho, let's just add "talking to myself" to the mix.

Instead of going out through the lobby, I push through the door at the bottom of the stairs and head around the side of the building to the front, where my car is parked. Of course elevator guy is parked right next to me and gives me a weird look when he sees me heading toward his car. He slips behind the wheel, not waiting to see what I'm going to do. As I pass him, he gives me a look and shakes his head. I pretend not to notice and walk to my driver's side door.

My car—which I like to call hunk of shit or beast—needs to be coaxed to start. I have to turn the engine over three times before it does anything. Even then, it pretty much grumbles to life. I leave my earbuds in because the radio doesn't work. Thank god it's not cold anymore, since my car's heat is almost nonexistent.

The church where group is held is about fifteen minutes away, and considering it's rush hour, it'll probably take me twenty-five minutes to get there, so I have no time to make a stop for food. I hope they still serve coffee and snacks at these things, but who knows. With budget cuts and whatnot, they probably have to beg, borrow, and steal to even get a room.

After a couple turns and a few miles, I pull into the church parking lot. I find a spot toward the back, since there are a bunch of cars in the lot and turning off the rust bucket is about as smooth as turning it on.

I stare at my reflection in the rearview mirror and take a couple deep breaths before I push my door open.

"Whelp, here we go again."

CHAPTER 2

Sara

Since I last came to group, the host church has doubled in size. That surprises me, because I didn't think many people went to church anymore. I don't know where the hell to go, so I follow a mother and daughter—I think—through the double doors and into the foyer. There are no signs directing people where to go for group, probably to protect the identity of the members, so I'm stuck. I don't want to assume someone's going to the same place as me, because I never want to learn that someone has gone through the same thing. Luckily I see Jacqui walking up to the door and puffing on a cigarette, which I fully intend to give her shit about.

"You know that shit will kill you and make you smell horrible!" I say as she passes through the door.

She almost jumps out of her skin. "For heaven's sake, Sara, you scared me! And I'm very aware that smoking could eventually kill me, but I'm sure one of my clients will cause my death first."

I slap my hands against my cheeks in a perfect *Home Alone* face. "Wow! Is that sarcasm I hear?" She keeps walking, so I follow.

"What can I say? I learned from the best."

"I'm a little shocked you would talk to me like that. Aren't you afraid that you'll damage me further?"

"You have a thick skin, and we're not on the clock right now, so I can talk to you like any other person." She bounces down a flight of stairs.

"Hmm, I guess in all the years I've known you, I've never thought of you as a person." I shrug and walk behind Jacqui to a circle of chairs.

"That's nice to know." She looks back at me. "You know, you don't have to sit by me."

"Wow, now I'm wounded. Here I thought we were making a breakthrough." I sigh with my hand over my heart. "Anyway, I wanted to know where your girl was sitting so that I can face her. I want to make sure she's paying attention to what I'm saying."

"You don't need to do that, but she's over there in the red-and-black top, next to her mother." Jacqui points at the young girl and her mother whom I'd followed in.

"Fantastic, then I'll sit over there." I point at the seat five down from Jacqui, directly across from the girl. "Check ya later."

"Okay, everyone, if we can all find a seat, we'll get started," some chick next to Jacqui calls just as my ass hits the cold metal of the folding chair. "My name's Sam. I'm a social worker who works with sexual assault victims. I know I've met a few of you, but I'm not familiar with everyone, so as an ice breaker, let's just go around the room and introduce ourselves. First name and age will be fine."

As the names and ages start flying, I get lost. Most of the girls were that—girls. Sadly, I'm one of the oldest ones. It wasn't like that when I used to come. I used to think I was alone before I started coming to group, and even then, there were only a couple girls around my age. The number has multiplied.

"Earth to Sara!" Jacqui's voice pulls me out of my head.

Giving a small wave to the circle, I say, "Yeah, sorry. Hi, I'm Sara, twenty-three."

As soon as the chick next to me opens her mouth, I retreat back into my mind, trying to figure out when Jacqui expects me to speak. Does she want me to tell my whole horrid tale or just the highlights? We didn't discuss logistics before I left the office. I guess I'll find out soon, since the introductions have made it back to Sam.

"So since we have a couple new faces here tonight," Jacqui takes over. "I'm going to ask you to share—only if you're comfortable, ladies. Remember, everyone in this room has been affected by sexual assault, so you shouldn't be afraid to talk. Sara, since I know you've been to group in the past, why don't you start?"

I look at Jacqui as my eyes bug out of my head, and she gives me a look that says, "Just go with it, will you?"

I suck in a deep breath. "Sure, Jacqui, I'll get right on that."

"Thank you," she replies with a hint of annoyance.

"So like I said, I'm Sara, and as Jacqui told you, I've been to group before, but it's been a long time. I'm not shy about telling my story anymore—well, not here—but I warn you, it's a horror story." I suck in a deep breath before I start.

"Eight years ago, my parents got me a plane ticket to Florida for my fifteenth birthday. The plan was for me to spend a few weeks visiting my aunt and her boyfriend while I was on my summer break from training—I used to be a swimmer, and I was good. Celia, my aunt, is a trauma nurse in Miami and had just moved into a new condo a couple blocks from the beach, so I was looking forward to spending time with her soaking up some sun.

"As soon as my plane landed, I took off to go find Aunt Celia and Trent. They were such dorks, holding up a sign covered in glitter, my name written in bubble letters across the middle. After we grabbed my bags, they took me out to lunch, then showed me a little bit of what was around their condo.

"Celia had to work from two pm to midnight Sunday through Wednesday, so we didn't have much time to spend together before she had to go to work, but Trent planned to take me out before we grabbed some dinner. So while my aunt got ready for work, I unpacked and changed. When she left, so did we, heading right for the beach.

"The rest of the days Aunt Celia had to work, she and I spent time together in the mornings, then I'd be on my own until Trent got home. The first four days I was there, I spent a lot of time by the pool, reading or tanning. From Thursday to Saturday, my aunt joined me. I remember one afternoon it was raining, so we decided to hit the movies and see a chick flick. It was the best vacation, even though Aunt Celia had to work, but that didn't bother me. Trent was cool and kind of fun to hang out with too."

I stop talking for a minute and breathe deeply several times. I'm not looking at the faces in the circle because I don't want to see their expectant looks. They know what's coming. This is about when the story takes a turn for shitsville.

"The second Sunday I was there, my aunt went to work early—which she planned to do the whole week so she could take the following week off for my last few days there. After we finished brunch, she got ready and left at about noon.

"Trent and I spent the day at the beach, then we walked around the shopping center near their complex. We headed back to the condo around dinnertime and picked up something to eat on the way. After we ate, the two of us hung out in the living room, watching TV until I got tired. Sometime around nine, I told Trent I was going to bed.

"About an hour later, just after I started to fall asleep, I heard the door to my room creak open. A few seconds passed before I felt the bed dip as Trent sat down. Thinking that something was wrong, I popped up in bed and faced him.

"'What's going on? What's wrong?' I asked, semi-panicked.

"'Nothing, just relax.' He pushed me back so I was lying down again. 'I just came in here to see you. That's okay, isn't it?'

"I was slightly creeped out but didn't think anything of it. "'Sure, I guess.'

"'Good.'

"His voice sounded weird. I can't really describe it, but it wasn't how he normally sounded. Then he leaned forward and kissed me.

"'I pushed him back. "What the hell are you doing?'

"'Isn't it obvious? I'm kissing you.'

"'Uh, yeah, I got that, but why did you kiss me? Not only are you dating my aunt, but you're, like, ten years older than me.'

"Actually I'm twelve years older than you, and because of that, I know you want this. I've seen it in your face all week.' He ran his hand down the side of my face, and I flinched.

"'What the hell are you talking about? I don't want anything from you. You're my aunt's boyfriend. I thought you were my friend.'

"'Please, Sara, I know you want this, so just let it happen.'

"Trent pushed me back again, only this time he placed his body over mine, trapping me beneath him. He kissed me again, so I pushed against him. I gave him a hard shove in the neck, which made him choke and lift off me. I thought he was giving up, maybe going to leave, but his fist slammed into my right eye. Pain shot through the right side of my head, and within seconds, I could feel it swelling shut.

"'That didn't have to happen, Sara. If you would just stop moving, I'll make sure that this is good for both of us.'

"I gave up on pushing—he had trapped my hands above my head anyway. Instead I cried and screamed, thrashing my body and trying to buck him off of me.

"Trent leaned down close to my ear. 'Do you want me to hit you again?'

"I shook my head.

"'Then I suggest you stop your shit and keep your mouth closed.'

"I didn't know what to do. I don't even think anyone would have heard me if I'd kept screaming, but I didn't want to get hit again. So I lay there with my hands bound above my head and tears flowing down my cheeks.

"Using his free hand, Trent worked as best he could to remove my top. I kept crying, but I kept my eyes closed as tight as I could. I was trying to keep still so I didn't piss him off again. But when he pushed things further, my eyes popped open and I wiggled and fought again. I knew what was coming. I'd seen enough movies with shit like that. I was a virgin, and that wasn't the way I wanted to lose my innocence.

"The wiggling didn't help me; it only seemed to help him. There was nothing I could do about what was happening to me. I squeezed my eyes closed again and tried to imagine I was anywhere but there. I wished I was back home, that I was just having a nightmare. I tried begging one more time before he took everything from me.

"'Trent, please stop. I won't tell anyone,' I sputtered through my sobs and tears.

"'You're gonna like it so much, baby. Don't worry, I'll make sure it's good for you,' he said with an almost dreamy voice that made me sick to my stomach.

"Then it was like my mind took a hike. I couldn't even process what was happening anymore. The next thing I knew, he was stealing everything from me. As I screamed, he grunted and whispered how I should enjoy it. I felt like my insides were burning.

"Emotionally, I was spent. Screaming and crying hadn't helped, so I just lay there and waited for him to finish, which thankfully didn't take more than another minute. With one last grunt, he collapsed his full weight on top of me.

"'God, that was amazing. I'm sorry it didn't last that long. Next time it'll be better for you,' he promised.

"I cringed and silently begged God not to let there be a next time.

25

"After his breathing returned to normal, Trent pushed off me and let go of my arms. I slid back and cowered against the headboard. I saw the evidence of my innocence on the sheets, and when I chanced a look at Trent, he was working on cleaning himself.

"'Go take a shower and clean yourself up. I'll take care of your sheets.' He stopped and looked at me for minute. When I didn't move, he snapped, 'Now move! I have to change your sheets.'"

I have to take another deep breath and swipe at the tears I didn't realize were slipping down my cheeks. It seems as if I've been talking forever, but I know it's only been minutes—kind of like the real experience. Another deep breath, and I lose myself in the story again.

"I got up and moved, in what seemed like slow motion, to the bathroom across the hall. Standing on the bath mat—my shorts around my ankles and my shirt twisted haphazardly—I turned on the hot water and waited. Once the room was full of steam, I took off my shirt and stepped out of the shorts.

"Without adding a drop of cold to the water, I stepped under the spray. I can only imagine I was in shock. Everything around me seemed normal as I stood still and watched it. Once the feeling wore off, I picked up the soap and rubbed my chest, then between my legs. No matter how long or how hard I pressed, I didn't feel clean. I couldn't tell if my skin was red from scrubbing or from the hot water.

"The bathroom door opened, and Trent came in, freezing me in place. I couldn't see him through the curtain, but I think he might have sat on the toilet seat.

"'Listen, Sara, when Celia calls, I'm going to tell her you fell and bumped your head, your right eye taking the worst of it. You *will not* tell her what happened here tonight. If you do, it'll only get worse for you, mark my words.'

"I didn't answer—I couldn't. I just kept trying to wash away the dirty feeling. Long after Trent left the bathroom and the water turned cold, I finally got out of the shower. I wanted to tell my aunt everything that had happened, and I prayed she'd believe me over him. I didn't give a shit what he threatened. But my plan changed when I walked out of the bathroom and heard Trent on the phone. He told my aunt I had fallen and bumped my head. He said he was worried I may have a concussion, because I was talking crazy. He thought maybe he should have taken me to the hospital, but I absolutely refused.

"I went back into my bedroom and shut the door. Instead of falling back onto the mattress like my body craved, I grabbed a blanket from the foot of the bed and headed outside to sit on the small porch connected to my room. Every time I tried to close my eyes, I saw Trent above me, holding me down, as he forced himself on me. So the next morning, when my aunt shook me awake to make sure that my head was okay, I was surprised I had actually fallen asleep."

Before I look at the faces in the circle, I rub my own. I look directly across the circle at the girl Jacqui told me about. From the look on her face, she knows exactly what I went through, but I need her to know I didn't escape after only one night.

I take a huge deep breath and sigh. "That was the first of four nights he came into my room and raped me."

27

Jacqui calls my name, so I turn my head toward her.

"I want to you to share the rest of your story, but I can tell that took a lot out of you," she says. "Why don't we get something to drink and then come back, okay?"

"Yeah, sure," I half mumble, then get out of my chair and head to the coffee table.

"Okay, everyone, get a drink and take a few deep breaths, then we'll continue." She comes up behind me and places her hand on the middle of my back. "Hey, you okay?"

I shrug off her hand. "I'm fine. It just always seems to last forever when I talk about it, but I won't give them the rest of the nitty gritty. They don't need to know that…"

"Sara, I think they do. Some of these girls have been through what you went through on the first night, and some of them have been through what you went through on the remaining nights. I want you to tell them the whole story, right up until you told me that Elaine is moving."

"Geez, Jacqui, I didn't sign up to read my memoirs, and I don't think we have enough time for all that." I turn away to fill a Styrofoam cup with shitty coffee.

"What you just talked about only took a little over five minutes. It won't take that long for you to finish. Trust me, it'll be good for them to hear."

Sipping my coffee, I pretend to contemplate her suggestion. "Whateves. As long as they don't sell my story to some Hollywood rag, we're good." From over my shoulder, I see Jacqui shake her head at me as I walk back to my chair. I plop down with my legs splayed out in front of me.

Jacqui gets everyone's attention with an ear-piercing whistle. After everyone sits, she calls the meeting back to order. "Okay, we're going to listen to the rest of Sara's story, then if she's comfortable, she'll answer some questions."

"Gee thanks," I say. "I didn't realize this was going to turn into an inquisition."

"I said if you're comfortable, Sara, it's not required."

"Gotcha." So back to the horror story I call my life. I sit up a little straighter in my chair and play with my coffee mug as I talk again.

"The first night was only a preview of what was to come. I was stuck at home with Trent for three more nights. The next morning, I had breakfast with my aunt. She laughed when she talked about me falling and conking my head, but only after she had checked a million times to see if I was okay. I never once corrected it. I could see in her eyes that she wouldn't believe Trent had raped anyone, let alone me. She thought he was the perfect man. Still does.

"After we finished breakfast, I grabbed a giant sun hat, my darkest sunglasses, and a book, shoved it into a beach bag with a towel and sunscreen, and told my aunt I was going to spend the day at the beach. I walked as far away from the condo as I could without thinking I'd get lost. I found a spot in the middle of the beach, far enough from the sidewalk but not too close to the water. Just enough room to let me get away if Trent tried to come find me.

"But there was no relaxing. I was facing the sidewalk so I could see Trent coming. I stayed there, switching positions throughout the day as my back started to hurt. When the sun started to lower, I knew there was no way around going back to the condo. I just hoped Trent was out. I didn't care if he was looking for me or if he'd gone out with friends. Just as long as he wasn't there.

"When I got back, I opened the door a crack, stood stock still, and listened to hear if anyone was inside. When I didn't hear anything, I crept in and went right to my room. On my way past the kitchen, I saw someone had been home at some point—there were dished scattered across the counter and pans on the stove.

"Despite the growling of my stomach, I walked through the apartment as fast as I could. When I hit my room, I locked the door behind me. My bed was still unmade from the night before, which was odd for me. My parents always made sure that my brothers and I made our beds before we left the house, but I just couldn't do it. I needed to get out of the house as soon as possible.

"After throwing my bag on the bed, I changed my clothes. I had to go to the bathroom, but I was afraid to leave the room. So I cracked the door, just a little, and listened. When I only heard silence, I took a chance and crossed the hall. I peed as fast as my body let me, flushed, then pressed my ear against the crack in the door. Still nothing, so I ran back to my room, shut the door, and turned the lock.

"The chair I was in the night before was the only thing inviting, so I grabbed my book and headed outside. The thought of locking myself out on the veranda crossed my mind, but I want to make sure I heard when Trent got home.

"The sound of a fist or boot crashing against my bedroom door woke me from a sound sleep. When it happened again, I moved into the room to see if I could hear what was going on.

"'Sara,' Trent said calmly, just a little louder than a whisper, 'open the door. Don't make me go find something to pick the lock with.'

"He sounded drunk, which made me more nervous. For a minute, I thought maybe he felt bad about what had happened the night before, until his boot, and most likely a good portion of his body, slammed against the door.

"'Come on, Sara! Quit fucking around and let me in.'

"'Just leave me alone, Trent.' I tried not to sound terrified.

"'Just let me in.'

"'No.' It was all I had. I knew he could get in if he wanted—he'd just told me he could—but I was hoping he'd be too drunk to work that hard.

"'Fine, we'll do this the hard way.' His voice trailed off as he walked away from my door.

'I didn't have anywhere to hide. If I went under the bed or hid in the closet, he'd find me and pull me out. My only option was the veranda. I pulled the curtain half closed, then slipped out the door, making sure I locked it before it latched closed. I ducked down on the other side of the chair and held my breath.

"It was only another minute before I heard the crash of the closet door hitting the wall behind me. Then I heard Trent's hands slam against glass. The sound of the lock popping and the slide of the door along the track weren't far behind.

Trying to make myself as small as I could, I cowered in the corner behind the chair. When I dared to look up, I looked right into Trent's eyes. His sly smile horrified me. He stepped out and leaned back against the far railing.

"'Did you really think you could hide from me?' he asked sarcastically.

"'Why are you doing this to me?'" My voice shook as I tried to get the words out.

"'What do you mean, why am I doing this to you? Don't you remember—you begged me for it. Every time you smiled at me or looked at me with my shirt off when we were at the beach. I could read it in your eyes, Sara. You want this as much as I do.'

"'No, I don't.' I sounded as small as I felt.

"'Sara, Sara, Sara, stop fighting it. No matter what you say, it's going to happen.' He raised his voice a little before he became scary calm. 'You've awakened a part of me Celia just can't fulfill.'

"'I thought you loved her?' I hoped asking questions would distract him and make him forget why he'd come out there. 'What do you think she would say about this?'

"'I do love her, very much, and I plan on marrying her. But I have needs too, for things she just can't give me, and I know you won't say anything. If you were going to, you would have this morning. But you didn't, because you know better than that.' He stepped toward me, uncrossing his arms as he moved.

"A tight grip on my biceps pulled me away from the veranda. I heard metal tapping against the floor as the uneven chair legs wobbled side to side..."

As I try to catch my breath, my eyes begin to focus again.

Jacqui is standing right in front of me. "There you are. You left us for a few minutes." Jacqui's voice is soothing as she tries to comfort me. When she reaches out to touch me, I flinch, and she backs away.

"Don't touch me," I almost whisper. "I can't do this." I stand, pushing the metal folding chair backward so it crashes to the floor.

The sound of Jacqui's voice follows me as I run out the door, up the stairs, through the lobby, and into the parking lot. I don't stop running until I reach my driver's side door. In one fluid motion, I open it, slide behind the wheel, and jam my key in the ignition while praying it'll start with the first turn. When the engine roars to life, I jam the shifter to reverse and peel out of the spot. As I drive by the front entrance, I see Jacqui standing on the curb with her phone to her ear. I don't know if she notices me looking, but she doesn't try to flag me down. I turn right and head out of the parking lot.

CHAPTER 3

Sara

"Son of a bitch!" I smash my hand into the bottom of the steering wheel.

I just want to escape into my apartment and hide for the rest of the night, but Elaine is sitting on the porch rocking back and forth over the smooth concrete floor, and there's no way in hell she'll let me slip by when she sees my face. Trying not to look toward her, I pull in the driveway and stop the beast right outside the garage door.

Taking two deep breaths and wiping my hands down my cheeks, I try to make myself look presentable. If the visor mirror hadn't fallen out right after I bought the car, I'd be in better shape. After a glance in the cloudy rearview mirror, I throw open the door and bite the bullet.

Elaine has never really pried before and I'm sure she won't now, but in the five years I've lived above her, I don't think she's ever seen me come home looking like a train wreck. As I move closer to the stairs, I hear a faint humming and the squeak of her rocking chair.

"Sara!" She sounds so excited to see me.

"Hey, Elaine, how's it going?"

"Not too bad. Just out enjoying the warm weather that's finally here." She pauses as I reach the bottom step. "Didn't you have to work tonight, dear?"

"I have the night off." I climb two of the three steps and lean against the iron railing, making sure not to look Elaine in the eye.

"Huh." Sara hears Elaine's huff out. "You okay?"

"I'm fine. Just tired. It's been a rough day."

"You know, I'll be here for a little while longer if you want to talk."

I look at Elaine and see only sincerity in her eyes. "Thanks, I'll keep that in mind." I head to my door, passing Elaine's chair.

"If you're hungry, I accidentally made too much," Elaine hints as I pull open the storm door.

"You know, for the last five years, you've always accidentally made too much…"

"Well, it happens."

"I just want you to know I always appreciate it. I'm going to miss your amazing dinners after you move."

"Don't worry, dear, Izach's a good cook too. He learned from his grandma!" She looks over the back of her chair with an eyebrow raised, looking so serious!

Unable to hold back, I giggle. "I'll remember that."

"You better go change into your comfy clothes, then come back down and eat. You're too skinny."

"Give me, like, five minutes." I thump up the wooden stairs two at a time and stop at my door. "And I'm not too skinny!" I yell down before stepping inside my apartment and pulling the door closed behind me.

My apartment's a wreck. Considering I have the night off, I should think about cleaning, but there's no way I can turn down Elaine. Other than Jacqui, she's the only other person I could call a friend. Just thinking about not having her downstairs makes me want to cry again, and despite my earlier waterworks, I try not to cry very often, at least not anymore.

On my way to the bathroom, I toss my purse on the couch and pick up the "I <3 Buffalo" hoodie hanging off the armrest. I pull it over my head as I make my way to the vanity.

I cringe at the light raccoon eyes looking back at me in the mirror. Armed with a makeup wipe, I remove the faint black stripes down my cheeks and the smears around my eyes.

I grasp the elastic band in my ponytail and pull it free, then I run my fingers through the mass of tangles. My once-blond hair, now almost black, is in serious need of a dye job, but I'm trying to wash out as much of the color as possible so I can change it to a lighter brown. Sadly, my piddly paychecks don't allow for much more than my rent, cell bill, car insurance and food—which sometimes is stretching it—so having my hair professionally done is out of the question. I gather my hair back up and tie it in a messy bun on top of my head. I don't even care if it looks like a hot mess.

Turning on my heel, I kick through the pile of clothes on the bathroom floor to find my black yoga pants, which of course aren't there. With my foot, I push the clothes back into a pile, and I make a mental note to do some laundry after dinner.

Leaving the bathroom, I catch my big toe on the carpet, where it's pulled up from the doorjamb, and go flying across my tiny living room, Superman style. In an attempt to catch myself, I throw my arms out and land on the heel of my left hand. My right arm slides across the indoor-outdoor carpeting, creating an instant rug burn.

"Son of a bitch!" I curl into the fetal position, hugging both arms. "I swear to god, the first thing Elaine's grandson is going to do is fix this goddamn carpet!"

Rolling to my back, I pull my arms away from my body and hold them up in front of my face. They aren't gushing blood, but the skin on both wrists and my right palm is shiny, which means I burned myself pretty good. Making my abs use their full potential, I strain to sit up without setting my hands on the godforsaken rug. Shimmying, I get to the coffee table—which I managed to miss in my fall—and use my elbows to push myself off the ground.

Still holding both hands in front of me, I return to the bathroom, flip the cold water on as high as it will go, and run my burning skin under the freezing stream. It only takes a few minutes for the pain to subside. I pat my arms dry with the towel hanging off the hook on the back of the bathroom door, then I set off to find my damn pants again, this time looking down to make sure I actually clear the door.

In the corner of my room is another pile of clothes, much bigger than the one in the bathroom, which cements the fact that laundry must get done. Right on the top of the pile are my pants. I pull the pants from the top of the pile and give them a sniff. They don't smell, so they're good enough.

The sound of the downstairs door squeaking open concerns me. Even though Elaine still gets around pretty well, the doctor forbade her from using stairs after she fell and broke her hip two years ago. To avoid another incident tonight, I fly to my door and throw it open. Peeking my head out, I see Elaine getting ready to climb upstairs.

"Freeze right there, lady!"

"Sara, you almost gave me a heart attack. Thank god I wasn't halfway up the stairs. I probably would have fallen backward and broken a hip or something."

"You could break your hip again from just trying to climb the stairs. What are you doing anyway? I told you I was coming back down," I say, stepping onto the landing and pulling the door shut.

"I heard a crash and then nothing. I just wanted to make sure you hadn't fallen and broken your neck."

"If you heard me fall, then you probably heard me swearing too." I take Elaine's arm to guide her back out the door.

"Well, yeah, but I was still worried that you had a broken neck."

"Thank you for being concerned about me, but don't try to climb the stairs. We don't need two broken necks around here." We round the corner, and I help Elaine back into her rocker.

She waves me away as she tries to get comfortable. "So what happened up there?"

"I tripped over the loose piece of carpet at my bathroom door," I say as I sit in the rocker adjacent hers.

"Why didn't you tell me there was some loose rug? I could have had someone come take care of it."

"I can take care of it myself. I've just been lazy and haven't gotten it nailed back into place. You don't need to hire someone when I'm capable of fixing it."

"Well, did you hurt yourself?"

"Just a couple of brush burns. I'll live."

"Put some tea bags on them. That'll take away the burn."

"Really? I'm going to have to try that because they hurt like a son of a bitch." As the words leave my mouth, I grimace at Elaine. I try my best not to swear around her out of respect. "Sorry."

"It's okay, honey, I've said worse in my time. So the food's in the Crock-Pot on the counter—pot roast. Go grab yourself a plate or two."

I hop up from the rocking chair. "I'm not that skinny! Stop trying to make me fat. I worked hard to have a swimmer's body, and just because I don't swim anymore doesn't mean I want to give up the body too!"

"Why don't you tell me how you got the swimmer's body? I'd love to hear the story," Elaine calls to my back as I walk through her living room to the kitchen.

I don't answer, and I don't have any plans to ever answer. Why I even throw little things like that out there, I don't know.

As promised, right in the middle of the counter is a Crock-Pot full of amazing-smelling pot roast. The scent assaults my nose, and my mouth waters. I fill a bowl and butter a couple of pieces of Italian bread before I head back outside to sit and talk to Elaine while I eat.

CHAPTER 4

Izach

Driving from Charlotte to Buffalo is quite possibly the most boring trip in the world, especially when you don't have a road trip buddy. I'm kicking myself for not heading to Buffalo after I graduated, but I wanted to spend some time with my friends in my hometown before I packed it all in and moved ten hours away for good. A month ago, I made a similar drive from college in Brockport, NY, to Charlotte—hauling pretty much the same load I have now—when I moved out of my apartment after I got my teaching degree.

Before I finished school, I applied for teaching jobs all over the state of New York—because New York state teachers are known to be the best paid. Luckily, I landed a job with the City of Buffalo school district. The job in Buffalo is perfect because my Gran-ma is moving to Arizona and leaving me her house. Well, half of her house. The other half she rents to some girl with issues—her words, not mine—which scares me a little. I'm not too keen on living downstairs from some weird psycho and having to worry about her trying to sneak in and kill me in my sleep. Although, Gran-ma reassures me she's not crazy, just a little fragile—whatever that means.

In the five years I lived in New York and all the times I went to see Gran-ma while I was in school, I never saw the girl. When I hung out with Gran-ma during the day, the girl from upstairs would be home, but she'd leave right after we went inside to have dinner. Gran-ma said she works the night shift at The Diner—weird name, I know—near the university. Just the thought of someone in their early twenties who isn't living it up kind of freaks me out. I'm not sure if I'm going to like what I find when I get there.

Glancing at the gas gauge in my Charger—a graduation gift from my parents—I decide I can get gas in the morning. I'm so tired from driving that I just want to get out of the car and walk around for a while. The drive was supposed to be ten hours long, but I got stuck in morning rush hour in Charlotte and afternoon traffic in Pittsburgh. By the time I reached the outskirts of Buffalo, the traffic wasn't bad, but people were driving like fucking morons. Add in the fact that my poor baby is towing a small U-Haul trailer, and ten hours turned into just about twelve.

Thankfully Gran-ma called and told me she would have dinner waiting for me in the Crock-Pot so it wouldn't get cold. She also informed me that her tenant was home, so I'll actually get to meet this mystery girl. Gran-ma made sure to tell me that her tenant is beautiful, but then again Gran-ma thinks everyone is beautiful, so I'm not sure if I can trust her judgment.

When I pull off the exit, my GPS goes crazy, giving me quick turn-by-turn directions. I've had about enough of its shitty directions, so I rip the power cord from the outlet, silencing the computer's babbling.

Making the final turn onto Gran-ma's street, I look at her house and see that she put up orange road cones to block anyone from parking in front. When I called earlier to tell her when I thought I'd be there, she told me as soon as the "asshole" from across the street left for work, she would go out and save me a spot. I didn't ask how she was going to do it—I didn't want to know. All I know is the woman is off her rocker and will go to bat with anyone who challenges her. I'm kind of scared for the people in the retirement community she's moving to. They have no idea what they signed on for when they accepted her application.

After stopping in the middle of the road, I hop out of the car and run to move the cones so I can pull into the spot. Looking at the house, I see Gran-ma sitting in her rocking chair on the front porch, so I give her a wave before I run back to the car. After maneuvering into the spot, I kill the overworked engine, grab my GPS from the window, and throw open the door. Standing up has never felt better. Lifting my arms above my head, I stretch my sore, tired muscles, then crack my back before stepping away and swinging the door shut.

Even though it's only the beginning of June, my Gran-ma's grass looks like shit. It's all burnt out and full of weeds, something I'll have to fix. Working for a landscaping business for the past five summers has become somewhat of a curse. I can't stand seeing a yard with good potential going to hell because no one takes care of it—not that I want my Gran-ma out working on the lawn. But her tenant is young and more than capable of helping her, probably just doesn't want to because it's not part of her lease agreement. Just another thing to add to my annoyance of meeting this girl.

"Hey, Gran-ma!" I sound like I smoke a pack a day after spending all day in an air-conditioned car without talking.

43

"Izach! I'm so glad you're finally here." She moves to get out of her chair, but I'm up the stairs and in front of her before she's halfway up.

"Don't get up, Gran-ma, I can give you a hug when you're sitting."

"Christ, between Sara and you, you'd think I'm an invalid. I can stand up to give you a hug. Now back up so I have some space to move." She shoos me with her hands so I back up a couple of steps. "Just because I broke my hip—what, two years ago now—everyone's got to treat me like I'm going to break at any moment."

"I didn't say you were going to break. You just look comfortable, and there's no need for you to stand—" The sound of a dish crashing in the house makes my head whip toward the door. "Is someone in there?"

"Yeah, Sara's fixing herself a plate to eat. Let me go see if she's okay. You stay out here. I want to ease her into meeting you. She's kind of skittish around new people, especially men."

"Are you sure she wants to meet me?"

"She really doesn't have a choice, since you're going to be living here. Oh, and she needs some carpet tacked down upstairs. She almost broke her neck earlier, has some pretty bad brush burns on her arms. Now, don't move. I'm going to let her know you're here."

Dropping into the rocking chair next to the one Gran-ma just vacated, I kick my legs out in front of me and lean my head back against the worn wood. Regardless of the fact that I just sat for twelve hours, it feels good to sit down and stretch out. Crossing my feet at the ankles, I clasp my hands behind my head and close my eyes.

Soft, almost whispered voices float out the door. I can't make out what they're saying, but I can tell the difference between Gran-ma's more mature voice and the voice of a young girl. The sound of broken glass being scraped across the floor grabs my attention, and I want to go in to see what happened despite my Gran-ma telling me not to move.

When I stand up, I hear Gran-ma's, voice much louder than a few seconds ago. "Izach, I'm going to fix you a plate. Do you want some bread and butter to go with your pot roast?"

"Gran-ma, you don't have to serve me. I can get my own," I call to her.

"You just stay out there and relax. I'm making you a plate, and I don't want to hear anything else about it. Now do you want bread or not?"

"Sure."

After some banging around, Gran-ma encourages her tenant to come outside and meet me. Knowing that I probably took Sara's seat, I move to the wide brick railing around the porch. Just after I get myself comfortable, Gran-ma bumps into the door, trying to hold my plate and her cane at the same time. I rush over to the door and pull it open.

She lets out a loud breath. "I would have gotten it, but thank you." She shoves the plate into my hand, followed by a fork and knife. "Eat before it gets cold. I'm going to run and get you and Sara something to drink. What do you want?"

"Just some Coke, if you have it."

"Izach, you're back in New York. We drink Pepsi up here."

"Sorry, I forgot, Pepsi's fine. Thanks, Gran-ma."

"You're welcome. Now eat."

Shaking my head, I move back to my spot on the railing. "So bossy!" I say to myself as the screen door slams behind Gran-ma's back.

Just a few minutes later, I hear her getting close to the door again. I turn and look as she pushes it open and walks through with Sara behind her.

As soon as Sara clears the door, I'm mesmerized. She's nothing like what I imagined. When Gran-ma told me she had issues, I pictured a homely girl—not necessarily bad-looking, but plain. With one look, I can tell Sara is anything but plain. Her hair is tied in a messy knot-looking ball on top of her head. She hasn't lifted her face, so I can't tell what color her eyes are, but from what I can see of her eyebrows her natural hair color is blond, not that washed-out, tired-looking black.

Moving my eyes farther down her body, I take in the over-sized hoodie covering her torso all the way past her butt. Her legs, covered in those amazing, tight, black pants, go on for days. They're not twigs either—I can tell she has some muscle definition. Maybe a runner? I'm kind of surprised that her shirt covers as much of her as it does. She's got to be almost as tall as I am, and I'm 5'10". I run my eyes back up her body to her face, which is still looking down, but I notice a hint of blush on her cheeks. I'm not sure if she's just embarrassed that my Gran-ma basically ambushed her or if she caught me checking her out.

"Sara, this is my rude-as-sin grandson, Izach, who doesn't stand when ladies come into the room," Gran-ma says, interrupting my thoughts.

"Technically you didn't come into the room; you came outside."

"I don't care if we went to the moon. You stand when a lady enters your vicinity, you greet her, then you sit back down only after she sits. You're a Southern boy. I know you have manners."

"Sorry, Gran-ma." I stand and set down my plate.

"Izach, this is Sara. She's my upstairs tenant—well, technically now she's your tenant. Which brings me back to that carpet you have to tack down for her…"

"Elaine, I can take care of it." Sara's voice is barely above a whisper, but the sound does something funny to my insides.

This chick is seriously messing with my head, and I still haven't seen her damn face. She keeps her eyes on the floor, or on her plate—I can't tell from where I'm standing—as she waits for Gran-ma to sit down. Sara takes the other rocking chair, pulling her right leg up and tucking it under her butt. I'm trying not to stare at her, but from what I can see, she's really beautiful, and I don't want to miss the chance to get a glimpse of her face. I bet her eyes are a light color. Maybe green or blue? No way with her alabaster coloring and blond eyebrows will she have dark eyes like mine.

Once they're firmly planted in their chairs, I throw my leg back over the ledge and prop my back against the brick pillar. Leaving my legs dangling on each side, I pull my dinner toward me and lean over it to eat. From this vantage point, I can sneak a peek at Sara without Gran-ma noticing.

"Don't worry about it. I can tack it down. Gran-ma, do you have a staple gun?" I ask, but only after I've chewed what's in my mouth. I don't need to be lectured for being rude again.

47

"I'm sure there's one in the garage. Your Gran-pa had at least two of everything."

"Good, I'll go see what I can find and take care of the rug when I'm done."

I get a smile from Gran-ma, but Sara never lifts her head. I'm starting to get paranoid. *Why the hell hasn't she looked at me? Is that her issue — is she a lesbian? Did she look up before she came out the door? Maybe she thinks I'm ugly? Good Christ, now who sounds like a girl?*

Finally, after I've spent the whole meal practically eating blind — because I'm a fucking creep and can't stop looking at this girl — she looks up, and I'm met with the most amazing blue eyes. *Shit, I'm a goner. I don't even care what the issues are. She could be a psycho or a sociopath and it wouldn't phase me as long as she keeps looking at me. Damn it, she caught me staring.*

Her eyes dart back to her plate as fast as they shot up.

CHAPTER 5

Sara

Shit, shit, shit!

Moving through a door with a plate of food in your hand while looking down isn't an easy feat, but it's necessary. After I creep through the apartment, I peek out the screen, and see Elaine's grandson sitting on the porch railing. I almost trip again, but not because of a loose piece of carpet. From what I can see he's really good-looking. No, not just good-looking—he's hot! With the way he's sitting, I can only see his profile, but I'm pretty sure when I actually have the full view of his face, I won't have to worry about tripping. I'll just fall flat on my ass.

Taking a chance as I walk onto the porch with my plate, I peek at him, trying to be as sneaky as I can. His too-long hair is stuffed under a baseball hat, and random pieces stick out at his ears and the back of his neck. It's dark and looks as if it may have a little wave. Moving my eyes back down, I catch sight of how tight his sleeves are against his arms. He's recently graduated from college, so he's probably a gym rat—not that I'd know. I see ink on his arms and try not to look too hard, but I'm curious about what he has.

The sound of the screen door slamming behind me makes me jump. I feel Elaine moving past me, so I look up to see which rocking chair she claimed, and I make a move toward the other one, which is farthest from Izach and closest to my door. Carefully I lower my butt into the seat—these old rockers have a tendency to slip when you sit too fast—and make sure I'm firmly planted before I slide back and set my plate in my lap. Once I'm settled, I look up at Izach from under my lashes. He's looking at his plate, but now I can see his face. I'm pretty sure that at this point, my mouth is hanging open with drool hanging off my lip, not that I'm paying any attention to it. Scanning his front, I bypass his eyes, because I don't want to be too obvious. In addition to pulling tight at his arms, his shirt is stretched to the max across his chest. His legs—straddling the railing—are covered in camo shorts that are pulled tight at his thighs. Dropping my eyes farther, I notice ink on his calf. It's a portrait, but because of his dark leg hair, I can't tell what it is. Finally I reach his black Converse.

"It just needs to be tacked down." Elaine's voice cuts through my perusal of her grandson's leg.

"I can do that. Do you have staple gun?" Izach's deep baritone voice rattles me to my core.

"Wait, what?" I ask, looking at Elaine.

"Izach's going to fix your carpet so you don't break your neck."

"I can fix it myself, we already talked about this." I chance a look at Izach and notice his smirk. "Don't worry about it." Gah! Those were not the first words I wanted to say to him.

"It's no problem. When we're done eating, I'll grab the staple gun, then you can show me what nearly took you out."

He's trying to crack a joke and it's really cute, but I start to panic. I feel my temperature rise and my pits start to sweat. I don't let guys into my apartment, not with me by myself. I always made Elaine tell me when she was having someone come fix something so I could be gone. I turn my pleading eyes toward Elaine and notice a small smile on her lips. She's enjoying this, and I'm freaking out!

"One of the positives of having a man live here is I don't have to call someone in to make repairs," she says.

"Don't give me too much credit, Gran-ma. I can tack down a carpet, paint, and maybe hang shelves, but when it comes to bigger things, like plumbing, I'm definitely not your guy."

"Please, honey, I know you can do anything you set your mind to."

I glance at Izach and see a hint of pink in his cheeks, just above his short beard. He's staring at his almost-empty plate, but as if he senses me looking at him, he looks up and catches my eyes. He looks surprised when his eyes meet mine. Those eyes, they're a whiskey color, and from what I see, I can tell they're darker toward the center and gradually get lighter, transforming to almost a yellow color.

After what's probably only a second, I drop my gaze to the plate on my lap and decide to eat something even though my stomach is tossing and turning with the wild butterflies flapping around in it. If I don't eat, I'll catch hell from Elaine, and I don't need her making another scene in front of her hot grandson. As I pick at my food, I plan how to get out of being alone in my apartment with him. I need to talk to Jacqui—guys don't affect me like this. I find them attractive, but I don't want to think that way about a guy who's related to someone I've come to love.

The sound of silverware scraping against glass pulls me from my thoughts.

"Let me get you more," Elaine tells Izach.

"No, I'm stuffed, but thank you."

"What do you mean you're stuffed? You only ate one helping, and I didn't even fill your plate."

I have to bite my lip to keep from giggling. At least she's not giving me shit about not eating enough.

"Gran-ma, I'll eat more later. Right now, I'm stuffed from all the junk I ate while I was driving."

Elaine huffs, but she doesn't nag him further. I'll need to remember that excuse for the future, not that I'll have much longer to use it since she's leaving in a week.

Elaine almost yells my name. "Sara, you're not eating. Don't tell me you spent the day eating junk too?"

Damn it, she's not satisfied with just giving him shit. "I'm eating," I state, and hear another huff.

"I'm afraid the two of you are going to waste away when I'm gone." She shakes her head and says to herself, "I better get to cooking things that can be frozen."

"Gran-ma, Sara and I are adults. We've both survived this long without your cooking, and I'm sure we'll make it once you move."

"You're both too skinny," Elaine snaps, then ends the conversation by standing and shuffling through the screen door.

"Well, I guess she told us," Izach comments, making me lift my eyes to his face as he stands up from the railing.

I feel heat in my cheeks and force a small smile.

"You done?" he asks, dropping his eyes to my barely touched plate.

I mumble, "Yeah."

He takes my plate before he walks across the porch and through Elaine's door.

"Elaine do not come up here." I snap over my shoulder.

"Stop arguing with me, Sara. I know you're not comfortable with guys, and Izach is no different. I can see it in your face when he's around," she says as she continues to climb the stairs.

Whelp, I guess I don't hide my feelings as well as I thought I did, or Elaine has just gotten really good at reading me.

"That's why I told you I would take care of it myself. Now I have to deal with you trying to climb the stairs and someone I don't know coming into my personal space. The only reason why I haven't locked you both out is because he's your grandson. I'm trying here, so please give me a few minutes to pick up my apartment. I'll come down to get him."

She stomps her foot against the stairs.

"Elaine, please, I don't want to be angry with you. You're moving soon and I already miss you, even though you're standing right in front of me. I don't want to be mad at you."

"Okay, honey, I'll just wait on the porch with Izach. You can show him what needs to be fixed." Elaine's voice sounds sweet and sad at the same time.

"Thank you." I watch as Elaine heads back down the stairs, gripping the rail with both hands. Glancing over her shoulder, I see Izach looking at me before taking a few steps up to help his grandma to the bottom landing.

Ignoring him, I go back into my apartment and close the door. *What the shit… seriously, can he not catch me having a moment?* I just want to slide to the floor and pretend that tonight didn't happen. What I don't want to do is pick up my apartment so hot Izach can come fix the carpet.

Shaking my head, I cross the living room and pull the hoodies off the back of my couch, then I head to the bathroom so I can shove them in the hamper. Since I'm doing laundry tonight, I drag the hamper to my bedroom and abandon it behind the door, pulling the door almost shut. If I close it all the way, I won't have any light in the living room since the light bulbs in the overhead light have needed to be changed for quite some time. I should probably let Elaine know that too, considering Izach will probably tell her the bulbs are out. Changing them before it came to this might have been a good idea, but I just couldn't bring my lazy ass to do something that wasn't really necessary.

Izach

After getting the staple gun from the garage I head toward Sara's door where I can hear her snapping at Gran-ma. Sara's eyes lock on mine just a second before she backs into her apartment and shuts the door lightly. I help Gran-ma shuffle off the final step and out the door, then she pushes me out of the way so she can swing around into her chair.

"She'll be down in a minute to get you," Gran-ma says as I lean my butt against the railing and continue to look up the stairs. "Don't push her, Izach, she's

54

fragile. Never told me what happened, but I suspect something bad that has to do with a guy, probably something she didn't want."

"Okay." I'm not sure why she told me that.

"I don't think she'll share it with anyone, considering she's lived here for five years and has never said anything about it to me." She looks at me to make sure I'm registering what she is saying. "Just let her come to you when she's ready. And before you make a comment, I know she will. I can see it in her eyes when she looks at you. You're different for her, and I'm pretty sure that scares the shit out of her."

At the sound of a door creaking open, Gran-ma shuts her mouth. My eyes lock on Sara's legs as she descends one step at a time. Trying not to look like a creeper, I meet her eyes for a second before she drops them. If her goal is to not make me curious, she's doing a pretty shitty job. The more she avoids me, the more I want to know why. I just met her today, but I can tell there's something different about her.

When she doesn't speak, I decide to take matters into my own hands. "Ready?"

"Uh, yeah, sure." She hesitates but walks back up the stairs in front of me.

Each time she climbs one of the steep steps, her hoodie rides up in the back, giving me a quick glance of the most perfect ass I've ever seen. Keeping my mouth shut, I follow Sara into her living room and toward the bathroom door. The carpet is lifted right at the jamb, and it's got a pretty distinctive fold that tells me it's been like that for a while. It's so dark though, I'm not sure I'll be able to see to get the carpet lined up right. The only light in the room is coming from a crack in her bedroom door and the small light above the sink in the bathroom.

"Can you hit the overhead light for me?" I ask nonchalantly, hoping I don't freak her out.

"Um, the light's kind of burned out."

"Kind of burned out?"

"Well, it is burned out. I haven't had a chance to get new bulbs yet," she says shyly.

"How many bulbs do you need? I'm sure Gran-ma has some downstairs."

"Uh, I think three."

"Okay, I'll check and see when I'm done with the carpet. Can you get me a chair to stand on? And maybe a flashlight?"

"Sure." Sara heads toward the kitchen in the back of her unit.

To pull the carpet tight, I have to kneel with my back in the bathroom. This also gives me a great vantage point to check out Sara's legs when she comes back. The sound of a chair moving across the floor pulls me from my fascination with her long-as-sin legs and back to the task in front of me. With one hand, I pull the folded carpet tight, and with the other, I press the staple gun into the floor and pull the trigger. I staple across the opening of the bathroom, even where the carpet is still tacked down, just in case it pulls up.

After I pull the trigger for the last time, I look up to see Sara standing with a chair in the middle of the room. She's trying to place it precisely under the light. I almost want to laugh because I'm just going to move it off to the side so I can get to the screw in the center of the fixture, but I don't want to make her feel bad. I can tell she's nervous about having me up here. I run my eyes up the side of her and notice her bottom lip is tucked between her teeth as she concentrates.

56

"All set."

She jumps when I speak.

"I might have to come back up and pound the staples in further, but you let me know if there are any sticking out. Maybe just run your foot over them. I don't want you stepping on one and cutting yourself." Christ, I'm rambling and she's just staring at me. This has got to be the most awkward conversation I've ever had with a girl. When it's clear she's not going to respond, I ask, "Okay?"

"Um, sure. I'll go find you a flashlight. I think I have one under my sink." Her voice drifts off as she hightails it out of the room.

Just to make sure there isn't anything sharp sticking out of the floor, I run my hands over the newly placed staples, then I stand and head to the chair. With the little bit of light available, I can see the screw for the fixture is right in the center of the glass, so I move the chair about a foot to the left and climb up. As I start to turn the screw, I see a beam of light coming from the kitchen. She must not be paying attention though, because the light shines right in my eyes, momentarily blinding me.

"Oh, sorry," she mumbles and moves the beam of light to where my hands are working on the screw.

"It's fine. Can you hold this?" I ask with my hand stretched out, holding the decorative screw from the middle of the fixture.

Sara looks up at me nervously but extends her other hand and lets me drop the small bead into her palm. Once her fingers close around it, I turn back to the glass and slowly slide it free.

"Looks like you need four bulbs, not three. I'll check and see what Gran-ma has. If she doesn't have all four, I'll just change what we have and run to the store tomorrow morning for a couple packages."

"I can go. I have to stay up so I don't mess up my sleep schedule for work."

"That's right, Gran-ma told me that you work overnights at The Diner. I'm not trying to be nosy, but why do you work overnights?"

"Drunk people, especially when college is in session, tip better."

"I can agree with that. There were definitely some nights when I swore I had an extra twenty before I opened my wallet the next morning and found it empty." I watch her for a minute, waiting to see if she's going to add anything. "Well, I guess I'll go see how many light bulbs we have downstairs. I'll be back in a few."

I jump off the chair, grab the staple gun from the floor, and head out the open door. Rounding the corner onto the porch, I almost run into Gran-ma.

Grabbing her arm to steady her, I ask, "Whoa, what are you doing?"

"Nothing. Did you get Sara's carpet all tacked down?"

"Yeah, but she has some light bulbs out. I wanted to see if you have any replacements before she heads to the store?" I keep walking toward the door to Gran-ma's unit.

"I'm sure there's a box under the sink. Are you going to go back up there and change them for her?" she asks before I pull open the screen door.

I turn and look at her. "Yeah, why?"

"Just wondering," she states.

I let it go, shaking my head as I head to the kitchen to check for light bulbs.

Sara

Standing by the door, I listen as Izach chats with Elaine. Just by her curiosity, I can tell she's going to become a major pain in my ass when it comes to him. Thankfully I don't have to worry about her pushing the issue for much longer. Considering Izach doesn't question her motives, I don't think he's caught on, or maybe he just doesn't want to give his grandma a hard time because she's moving so far away. Either way, whatever she seems to be planning isn't going to happen. I just need him to change my light bulbs so I can get on with my life and pretend nothing's changed.

At the sound of the first footfall on the stairs, I run across the room to my futon and lean against the arm, picking at my nails to make it look as though I wasn't listening. Not that there had been much to hear.

Izach twists around the door frame, locking eyes with me for a second, then flashing me a dazzling smile. He beelines to the chair and steps up. Pushing my butt off the futon, I reach out to take the box of bulbs. I know I wouldn't be able to manage holding them while unscrewing old bulbs and screwing in the new bulbs.

Without a word, he hands me the flimsy package and slips one of the small white globes from the fixture. He changes three of the four blown bulbs, and when he's done, he jumps down, goes to the switch on the wall, and flips it up.

"Let there be light!" he jokes, looking like a little kid with his arms out to the side.

I can't help the little giggle that escapes my lips, so I bite them to stop myself from laughing more, and I look at the floor.

"Your laugh is like a squeak. It's cute."

I lift my eyes toward Izach. "I hate my laugh."

His face goes from smiling and happy to closed and sad. "You shouldn't, and you should laugh more. It's good for the soul, or so I've heard."

"I'll keep that in mind."

"All right, I'm going to go unload the trailer so I can get it off my baby and turn it in tomorrow."

I stand there and look at him, unsure if I'm supposed to offer to help or just say okay.

"So I guess if you need anything, let me know?" Izach asks as he steps closer to the door.

"Sure." I don't move from my spot, standing with the chair between us.

"Okay, well, have a good night."

"You too."

Izach backs out the door to the top of the stairs. He waits a beat, probably to see if I'm going to say more, before he bounces down the steps. I keep listening until I hear the screen door creak open, then slam closed.

Sucking in a deep breath, then blowing it out with a sigh, I grab the back of the chair and haul it into the kitchen. On my way through the living room, I rummage through my purse, pull out my phone, then hold the power button to bring it back to life. As soon as the screen lights up, the voicemail and text message indicators sound. I check my texts first and see two from Jacqui, just checking to make sure I'm okay.

Am I okay? Hell no, I'm not okay. I didn't expect to have to deal with Elaine's grandson for at least another week, and of course when I have a shitty day, he rolls up in his hot car, looking all hot, and I couldn't even be bitchy with him because I couldn't even talk! What the fuck is wrong with me?

After my internal rant, I fire off a text to Jacqui, basically saying what I'd thought. Considering she's my shrink, she doesn't mind my brand of crazy. Despite that it's after seven at night, I know she'll either call me or text me back. As that thought crosses my mine, my phone vibrates with an incoming call.

"Hey, how are you holding up?" she asks when I answer.

"I'm freaking the hell out!" I start to pace in circles around my living room. "Not only did I have a freak-out at group, but I come home to have Elaine guilt me into having dinner with her, then I get surprised by her hot-as-hell grandson."

"Okay, let's go back to the meltdown during group. You haven't done that in a long time, and I want to make sure you're coping in a positive manner?"

"No, I didn't cut, if that's what you're getting at in a round-about way. Although I'm thinking it's time for a new tattoo." Now I'm adding a loop around the coffee table.

"Did you try doing some of the things we've talked about?"

"No, I didn't freakin' meditate, Jacqui!" I yell. "I got home and had just enough time to wipe most of the mascara off my face before Elaine came to look for me. She was waiting on the porch when I got home. She totally planned the ambush!"

"Sara, you're all over the place. Please focus on what happened at group."

"Gah! I'm okay with what happened at group. I plan on discussing my fucked-upness with you on Friday. Right now my concern is this guy, who is hot, who I'm attracted to, who is moving into the apartment below me as we speak. He was just in my apartment, fixing my carpet and light."

"Okay, remember I told you to have an open mind about him. Get to know him. Clearly from what you just said he seems helpful. You can read people, Sara. What kind of vibe did you get from him?"

"I don't know. He didn't really say much, and when he was talking, I was so fixated on staring at him that I didn't even hear what came out of his mouth." I'm concentrating on the path I've created around the perimeter of the room.

"So you're attracted to him. It was bound to happen again at some point."

"You don't understand. I've never been this attracted to a guy. It's more than just physical. He was trying to joke with me, and I completely clammed up. I couldn't say more than two words to him. This is why I need to move. I can't do this. I don't do this—"

"Sara, calm the fuck down!"

I halt my pacing and scrunch up my face even though she can't see me. "Geez, way to give it to me straight."

"Sara..." she says softly. "Get to know him. Take a chance and let someone else in. Elaine's leaving, it's not healthy that you don' t have any other friends."

"I do too have other friends. There's Cheryl and Miguel at work. They're my friends."

"They're not your friends; they're your coworkers. Friends are people you have a personal relationship with, people you've allowed yourself to trust."

"Well, if that's your definition, then Elaine isn't really my friend. I've never told her a damn thing about me, except where I work and my schedule."

"You trust Elaine, and you've come to rely on her. The fact that you wiped your face and had dinner with her after a major meltdown tonight makes that pretty clear."

"Okay, so maybe she's my friend." I start my laps again, only slower this time, with one arm wrapped around my middle to hold myself together.

"And now she's leaving, but she's not leaving you alone. She's leaving you with her grandson. Take that opportunity and get to know him."

"Ugh, I'm not ready for that."

"You are. I know you are. So stop fighting it, and let him be your friend." She pauses, but I don't have anything to add. "You said he's moving in right now?"

"Yeah."

"Then go see if he needs some help."

"I have to do some laundry," I say, making up an excuse.

"Throw a load in the washer, then see if he needs some help. He helped you tonight, so return the favor. It's give and take. He gave. Now it's your turn."

"I'll think about it."

"All right, well, I won't beg you, so do what you're going to do."

"Hey, you don't have to be mean about it."

63

"I'm not being mean; I'm just giving you some advice. Now, I have my own laundry to do. If you start to feel like you're losing control, try doing one or more of the things we've talked about. If that doesn't work, then call me back. I'll be up for a while."

"Okay, thanks, Jacqui."

"You're welcome. Have a good night. Maybe take a little step forward."

"We'll see. Night, Jacqui."

After hitting the red circle on the phone screen, I toss the phone onto the futon, then head to my room and drag my overflowing hamper into the living room so I can sort through the colors. The empty laundry baskets with my detergent are stacked behind my bedroom door, so I grab them after I've situated the hamper.

As I separate the white clothes from the dark and the colors from the blacks and blues, I think about the first thing that came to Jacqui's mind. Something that hadn't even crossed mine. I didn't think about cutting—until she mentioned it. It's been nearly a year since I had my last slip up, or relapse, whatever you want to call it. For the most part, I've been able to fill that craving with tattoos or rubber band therapy. Jacqui prefers that I keep a journal or draw a butterfly on my skin where I would have cut, but instead of drawing the butterfly, I have it tattooed on. She not a fan of the ink because it's too close to the real thing, but sometimes it's the only thing that helps.

The basket of jeans is full and the first one I should wash since I don't put them in the dryer and I'll need a pair to wear in the morning. Putting aside the thoughts of cutting and therapy, I set the detergent and fabric softener on top of the pile, stand, and hoist the basket onto my hip. Before heading to the door, I look back at the futon and think about grabbing my phone, but I decide against it. I'm fine. It's only laundry, and maybe offering to help Elaine's hot grandson unpack his trailer. I got this shit.

CHAPTER 6

Izach

Pulling things out of the trailer and stacking them in the yard was probably not the best idea I've had. Not that Gran-ma's house is in a bad neighborhood, but it's the city, and I'm not sure I should leave my shit just sitting on the side of the road. Gran-ma's watching it, but she can't really walk that well. When I hear Gran-ma's voice, I look up to see Sara on the porch with a laundry basket in her arms. Not going to lie—it's a little weird to see her starting laundry this late, but I get that she needs to stay up late. I just hope she doesn't hide all day and I get the chance to talk to her once in a while.

With the lack of details I was given about Sara before I got here, I should have known Gran-ma had something up her sleeve. It's quite apparent she wants to see something happen between the two of us. The biggest obstacle so far is that Sara doesn't talk. I mean, we heard her yelling at someone—I'm assuming she was on her phone a little while ago—so I know she can talk, but she hasn't said more than five words to me. It's starting to give me a complex.

"Hey, Gran-ma?" I call, then walk back toward the porch, which makes Sara stop her conversation and take off down the stairs. She rounds the side of the house toward the outside basement door. "Well shit, there goes my plan."

"What's that, sweetheart?" Gran-ma asks. Too bad her hearing isn't failing.

"Nothing. I was just going to see if Sara would watch the stuff I have piled up so I can start moving it into the house."

"Well, she's only throwing in a load of laundry. I'm sure she'll be back in a minute." She waits for a response that I don't give her. "I'll ask her for you."

"Don't worry about it. I don't think anyone's going to take anything with you sitting on the porch," I call over my shoulder as I head back toward the pile I've created in the yard.

"Nonsense, I'll ask her when she comes up."

"Fine, but for now, can you keep an eye on my things?"

"Yeah, I'll watch them. You go ahead and take a load in."

On the sidewalk next to the trailer, I grab the handles of two duffle bags and lift them together, slinging a strap over each shoulder to make sure I'm balanced. Instead of walking across the uneven lawn, I follow the driveway toward the house. The last thing I need is to wipe out right when Sara comes out of the basement. Gran-ma gets up out of her chair to get the door for me, and I turn to the side, shuffle past her, and straighten out to make sure I don't hit anything on my way through the living room.

Since Gran-ma is still in the master bedroom, I have to take the smaller room directly behind the stairs to Sara's apartment. The thought of her coming home from work in the middle of the night annoys the hell out of me. I'm not a sound sleeper and the smallest noises wake me up. But the positive to hearing her come home is that I'll know she's home safe. I'm not sure why, but between what Gran-ma said about Sara and meeting her tonight, I have this overwhelming urge to protect her. Maybe it's because she looks so young but also like she carries the weight of the world on her shoulders.

After dumping my shit on the bed, I head back out to get another load. The closer I get to the door, the more distinct the voices on the porch become, and I know Sara has come back up from throwing in her laundry. I stop close enough to hear them but far enough back that they won't see me. I want to know if they're talking about me, but when I hear nothing more, I push the storm door open with a squeak.

"Here he is." Gran-ma gives me a wide smile. "I was just asking Sara if she wouldn't mind watching your things, but she's offered to help. I guess you're stuck with me as your watchdog."

"You don't need to help," I say to Sara. "I just wanna make sure no one comes by and snags anything while I'm in the house."

"Izach," Gran-ma cuts in, "if she helps, you'll get it done twice as fast. The criminals in this neighborhood don't come out until it's good and dark."

I can tell she's joking—the neighborhood really isn't bad. But when you come from the suburbs, you think any part of the city is the 'hood.

"Geez, Gran-ma, way to make me feel secure," I say just as sarcastically.

"If you don't bother them, then they won't bother you. We have an understanding on this block."

"I'll keep that in mind." I make my way to the stairs. "I have a couple bags and a bunch of boxes left. If you want to grab the bags first, I'll take the boxes."

Sara abandons her laundry basket and moves to follow me down the stairs. We stop on the sidewalk next to the trailer. I pick up one of the bags and go to place it on Sara's shoulder, but she shrugs away and holds out her hand, so I let her arrange the bag so it's comfortable for her. I figure she'll head back toward the house after she picks up the other bag, but she picks it up and waits until I lift a stack of two boxes. We head to the stairs, where Gran-ma is waiting with the door held wide. Sara stops at the bottom and lets me move past her.

"Thanks," I whisper as I pass Gran-ma. "I'm in the second room in the back," I call over my shoulder to Sara, even though she's following me.

I think she whispers okay, but I'm not sure I actually heard her. I'm kind of confused, considering I heard her yelling at someone on the phone not fifteen minutes ago. I know she talks, but apparently she won't talk to me.

Turning into my room, I head toward the far wall and set down the boxes with a thud, then I turn to Sara. She's standing in the middle of the room, looking at the bed where my other bags are. Instead of telling her to put them with the others, I walk over to her, grab one of the straps from her shoulder, then swing the bag onto the bed. She deposits the other bag before she spins and practically runs out the door and through the house.

In three more trips, we've emptied the trailer. Once I have it locked up, I back into the driveway, basically blocking in Sara's car. Since I have to leave early in the morning to turn it in, I'm sure she won't care. The sooner I return this stupid trailer, the better for my poor baby. She's suffered so much from having

to haul this hunk-of-shit for so long. Knock on wood—
after this trailer hitch comes off, it'll never go back on
again. I lock the Charger and head back to the porch
where Gran-ma is sitting by herself.

"Where'd Sara go?"

"Back upstairs. This has been a lot for her. She
usually makes herself scarce when I have people over,
so my throwing the two of you together was probably
pretty tough on her."

"She doesn't talk much, does she?" I ask.

"She does, but she's not comfortable with you. It
took her a while to open up as much as she has to me,
and that's not very much. Don't worry though. She'll
get there. You just have to give her time."

"Well, I'm not going anywhere, so time is what
she'll get. I'm going to crash. I'm exhausted, and I have
to turn in that trailer in the morning."

"All right, honey, I'll be in in just a few minutes."

"Night, Gran-ma." I lean over and plant a kiss on
her cheek.

"Good night sweetheart."

Sara

The window in my bedroom is open, and I hear
Elaine and Izach talking about me. Elaine thinks that if
he gives me time, I'll open up to him, but I won't. I
don't open up to anyone except Jacqui, and the only
reason I've opened up to her is because she keeps her
mouth shut. It helps that I keep her well stocked with
wine and gift cards to her favorite restaurants— she
won't let me pay her in cash— because we're more
friends than doctor and patient and it's not ethical.

71

But, she still wants to be there and help me, so I keep my regularly scheduled appointments. Several times over the past few years she tried to get me to talk to the authorities about what happened, but I can't. I won't. My own parents didn't believe me, so I'm not sure why she thinks the police will, especially after so much time has passed.

Heading back into my living room, I grab another pile of clothes to throw in the washer. Since I heard Izach say good night to Elaine, I know I won't run into him on the way down, but unfortunately for me, Elaine is still sitting on the porch. Good thing I've learned how to handle her. Holding the basket in front of me, I head back downstairs, through the door, and smash right into her, dropping my laundry to catch her so she doesn't fall.

"Hey, you weren't going to come up, were you?" I ask as she moves away from my front door.

"I was thinking about it. I'm sure the washer's stopped by now," she says quickly, changing the subject.

"Elaine, don't climb the stairs, especially at night. They're steep and not well lit."

"You know, listening to you yell at me about climbing the stairs is one thing I won't miss when I move."

"I'm not yelling at you; I didn't raise my voice at all." I lean against the rail.

"Thanks for helping Izach." She returns to her rocker. "I know being around him isn't easy for you. I wish I knew why, but I'm not going to push you the last week we're together. I'm just glad that I'm leaving you here in good hands."

"I'm fine by myself, but you're welcome, and thank you. With our work schedules being opposite, I'm not sure I'll see your grandson again after you leave, but I'm glad you made me meet him."

"He's a good-looking boy, isn't he?"

"Elaine…" I drag out her name. "I'm not going to answer that, but he seems very nice."

"Your lack of answer tells me everything I need to know."

"Think what you want. I gave up trying to convince you of things a long time ago." I push off the rail and head toward the porch stairs. "I'm going to switch out my laundry. You going to be up for a bit?"

"No, I'm heading in to watch some Criminal Minds before I fall asleep."

I stop at the top of the porch stairs and turn to look at Elaine. "You and that show. I'm not sure how you sleep after watching it."

"It's not real. If I thought it was, it would scare the pants off of me."

"Well, thank goodness you know it's not real. Wouldn't want you walking around without any pants."

"Ha, ha, you're such a comedian," she says, waving as she walks to her front door.

"I'd like to think so. Good night, Elaine."

"Night, honey. Don't stay up too late."

"I won't." I step down the stairs and wait around the side of the house for the door to close behind Elaine.

If she wasn't such a pain in the ass, I wouldn't be so sad that she's leaving, but because she meddles so much, she's gotten to me, and I'm going to miss her so much. That's the only reason I didn't put up much of a fight when she cornered me into meeting Izach tonight. I shake off the thought of her leaving and go switch my laundry.

Before I crash at four in the morning, I finish three loads and put it all away.

CHAPTER 7

Sara

It's been two days since Elaine's sneak attack introduction of Izach, and I've managed to avoid both of them, not that I want to avoid Elaine. My work schedule is heavy on Tuesday, Friday, and Saturday, with the occasional Wednesday; I usually pick up the long shifts my coworkers don't want on the weekend. The tips from the drunk, hungry fools allow me to have the majority of the week off, not that I actually do anything on my days off. But if I want to, it's an option. If I leave The Diner with anything less than $200 in tips in my pocket on a Saturday morning, it's a surprise. Rent, along with all my other bills, in addition to gifts for Jacqui doesn't come cheap.

Just after I moved into my apartment, I found my job. They weren't looking for someone for overnights—especially an eighteen-year-old girl—but I offered, more like begged, and after a few weeks they added me to the rotation. The rule was, and still is, I wouldn't be left alone, no matter what night it was, unlike the older servers. Although, no one is left alone on the weekend overnights.

My bosses, the owners of The Diner, are just as likely to come in drunk as the patrons, particularly on party nights. I'm pretty sure they decided to open a diner when they were in college and looking for a place to satisfy the drunk munchies at four in the morning. Since the bars in Buffalo don't close until four, I'm usually busy throughout my whole shift.

The only shitty thing about my job that I can come up with is the horrendous "diner" uniform I have to wear. It's a pale blue dress trimmed in black piping, has my name on the left just above my tit, and "The Diner" is written in script across the back. It's the most ridiculous thing to wear around drunk people and food.

Last night a table full of guys ordered French fries smothered in gravy, and they thought it would be fun try to play catch across the table. I got caught in the cross fire while attempting to stop an all-out food fight from starting. Thank god it was nearly four thirty when they came in, so I didn't have to spend hours in my gravy-soaked dress. The crappy part was coming home and pretreating it so I wouldn't have any stains. I refuse to spend another dime on uniforms when it's the customers' fault I'm always a fucking mess.

When I rolled in the driveway at just about five in the morning, the last thing I wanted to do was laundry, but if I didn't, not only would the gravy leave a stain, but the smell would never leave the fabric. After spending a good half hour scrubbing the brown mess out of my dress, I was satisfied that it had lightened enough that I could throw it in the machine and hope for it to come out completely.

That was just about ten hours ago, and quite honestly, I'm surprised I slept that long for the second night in a row. Now I have to drag my ass out of bed, get something to eat, then get ready to go spill my guts to Jacqui.

Hauling myself up, I swing my legs off the bed, then I shuffle across the carpet. The build up of static electricity makes me zap my toes on the metal cover separating the rug from the linoleum kitchen floor, and I nearly jump through the roof.

"Son of a bitch, why do I do that every fucking day?" I hop across the room and dump myself in a chair so I can rub my poor electrified tootsies. "Stupid metal cover thingies. One of these days, I'm going to rip your ass right off the floor."

When I get my bearings back, I head to the cupboard above my sink, grab the biggest clean bowl I have, and reach for the box of Cocoa Flakes on top of the fridge. I fill the bowl almost to the top, then slosh in milk so fast that a good amount of flakes fall over the side of the bowl. I just pick them up and throw them back in with the rest. As I'm getting ready to lift the spoon to my lips for my first bite, I hear the door at the bottom of my stairs squeak open. Elaine must be about to try to make a trip up the stairs.

After throwing the spoon on the table, I stomp over to the door, throw the lock, and pull the wooden beast open with a thud. Before I yell, "Elaine, if you're even thinking about coming up here, I'm going to beat you!"

"It's okay. Gran-ma sent me up to check on you. Are you all right?" Izach looks at me with concern on his face.

"Huh?" I think for a second while focusing on his face. "Oh, I'm fine. Just zapped my toes on the metal thing between the living room and kitchen."

"Okay, is there a reason the metal cover is electrified?"

"Static electricity. I'd just gotten out of bed and was shuffling my feet across the carpet."

"Well, as long as you're okay and nothing is shooting sparks that shouldn't be—"

"I'm fine." I want to end this awkward conversation, so I back into my apartment. "I need to get ready for work."

"All right, I just wanted to make sure you were okay." Izach follows my lead and backs down the stairs.

"I'm fine."

"Have a good night at work," Izach calls over his shoulder just before he opens the downstairs door.

Shutting my own door, I lean my forehead against the wood. "What the shit. Could I sound more stupid? 'I shuffle my feet across the carpet.' Durh, I'm such a dumbass!"

Izach

"Is she all right?" Gran-ma asks from the rocking chair closest to the door to her unit.

"She's fine, just some static electricity from shuffling across the floor." I take a breath and wait to see what's going to fly out of Gran-ma's mouth next. "Any other way I can embarrass myself in front of Sara before she heads to work today?"

"Why are you embarrassed?"

"Gran-ma, clearly she was fine. You didn't hear her fall, so I'm not sure why you had to send me up there?" I lean against the railing in front of her.

"Because you haven't talked to her since the night you got in."

"So? It's not like we're dating, I wouldn't even call us friends." I throw my hands out to the side. "She's my tenant. Well, technically she won't be until next Wednesday, but that's just a formality."

"I'm sorry that I'm just trying to make sure my grandson and a young woman who means a lot to me are close before I move across the country."

"It's not your job to meddle in Sara's life. It's bad enough you meddle in mine and I can't stop you because you're my gran-ma."

"I'm not meddling in either of your lives. I'm just making sure you take care of each other when I'm gone."

"It's meddling, Gran-ma, and you have to stop. If Sara and I end up friends, or even something more, it'll be on our own terms, not yours." I stare at her pouting for a minute. "Now, I'm going to work on this yard, since I know Sara isn't sleeping anymore."

"Fine, I'll just sit here and mind my own business."

Ignoring her comment, I place a kiss on her soft, sagging cheek. I run down the stairs and head for the shed to get the lawnmower. While I'm pushing the mower down the driveway to cut the front yard, Sara rounds the corner of the house, wearing a blue uniform dress. She looks so ridiculous, it's cute. I smile but don't say anything as she folds herself into her car and cranks the engine, bringing the rust bucket to life. I'm kind of surprised the car runs as well as it does, since I think she has just about the same amount of duct tape as paint on it. She backs out the driveway, stopping at the end, and looks back at me with a smile before she pulls away onto the street.

CHAPTER 8

Sara

The lot at Jacqui's office is nearly empty when I pull in, as it usually is on a Friday evening. I'm pretty sure she's the only one in the building with office hours past five on Friday evening, which is probably just for me, although she's never said that. I park in the first row, then cross the lot to the door. Heading right to the elevator, I hit the up button and step back, not knowing if the car will be full of people rushing to start their weekend. Once the last person clears out of the elevator, I get in and hit the button for the third floor.

In Jacqui's office lobby, I notice the lights have been dimmed and the ever-bubbly Jill isn't sitting behind the sliding-glass window. Regardless, I write my name on the waiting list. As I'm setting the pen back in the holder, a knock at the window makes me jump. I look up to see Jacqui waving for me to come in. When I swing open the door that separates the waiting room from the inner offices, Jacqui's standing at the corner.

"Hey, where's the gatekeeper?"

"Jill?" She sounds slightly confused.

"Uh, yeah, Jill. Did she go home early or something?" I follow Jacqui toward her office.

"Yeah, she's heading out of town for the weekend and wanted to hit the road before traffic got too bad."

"Good for me. I didn't have to put up with her nasty looks."

"Sara, maybe if you were a little more pleasant to her, she wouldn't be so cold to you." She holds the door open for me to pass through.

"Maybe. It's too bad we'll never find out." I put a gift card on Jacqui's desk, then cross the room and take my usual spot on her leather couch.

"Well, I'm glad to see your mood has changed since Wednesday."

I look at where Jacqui has taken a seat in her usual chair. "What are you talking about? I'm in a fantastic mood! I've managed to make an ass of myself several times this week—once that you witnessed, even more that you didn't—and now I'm here after yet again making an ass of myself. All in all, I would say it's been a grand week." I throw my arm over my eyes.

"I'm taking it things haven't gotten better with Elaine and her grandson?"

"Izach, and not really, although I did manage to squeeze out a smile for him as I backed out of the driveway. If he had actually talked to me, he may have seen the drool hanging off my lip."

"Um, okay. Why's that?"

"He was cutting the grass. With no shirt on." I hold my hands up in front of my face. "I mean really, when a guy looks as good as he does with clothes on, it's almost indecent when he doesn't have them on." I drop my arm back over my eyes.

"So you're attracted to him. What's the big deal?"

"The big deal is I can't be attracted to him! I don't date. I don't want to date. I'm perfectly miserable being alone. I don't need to drag some hot guy down with me."

"What makes you think you would drag him down?"

"Are you asking as my friend or my therapist?" I almost mumble. I don't want to know her answer.

She taps her pen against the side of her tablet. "Considering I am a therapist and we're here, that's what I'm asking as."

"Fine, because you're a therapist, I guess I'll answer. I don't have any happiness left in me. Most of it was taken by Trent, and the rest was taken by my parents. I'm not sure I know how to be happy anymore—it's been so long since I've felt that way."

"Sara, you can't really believe that?" Jacqui sits back in her chair and raises her pen to her mouth. She chews on pens during sessions because she can't smoke.

"I do. I don't know what happiness is anymore. I remember what it was, but I haven't felt it since I was fifteen."

"I think you're wrong. I think you've found happiness in your relationship with Elaine, and that's why you're going to miss her so much."

"Elaine is a pain in my ass. Have I grown to care about her? Yes, because she took a chance on me when I had no one else." I take a cleansing breath so I won't cry. "She didn't have to, but she did. I am going to miss her. But I won't miss her trying to throw me and Izach together. She's been relentless since the minute he pulled up in front of the house."

"Maybe she's doing it because she doesn't want either of you alone, and she knows he might be good for you."

"How could she know that? She barely knows me."

"Sara, you've been living above her for five years. I'm sure she knows you, probably better than you think."

"Maybe you're right."

"I know I am. Now, time for some Izach homework." Jacqui sounds hopeful.

"Good Christ, I knew this was coming," I mumble. "Okay, hit me with your damn homework."

"I want you to talk to him, get to know him like you would a friend. Guys love to brag about themselves. I'm not asking you to tell him everything about you, but maybe start with what you do for work, ask him what he does. Just get to know him and give friendship a chance."

"He already knows where I work. When he was helping me with my light bulbs, we kinda talked about it a little. It was weird. I got all tongue-tied."

"What do you mean?" She pauses expectantly with her pen resting on her lips.

I turn my head and look at Jacqui. "I got all shy and shit. I can't seem to form a whole sentence when I'm talking to him."

"That's because you like him," she says. "It's normal, but push your fear aside and get to know him. It's not only your homework, but it's something that will make Elaine happy."

"Gah, you and Elaine, you're both pains in my ass!" I knife up into a sitting position and kick my legs off the side of the couch—not caring that I'm wearing a dress—so I'm facing Jacqui. "What else is on the agenda for today?"

"We need to talk about group on Wednesday. It's been a really long time since you've reacted that way to telling your story. What happened?"

"It was that girl. When I looked up, she was staring at me, and all I could see was the emptiness in her eyes. It freaked me out, and I couldn't shake it. That, and her mom was with her. Her mom believed her. It's just not fair." I tuck my chin into my chest and take a couple deep breaths.

"Did you cut when you got home?"

"Way to be blunt, Jacqui, and no, I didn't. I told you I didn't when we talked that night."

"Yeah, but I couldn't see your face to see if you were being truthful."

Rolling my eyes at her lack of trust, I give her what she wants. "Well, I didn't really have time to, considering Elaine was practically up my stairs two minutes after I got home."

"Did she see you crying?"

"No, I tripped, and apparently the house shook like an earthquake was rolling through Buffalo."

"Despite your fall, I'm glad to hear you didn't end up doing it."

"I told you I was going to make another tattoo appointment."

"I know. Even though it's not the same thing, you're using it as a cover, and I'm still not comfortable with that decision. Did you make an appointment?" Concern is evident in Jacqui's voice.

"No, I didn't have time."

"Are you going to?"

"I don't think so, not right now. I'm feeling better."

"Good. I want you to get tattoos not because you're trying to cover your internal pain, but because you want to add to the beautiful ink you already have." She stares at me for a minute. She looks at my left wrist where I have three rubber bands instead of bracelets. "How about the rubber-band therapy?"

"They're there, but I haven't used them in a while."

"That's really good. I'm proud of you."

"Well, gee thanks. Are you proud enough to give me the night off of work and go in my place?"

"Not that proud." She chuckles. "We're almost out of time. What are your plans for the weekend?"

"I have to work tonight and tomorrow, but I have Sunday and Monday off, so I might lay out in the sun for a while, if the weather's nice."

"Sounds like a relaxing plan. You know I'm here if you need me."

"Don't you ever get tired of being on call all weekend?"

"See, that's where I turn into your friend. I don't make myself available for all of my patients." Jacqui tosses her pen, then her tablet on the table, and moves to stand.

"Aww, we really are friends! I knew deep down inside it had to be true!"

"Okay, smartass, get out of my office so I can start my weekend and you can go earn that moolah."

Standing, I click my heels together and salute Jacqui. "Yes, sir!"

She rolls her eyes as I giggle.

"Want me to wait and walk out with you?" I ask.

"If you don't have to go to work right away, I'd like that."

"Nah, I've got, like, an hour before I have to be there."

I pull open her door and lean against the jamb while Jacqui packs her bags and straightens up her desk. After both her arms are loaded, I flip the light switch. We walk through the halls quietly, and Jacqui stops to lock the main door. In the parking lot, we stop at the curb and wish each other a good weekend. Jacqui reminds me of my homework, and I roll my eyes at her. I walk to my car but keep an eye on her as she moves to hers. We come to a stalemate when it's time to leave, so I throw my beater in gear and head toward the exit, Jacqui following not far behind me.

Sara

I bang on the back door of The Diner and wait for one of the cooks to come let me in. I'm not really sure who it'll be, but I'm sure they'll bitch about doing it. I take a couple steps back to make sure the door isn't thrown open into my face—it's happened before. Of course, that would get me out of work tonight, but I'd lose out on my biggest night of tips. After I bang on the door again, someone finally sends it flying by my face.

"Hey, Miguel," I say.

"You couldn't use the front door? Had to wait for me to stop what I was doing and come let you in? Can't you see we're busy?"

"Can it, Miguel, you're not busy. Your shift doesn't start until mine does at eight. We still have another half hour, so stop giving me shit."

"Such a big fighting attitude for such a small, little, white girl."

"Whatever. Get out of my way. I want to get something to eat before I start." I push past him and pray I was right about him starting at the same time as me, or else I'll be cooking my own dinner.

After dumping my bag or purse—whatever you want to call it—in my locker against the back wall of the kitchen, I head out to the floor to grab a seat and get some food. Before I push through the swinging door, I peek through the round window and see Cheryl, my partner in crime for the evening, sitting at the bar counter. She's got a drink but no food, so I decide to grab the seat next to her.

"Hey, Sara!" she calls as soon as I push through the door. "Did he give you shit?" She nods toward the kitchen where Miguel's head can be seen through the pickup window.

"Of course. He's such a grumpy pain in the ass. I'm sure he's going to make our night just as happy as can be."

"I bet. You getting something to eat?"

"Yes, I'm starving. Is Jen on now?"

"Yeah, she just bounced by before you came out. Going to refill some coffee, then she can take our orders."

Cheryl and I each pig out on a cheeseburger and fries with a chocolate shake before our shifts start. It's a Friday, so we serve a constant stream of drunk people until four in the morning. Cheryl, Miguel, and I all get off at the same time, and regardless of his attitude problem, Miguel always waits to walk us to our cars and make sure they start. I roll into the driveway at just about four thirty. Not thinking about

Izach sleeping below me, I run up the stairs, tear through the door, and slam it behind me. After a quick shower, I set my alarm to do it all over again that night.

CHAPTER 9

Izach

It's Sunday afternoon, and I haven't seen Sara since Gran-ma made me go check on her after she shocked her toes. I'm starting to feel kind of obsessed with her—maybe because Gran-ma talks about her nonstop and I don't have any friends in the area. Although, I did find out that a couple of my buddies from school are now living in Buffalo, so we've planned to get together soon.

I do know that Sara isn't working today or tomorrow because Gran-ma has her schedule written on the dry erase board on the fridge. I don't know what's worse: that Gran-ma practically knows her every move, or that I'm paying attention so I can run into her. This morning, just like the morning before, she stomped up the stairs and woke me before six o'clock, something I plan to bring up when I see her.

In an attempt to keep busy, I've decided to clean out the gardens surrounding the house. At first glance, they don't look too bad, but up close, I can tell they haven't been touched in years. Thankfully, the last time Gran-ma was able to work in them, she laid down garden plastic and it managed to stay in good condition. I worked in the front of the house until lunch; now I'm heading to the backyard.

Pushing the wheelbarrow full of weeds I pulled in the front, along with shovels and my drenched shirt, I head out back. Rounding the corner of the house, I stop in my tracks.

"Sara," I whisper, unable to move.

I run my eyes over her, taking in the small black-and-blue bikini covering very little of her body. Her flip-flops are hanging off her feet in a way that indicates she might be sleeping. I can't tell though, because large dark sunglasses cover her eyes. Her right arm is tucked up behind her head while her left arm is lying across her stomach. She's got tattoos, lots of them, covering most of her left arm and a good portion of her right forearm. I see more on her leg and one going up her right side.

Her right arm moves and she snaps up into a sitting position, pulling out an earbud. Without removing her sunglasses, she turns her head toward me. "Hey."

"Uh, hi. I didn't know you were up yet."

"Yeah, I got up a little while ago, and I decided to come take advantage of the sun. What are you doing?"

"Cleaning out the gardens." I lift the wheelbarrow, push it over by her chair, and drop it again. "Were you sleeping?" I feel as though I'm grasping at things to ask her just to keep her talking.

"I must have dozed off. It's probably a good thing you woke me, or I might have fried."

"We wouldn't want that." I drop to my knees in front of the garden beside Sara. For a minute, I think she's looking at me, but I can't tell with her eyes hidden. "Do you have sunscreen on those tattoos?"

"Yeah, I'm kind of psycho about the color, so I slather it on anytime I'm out. What about you?"

"Yeah, Gran-ma freaked when I took my shirt off and threw me the bottle she had on the porch. She watched to make sure I didn't miss a spot."

"Typical Elaine, always making sure everyone is safe from the sun. I'm actually surprised she hasn't come out to check on me yet. I saw her peeking through the window shade about ten minutes ago."

"This is nice," I remark about the two of us talking.

"What?" Sara leans back in her chair, hooking her arm back around the top.

"Us talking, instead of dancing around each other with one-word comments."

"Oh, yeah, sorry about that. I'm not really much of a talker, especially with people my own age. But it's my homework, so I thought I'd give it a try."

"Your homework is to talk to me?" I sit back on my knees and raise my brows at her.

"Um, okay, maybe I should have kept that to myself, but I'm trying, so things might come out of my mouth that don't really make sense to you. But they make sense to me, so just ignore them or go with it," she rambles.

Chuckling, I wipe my forearm across my brow, "Okay, I guess we'll just go with it?"

"Sounds good to me. Do you want some help?"

"Only if you want to."

"Sure, let me grab a pair of old shorts to throw on and maybe find something to kneel on." Sara swings her legs to the side and stands, then wrinkles her nose at me kneeling in the dirt.

"Gran-ma has this garden pad thing in the garage you can kneel on. I'll get it while you go get changed."

"Thanks, be back in a minute."

Sara

Pretending to jostle myself awake, I lift my sunglasses so Izach can see my eyes. As he keeps appraising my body, Izach tells me he's going to work on getting the gardens cleaned up. Keeping my "homework" in the back of my mind, and apparently letting it slip through my lips, I offer to help him, but there's no way in hell I'm going to kneel in the dirt—or touch it. So I'm running up to my apartment to grab not only an old pair of shorts but also the pair of garden gloves I bought on a whim because they were cute. Forgoing a shirt, with my gloves in my hand, I skip—yes, skip—back downstairs and out my front door, where I run right into Elaine.

"Hey," I say, slightly out of breath.

"Where you running off to?" she asks me with a smirk and one of her eyebrows raised.

"You know exactly where I'm going, so don't pretend you don't, and don't make anything more of it than it is." I bring my hands to my hips.

"I didn't say anything. Oh, but I wanted to make sure you're going to be here for dinner tomorrow night?"

"I should be. I have my normal appointment at four thirty, but I'll be home by six. Why? What's going on?"

"I'm making dinner."

"You make dinner every night. What's so special about tomorrow?"

"It's the last time I'll be able to have dinner with you before I leave. Izach's mom will be here on

Tuesday night, and we're leaving Wednesday morning."

My breaths start to come a little faster, but I try to keep control so Elaine can't tell I'm freaking out. "I didn't realize you were leaving so soon."

"Well, it takes three days to get there if you drive straight through, which we aren't. We're taking a week to drive across the country. We'll get to Arizona on the 27th, spend a few days with family, then I'll move into my new place on July 1st. It's too bad you're working on Tuesday. I'd love for you to meet my daughter."

"Wow, I'm still stuck on the fact you're leaving in a few days."

I know Elaine can see that I'm scared, because she touches my forearm, then wraps her hand around my wrist and gives me a reassuring squeeze. "You'll be fine, and you can call me whenever you need me. Just think, now you have someone to visit when you need to get away from the winter weather."

"I know, but I'm going to miss you." I sniffle even though I'm fighting it. I know tears are gathering in the corner of my eyes.

"We're not doing this now, Sara. We still have today, all day tomorrow, and most of the day on Tuesday to spend together. You go help Izach, and I'll bring the two of you some iced tea, okay?"

"Yeah," I say softly, and she lets go of my arm.

Elaine turns away and disappears inside, where I'm sure she's going to get the iced tea started. After I give my head a shake, I unglue my feet from where they became stuck to the porch and head to the backyard. I started to run when I hit the pavement, then I all-out sprinted to get back around the house.

Maybe this way I won't look as if I was on the verge of crying.

Rounding the corner, I see Izach has moved my chair to the center of the yard, then moved the wheelbarrow to where it was. He's kneeling at the edge of the garden, pulling weeds and throwing them over his shoulder as he goes. The garden mat is right next to him. I pick it up and moved about five feet away. I figure if I left it there, we'd end up getting in each other's way.

"Where are you going?" he asks.

"Just down here. This way we won't run into each other as we move down."

"Oh, okay, I thought it was because you thought I smelled."

"How would I know if you smelled? I just got out here, and you were standing really far away before I went to change." I'm kind of snotty sounding.

"You okay?"

"Yeah, I'm fine. Why?" I ask as I drop to my knees and pull on my gloves.

"I don't know. You just seem a little tense, maybe upset."

"I'm good." I bend over the garden to remove the weeds blocking the light from the flowers. When I can't tell what's a flower and what's a weed, I sit back on my knees. "Do you know if there are actually flowers growing in this garden, or are they all weeds?"

"Not sure. I'm just pulling everything that doesn't have a flower on it. We can always run to the store and get some to plant when we finish."

I shrug one shoulder and lean back into the garden.

A few minutes of silence go by before Izach talks again. "Do you wanna play a game?"

"I thought we were weeding the garden?"

"We can play a game while we weed."

"Not sure I'm following. What kind of game can you play while weeding the garden?" I ask.

"How about twenty questions?"

"How about no. I'm not really comfortable with sharing a lot."

"That's okay. We can keep it general, nothing too personal."

I stop weeding and look at Izach, who is sitting on his knees and looking at me. "You're gonna have to give me an example."

"Well, to start, how old are you?" he asks.

"I'm twenty-three, not that I can believe Elaine didn't share that with you already."

"You're right, she did, but that's the kind of question we can ask each other. You okay with that?"

I shrug. "Yeah, that'll work for me. How old are you?"

"I'm twenty-five. Actually my birthday was in May, so I just turned twenty-five before I graduated. My turn. Do you want to go to college?"

"Maybe someday when I have the money I might get my high school equivalency diploma, then I can go to college. But right now, that's not an option for me."

"You dropped out of high school?"

"That's two questions, and yes, I dropped out of school. No, I'm not telling you why. My turn. Why become a teacher?"

"Ah, so Gran-ma told you more about me than I thought. Okay, ever since I was little, I always had a thing for teaching. When the neighborhood kids got together to play a game, I was always the one who stepped up to make sure everyone knew the rules and how to play. I guess you could say I was born to be a teacher. My turn—"

"Not so fast, mister! You asked two questions and I answered them, so I get another. Why in the world would you move to Buffalo when you could stay in Charlotte and not have to put up with snow?"

He laughed. "Well, not only is the pay better in New York, but this is where I learned to be a teacher, so it felt right to come back here. Why do you work overnights?"

"I already told you. Drunk people are stupid, they tip good, and they can be entertaining," I finish with a laugh.

"I know it's your turn, but that doesn't really answer my question. Why overnights? It's not like you have school or anything during the day."

"It's just easier. I don't do people well, so I choose to be around them when they're not in their right frame of mind. My turn, and again I get two questions." I stop to give myself a minute to think. "What are you planning on doing for the rest of the summer? Are you going to work?"

"I'm not sure yet. Right now I don't have to work because I don't have any bills, and I have a lot of money in savings. So to answer your second question, if I get too bored, I'll find a summer job. If not, I'm going to enjoy my time off and relax." He stops pulling weeds and sits back.

When his eyes don't leave me, I sit back too.

"What about if I help you get your equivalency diploma?" he asks.

I look down at my hands as I twist my fingers together. "I don't know about that. It's been a long time since I've done the whole school thing."

"True, but I'll help you. It'll be like riding a bike. Even though it's been a long time, learning never leaves you." He waits, assessing my reaction. "How about I just get the info? We can look it over, and you can decide after that."

After a minute of trying to calculate his seriousness, I relent. "Fine, but I'm not making any promises." I go back to working on the weeds farther down the garden.

"If you don't mind me asking, how did you get a job without a high school degree?"

"I'm a waitress, Izach. Most of the people I work with are illegals who don't speak much English. They weren't too choosey when they hired me." I look over to see him still sitting on his knees and looking at me.

"I'm sure that's not true. They must have seen something in you."

"Don't you have some weeds to pull?" I throw a weed at him over my left shoulder.

"I'm working on it."

Izach goes back to volleying questions, and a few minutes later, Elaine appears at the corner of the house with two glasses of iced tea. Considering the ice is half melted, I'm sure she's been there much longer than she let on, but I don't say anything. Since we're almost done with the garden running along the back of the house, we keep our break short and get back to it.

Izach

We're almost done cleaning out the gardens, and I'm not ready for it to be over. As Sara moves farther away, I follow her, asking questions as we go. After we talked about her getting her high school equivalency, I moved on to more simple questions: favorite food, favorite color, favorite flower. What she didn't realize was that I was making a mental list for future reference, particularly about her food and flower choices.

With one knee in the dirt and the other bent up in front of me, I work to clear weeds next to the house's foundation. I've stopped looking at Sara because every time I do, I stop working and she ends up getting more done and moves again. All of a sudden, she screams at the top of her lungs. I'm not ready for it and almost fall over. Managing to get both feet under me, I push off the ground, moving back as she flies toward me. She launches herself into the air when she's about two or three steps away.

I grab her as her legs wrap around my waist. Thank god I'm paying attention so I don't fall on my ass with her on top of me, not that I would mind. She's still screaming and wiggling around so much that I have to take a couple steps back to make sure we don't go down anyway.

Sara finally calms enough for me to understand that she's saying, "Snake!"

Holding on to her ass, I walk us over to where she was weeding and see a small garden snake in the back, next to the house. "Sara, calm down. It's just a garden snake. They don't bite."

"How the hell do you know that?" She's still freaking out and hugging my neck tighter. "Get me away from it!"

"Okay, we'll move over by the fence. Is that far enough?" I walk toward where I started earlier, trying my hardest not to burst out laughing.

"No, the next state still wouldn't be far enough."

A noise catches my attention, and I look at the house to see Gran-ma looking out the window with a smirk. The old lady is totally enjoying this. I shake my head and move so we're right next to the fence with the wheelbarrow blocking the snake from getting to us.

"It's okay." I try to soothe her with words. "I'll get rid of it when you've calmed down." I feel her breathing change as if she hasn't realized she jumped in my arms. "You're okay. It's not going to bite you." I keep talking as her weight shifts and she pulls back from my chest.

"Izach," she says softly, "you can put me down." She looks deep into my eyes while her fingers loosen on my neck. I feel her thumb move up and down across my skin.

"You sure? I don't want to let you go if you're not ready." The truth is I don't want to put her down at all. She feels pretty damn good in my arms.

"I'm sure, and you need to go make the snake disappear." She moves one hand from the back of my neck and runs her thumb down my jaw. "Thank you for not laughing at me, and for saving me."

"You're welcome, but I have to admit, I kind of laughed a little when I figured out what you were running from." I smile as the corners of her eyes crinkle with a smile that doesn't actually reach her lips.

"I didn't notice, so I'll let that go. Now go get the damn snake!" she demands.

I let my hands slip over her ass to her lower back as she slides down my front. When her feet hit the ground, we're standing with our bodies pressed together as she looks up the couple of inches that separate our faces, and I gaze down at her.

We're both stuck, not moving, until I break the moment. "I'm gonna put the snake in the neighbors' garden."

Sara nods and a soft okay slips through her lips. Reluctantly I let her go, and she moves a couple feet away as I step by her to move the snake. After I get it in my hands, I look over at Sara. She's turned her head so she doesn't have to look at the beast that threatened her life. Biting the inside of my lips, I try really hard not to laugh at how cute she is, then I shake my head and wander around the corner of the house. Gran-ma is standing at the top of the porch stairs with the same smirk she had when she was spying on us through the window.

"It's a good thing you were out there to save her," Gran-ma says with humor in her voice. "I'm not sure she would have made it without your strong arms."

"Gran-ma! Really? I think you need to stop before Sara hears you and you embarrass her."

"Nothing to be embarrassed about when you find a hero who rescues you from a snake."

"Christ," I whisper as I set the snake in the neighbors' flowers. "Stop, Gran-ma, I mean it."

She holds up her hands in surrender.

Stomping past the porch, I ignore her and head back to make sure Sara didn't hear us and she's still okay—not that I mind being her hero.

CHAPTER 10

Sara

Tipping my face up into the spray, I let the hot water wash over me. I'm still kicking myself in the ass for acting like such a freak about the snake. God, I'm such a little girl! I've gone over the whole scenario in my head about a million times since we finished up in the backyard and I decided I needed to escape and shower. Now I'm wishing I wasn't so ridiculous!

Izach and I were talking, having an actual conversation—granted it was mostly just going back and forth asking dumb questions, but it was still a conversation. I almost felt like running upstairs and texting Jacqui to let her know I had completed my homework. Then I reached for a handful of weeds and saw something move. After that, I went into a full-on freak-out that included not only running away but jumping into Izach's arms.

"God, I'm such a freakin' idiot!" I slap one, hand then the other on my forehead and squeeze as if that will take my stupidity away. "Who does that? God, it was just a fuckin' garden snake! And I jumped into his arms! I'm such an asshole!"

There's no coming back from being so ridiculous, so I just have to hope he doesn't think I'm some stupid girl who's scared of bugs and horror movies, because I'm not. I love horror flicks, especially Elli Roth movies like Hostel. The gorier, the better. I'm not sure whether I'm thinking of ways to convince Izach or myself that I'm not a wuss. It's not as if he acted any differently toward me afterward. Why am I worried about what he thinks anyway?

Because we were getting to know each other—well, as much as I let someone know me—and I did agree to think about getting my equivalency diploma with his help. That's a pretty big step.

I kill the spray of water, then reach around the curtain to grab my towel. After running it over my body, I wrap the fabric around my chest and tuck it in like a dress. Stepping out of the bathtub, I grab my small towel from the rack and go to town on my hair, which still looks like shit. I really need to run to the beauty supply store and grab some hair dye soon—as in today. It could be my excuse later when Elaine insists I spend more time with Izach, because I know that's coming. I saw her wheels turning when I walked by her on the porch. Jacqui thinks Elaine knows more about me than I think, but I also know more about her, and she's up to something.

For now, I head to my bedroom and rummage through my dresser for a pair of shorts and a flowy off-white peasant-style top. I run the brush through my hair to get the snarls out, then I finger-comb it a couple times to make it messy. I can't really make this mop look any better. Not that I'm trying to look good. But I've spent the whole day looking like a bum and I never have a reason to dress nice, so I might as well go for it. So I add some eyeliner and mascara.

After I slide my feet into my flip-flops, I bounce back down the stairs and find Elaine in her usual rocking chair. Izach is sitting across from her on the railing, sporting a clean white T-shirt with tan cargo shorts. He's clearly fresh from the shower too. I give him a small smile before I sit in the chair opposite Elaine, bringing my right leg up under my butt as I sit.

"Hey." Izach's eyes follow my body. "We're thinking about getting a pizza and maybe some wings for dinner. You in?"

"I could eat pizza." I look over at Elaine, whose giant smile makes her soft wrinkles more prominent. Looking back at Izach, I say, "I don't do hot wings though, so if that's what you're getting, I'll get a small order of medium."

"I was going to get half hot, half mild. Gran-ma doesn't eat hot wings either."

"That works for me. I can always add some hot sauce if they're too bland."

"There's hot sauce in the fridge. I'll get it while you two go pick up the food," Elaine joins the conversation. "Do you mind stopping for some pop too? All I have to drink is iced tea, and I like a nice cold glass of Pepsi with my pizza."

"Sure, Gran-ma, I can stop at the corner store. Sara, do you want Pepsi too, or something different?"

"Pepsi's—"

"She's going with you, honey. She can pick out her own," Elaine says.

"Why don't we find out if Sara wants to come before you assume she is?" Izach almost reprimands Elaine, and I giggle under my breath. He turns to me. "You don't have to go with me, but if you want to, you can."

I take a few seconds before I give him an answer. "Uh, I guess I can go. Do you mind if we stop at the bank so I can deposit my tips from this weekend?"

"No, I don't mind, but you'll have to tell me where it is. I'm not really familiar with the area yet."

"That's a great idea!" Elaine cuts in again. "Why don't you two go now so Sara can show you around a bit?"

"Gran-ma," Izach almost growls.

"Don't Gran-ma me. It makes sense. She's lived here for five years and knows where everything is. You can kill two birds with one stone."

"You know, if we don't give in, she's going to keep pushing it," I say, trying to calm Izach—who's getting a little bent out of shape—down.

"See, Sara's a smart girl. She knows I'm relentless."

"Sara, only if you want to, I don't want to force you into something you don't want to do."

"I don't mind. Elaine, why don't you call and order so we know how much time we have? I'm going to run upstairs and grab my bag."

"Okay, honey. Izach, run and get me the menu and the phone please?"

"Sure, Gran-ma." Izach looks at me one more time before he jumps off the rail and heads inside.

I swing my door open, then run up the stairs. I'm not really sure what I'm doing, going for a ride with Izach to get pizza, but I'm trying to think of him as a friend. Like how I would think of Jacqui if she wasn't my therapist. So what if he's a guy? I can have a guy friend. It's just an added bonus that he's good-looking, and maybe I might have a little crush on him.

I cross my living room to the futon, where I threw my bag this morning when I got home from work. I sling the handle around my neck and over my chest, then I go into the bathroom to give myself a once-over before I head back downstairs to meet Izach.

Izach

I'm not sure what to think about what's going on today with Sara and me. First she spends the day with me in the garden, and now she's going to show me around before we get pizza. It almost as if she's done a complete one-eighty from the first couple of times I was around her. I'm not going to complain, but it's weird. I'm sure Gran-ma didn't convince her to hang out with me. I guess I should just be glad Sara's come out of her shell and wants to spend time with me. I can't say I don't have a thing for her I'd like to explore, especially after today, but I'm worried that I'll push her too far and she'll just stop talking to me.

The phone is on the cradle right above where Gran-ma keeps the takeout menus. I dig though the pile until I find the only pizza menu, then I grab the handset. Outside, Gran-ma hasn't moved from her rocking chair, so I hand her the phone and menu before taking my spot on the railing.

Without a word to me, she dials the number and places the order. I pay attention until she repeats forty minutes. That gives Sara and me almost an hour of alone time before we have to be there. Immediately I start to think of things for her to show me. The city isn't horribly big and I know where some of the things right around the house are, so I hope Sara has some suggestions.

"The pizza will be ready in forty minutes," Gran-ma says as I hear Sara's footfalls on the stairs. "That'll give Sara time to show you where the grocery store is, and maybe where she works."

"I know where The Diner is. You forget we went there for breakfast when I was visiting?"

"Oh, you're right, maybe I did forget. Anyway, she can still show you quite a few things. Maybe you two could pick up a movie or something to watch after dinner."

"Gran-ma," I say quietly so Sara won't hear, "you have to stop trying to force us together. I don't want to push her—"

"A movie would be okay," Sara interrupts me from the door.

"Sara, I don't want you to feel like Gran-ma is forcing you to do something you're not comfortable with," I say.

"I'm okay with it."

"See?" Gran-ma says. "Now go and get a movie. You can watch it down here or in Sara's apartment. Don't worry about me. I'm exhausted and heading to bed shortly after we eat."

I blow out a sigh. "Fine, we'll get a movie too." I stand and turn toward Sara. "You ready?"

"Lead the way."

Pulling my keys from my pocket, I bounce down the stairs and peek over my shoulder to make sure Sara's following me. I hit the locks on my Charger, but I don't go to the driver's side. Instead I open the door for Sara. I've never done that for a girl before, and I never wanted to until now. She gives me a small smile, then slides onto the seat. After shutting her door, I round the back of the car, deposit myself behind the wheel, and crank the engine. My car comes to life with quite a bit of noise, and out of the corner of my eye, I see Sara looking at me with wide eyes.

"What?" I ask.

"It sounds like my car when I start it, and mine's a piece of shit."

"This is a muscle car. They're supposed to sound like that. It's part of the appeal." I give her a smirk, then throw the car into reverse. Stopping at the end of the driveway, I look over at Sara. "Where to?"

"You can head toward Main Street. Pretty much everything you're going to need is over that way."

As we get farther away from the house, Sara shows me the cheap grocery store— where we stop at Redbox— the post office, and then the bank, where we stop so she can deposit her tips. Before we realize it, we've been driving for almost the full forty minutes. Since we're heading the wrong way, Sara has me turn into the parking lot of The Diner so we can head back toward the pizza shop to grab the food and drinks. She fights me on paying for the food, but gives in by stating she'll pay next time, which only makes me happy that there will be a next time.

When we turn into the driveway at home, I can see Gran-ma stand from her chair and head into the house. By the time we make it to the porch with our boxes, she has glasses and plates ready for us. We all grab a slice and a drink, then we take our usual chairs: Gran-ma by her door, Sara opposite her, and me on the railing with my feet kicked out in front of me.

To my surprise, Gran-ma doesn't ask about our trip or if we got a movie. I think she knows we're both going to do whatever she wants because we only have a couple more days with her. I'm not at all surprised when she finishes her slice of pizza and heads in the house instead of hanging out with Sara and me. I'm not sure if Sara even notices, but if she does, she doesn't say anything about it.

Sarah

Shit, shit, shit!

Clearly Elaine doesn't play around. I thought she was joking earlier when she said she would leave us alone after dinner. But sure enough, as soon as she finishes her pizza—one slice, I might add—she heads into the house without a word. Now Izach and I are sitting out here and picking at our food. Well, I'm picking at my food. He's outright eating, not speaking. I know I encouraged the whole movie thing earlier, but that was because Elaine is only going to be here for a few more days and I don't want to upset her. But now I'm not really sure what to do.

With a long, stringy piece of cheese hanging from between my thumb and index finger, I dangle it over my mouth and drop it in. I always eat pizza cheese first. Sometimes I don't even eat the crust. It's not really normal and I probably should have thought about the fact that I'm eating with someone who really doesn't know me before I brought out all of my weirdness. When I chew on the cheese, I look across the porch at Izach, who is staring at me with his mouth open.

"What? I like to eat the cheese first."

Apparently I've interrupted his thoughts, because he shakes his head before he responds. "Huh, nothing. I mean, okay."

"You okay?"

"Yeah, fine. This pizza's really good." Izach's face has become a nice, bright red.

"Okay."

"I mean, we don't have good pizza in Charlotte. Well, it's okay but not like this."

"So pizza is another reason you moved to Buffalo?"

"No, but maybe it should be. I'll have to add it to the list when people ask me why I moved here." He seems to have recomposed himself. "Um, so I guess Gran-ma wasn't kidding about leaving us alone."

"When does Elaine ever kid? She sets her mind to something and does everything in her power to make it happen, and apparently pushing us together is on her agenda."

"You caught that too?"

"Um, yeah, it's been obvious since day one." I purse my lips and look at him with my eyebrows raised. "I'm kind of glad she did though, because it would be really awkward for us when she leaves if we didn't get to know each other a little first."

"Right, if she hadn't introduced us, I'm not sure if I would have just come out and talked to you."

"That doesn't make sense. Why don't you think you would have talked to me?"

He turns red again. "Shit, I've talked myself into a corner, and now I have to either lie to you to make myself look like a dude or come clean and make myself look like a jackass."

"Look like a dude? What the hell does that mean?"

"I didn't want to say 'make myself look a man' because clearly I'm a man, so I said dude."

I smile at him. "I'm kind of glad I'm seeing your weird side tonight. Makes me feel a little less alone in the world."

"You're not weird. You're sweet and gorgeous, and you work hard to give yourself a life when you could have just given up."

"How do you know?" I ask, trying not to get upset with Izach.

"Know what?"

"That I could have given up."

"I don't, I'm just assuming."

After a minute, I decide to ask, "So why wouldn't you've talked to me?"

"Because sometimes I get shy around girls."

"You still don't make sense. You get shy around girls? How do you plan on being a teacher, or are you working at an all-boys' school?" I smirk because I know exactly what he means, but I want him to admit it.

"You are so not going to make this easy for me. No, I'm not working at an all-boys' school. I get shy around beautiful girls, girls I'm attracted to." Izach lets out a loud sigh and turns his head away from me.

"Look at me, Izach." I wait for him to turn his face toward me. "The first night we met—hell, the second day we saw each other—I couldn't get more than two words out when I was talking to you. I have the same problem."

"What, you can't talk around beautiful girls?" He shoots me a shit-eating grin.

"No, smartass, I think you're good-looking." I lift my hands in front of my face. "And I can't believe I just admitted that to you." Separating my fingers a little, I peek through them to see Izach smiling at me. "Stop smiling! I'm so embarrassed right now!"

"Don't be. I just admitted the same thing to you and I did it first, but you don't see me hiding."

Closing my fingers tight, I try not to look at him, but I hear his feet hit the porch and sense him getting close.

He wraps his fingers around my wrists and brings my hands away from my face. He looks directly into my eyes. "I'm glad you decided to get to know me, because I was afraid to push you too hard."

"What'd you mean?"

"I mean, I want to know you, and you weren't really giving me the opportunity. So when you started talking to me earlier today, I was happy you made that move." He lowers my hands to my lap and crouches in front of me.

"I wouldn't really call it a move."

"Call it what you want. I'm just glad you did it."

"What's going on here?" I ask, looking into his beautiful whisky eyes.

"Well, I'm pretty sure we just admitted to being attracted to each other, and now we're going to go watch a movie and get to know one another better. What'd you think about that?" His thumbs move back and forth over my pulse points.

"Okay." Honestly, that's probably the only word I could get to come out of my mouth.

CHAPTER 11

Sara

What the hell did I get myself into?

After admitting I have a thing for him, I invited Izach up to my apartment to watch the movie we picked up. I don't know if I'm ready for this, but being around him feels different. I usually feel uncomfortable and threatened by guys, but I don't feel that at all with Izach, and I'm not sure how to handle it. I only agreed to talk to him, and now I feel like this is so much more. I'm not sure how he got me to admit I liked him. Maybe it's because he admitted he's attracted to me too.

Well, he's probably done setting up by now because I'm stalling while I have my internal freak-out. I should've told him to come up in a little while, then I could text Jacqui. I need some pointers. I've never been alone with a guy in my apartment, and he wants to get to know me better! Other than what I've already told him, there really isn't much more to know. Okay, I'm lying to myself—there's a lot more to know—but I'm not willing to share that part of me. Jacqui's the only one, other than my parents and Trent, who knows about that part of my life.

This is so not a good idea!

I can't let him get any closer to me than he already has. I'm poison. Everything I touch turns to shit. I mean, even Jacqui! When I met her, she was a non-smoker, and now she's back to smoking—a lot. I can't ruin Izach. We can watch the movie and he can be my landlord, but it can't go any further.

Pulling up my big girl panties, I head back into the living room with the two glasses filled with ice. When I round the corner, I see Izach sitting on the far end of my futon with his legs spread out under the coffee table. The two-liter bottle of Pepsi is in front of him. I cross the room and set his glass on the table before I move to the other side of the futon and drop onto the cushion. After tucking my right foot under my butt, I reach for the TV remote and hit the play button.

"I can't wait to see this movie. I heard it's funny as shit," Izach says, breaking though my run-away thoughts.

"I hadn't heard of it until tonight."

"Seriously?"

"Yeah, I don't watch much TV. When I'm home, I'm sleeping. When I'm not sleeping, I read."

"Well, prepare to laugh until you pee! These guys are hilarious."

About five minutes into the movie, I have to agree with Izach—I haven't stopped laughing since the beginning credits ended. The story isn't that funny, but the actors play morons so well, I can't help but laugh at them. As the movie continues, I pull my other leg up and sit cross-legged, and Izach pulls his left leg up. Only a few inches separate our bodies, and while I'm trying to focus on the movie, I can't help but notice that he's inching closer to me.

"Do you think we can pause it for a minute? I wanna get a hoodie," I say.

"You're cold?" He takes his eyes off the TV and looks at me with his brows raised.

"A little." I reconsider the words as soon as they leave my mouth.

"Okay, yeah, go ahead and pause it."

After I hit the button, I toss the remote on the coffee table, then jump up and walk a little too fast toward my room. I glance back at Izach and notice his eyes following me. The first thing I do in my room, however, is snatch my phone off my nightstand and fire off a text to Jacqui.

Me: Um so Izach's in my apartment, we're watching a movie and I'm freaking the fuck out! HELP!!

Ditching my phone on the nightstand, I go to my laundry basket and dig to the bottom to get one of the hoodies I washed the other day. Just as I grasp the fabric and begin to pull it out, my phone goes off, vibrating across the wood. I cross my room to see what Jacqui's advice is.

Jacqui: Just go with it.

Me: WTF Jacqui! That doesn't help me!

Jacqui: Sara, you know what to do with a guy... If you like him then go for it! ;-)

Me: winkie face, really? Ugh, you're no help!

Jacqui: :-)

Giving up on Jacqui, I toss my phone back on my nightstand, pull on my hoodie, then head back to the living room. The first thing I notice is that Izach has moved closer to the center of the futon, which means that I'll have to practically touch him if I want to continue sitting with my legs crossed. Which I have to do so I don't look like I'm trying to get away from him.

"Better?" His eyes follow me as I cross the room.

"Yep." I plop down next to him and bring my legs back up under me.

Leaning forward, I snag the remote from the coffee table and hit the play button. I'm trying so hard not to notice how close Izach is and how I can feel the heat from his body. He's sprawled across the futon with his elbow next to my knee and his head right next to my left shoulder. I can't even watch the movie because I keep peeking at him from the corner of my eye. He's back to laughing and doesn't seem to notice how tense I've become.

Taking a deep breath, I kind of shake my shoulders and try to relax back into the cushion. This grabs his attention, and he looks at me, giving me a smile before he straightens and moves even closer, plastering his body to my side. He sits up and moves my knee up and over his leg, then doesn't even try to be sly about putting his arm around my shoulders. Don't guys usually do some awkward stretchy thing? This just seems kind of forward. I mean, the movie practically just started, and now we're going to sit like this for the rest of it? Izach obviously has no idea I'm spazzing out because he's right back to laughing at the dumb movie.

"Just go with it. Just go with it. Just go with it..." I say under my breath so he won't hear me. Stupid Jacqui and her damn homework!

Izach

The movie's coming to an end, and I finally feel the tension roll out of Sara's shoulders. She's been sitting unbelievably still since I put my arm around her, but she never fought it, so I stayed put.

The remote is still in her lap, so she picks it up and stops the movie, putting us in complete darkness. "Maybe I should have turned on the light before I did that." Her voice cuts through the silence, but she doesn't move, and I don't want to offer.

With my free arm, I blindly grab the remote from her hand and put it next to me. When her body doesn't tense further, I reach back over. But instead of reaching for her hand, I grab her chin and pull it toward me slowly. I have to turn my body a little so she doesn't get my cheek and I can look at her face. We're so close her nose brushes mine, and I feel a shiver rip through her body.

"Sara?" I whisper.

"Yeah?" She speaks just as softly.

"I'm going to kiss you."

"Okay."

Once I have the green light, I touch my lips to hers. My kiss is soft and quick, but I'm testing the waters. I don't want to go too fast and push her away. I pull away, and she lets out a dreamy sigh. I try to pull away farther, but she follows me.

"Can we do that again?"

Instead of answering, I touch my lips to hers again and move them slowly. She breathes heavily through her nose, then tentatively runs her tongue against my lower lip. I open and push my tongue back against hers, following it right into her mouth. Almost as soon as I start, I feel her pull back, so I let her go.

"Maybe we should turn on the light." She breaks away from me and stands.

Expecting the overhead light to go on, I put my hand over my eyes to shield them. I wait a few seconds, but nothing changes. "Sara?"

"Yeah?" Her voice is farther away than I expected, then the light in the kitchen goes on, sending a beam into the living room but not lighting the whole area.

"Oh, I was wondering where you went."

"I didn't want to blind you, and the light on my end table is burnt out."

"Another one?" I ask with a smile.

"Yeah, it blew last night sometime. I usually leave it on when I go to work, and when I got home this morning, it was out," she explains as she walks back into the living room.

"I can go get a bulb for you?"

"Nah, I can get one tomorrow morning." She sits on the futon, facing me with her legs crossed under her butt.

Drawing my leg up, I move so I'm facing her too. "Are you okay?"

"Yeah, why wouldn't I be?"

"I just thought because you pulled away... I don't want you to feel pressured."

She smiles. "I don't feel pressured. If I did, I wouldn't have asked you to kiss me again. I just can't do it with the lights off, and before you ask, no, I'm not going to explain. Not now. Maybe someday, but not now."

"It's okay, you don't have to. I just want to be sure you're good with it—I mean, with me kissing you—because I really want to do it again."

"Would a dude ask to do it again?" she teases.

"No, but a gentleman would." I move and take her lips again.

Sara slips her hands around my neck, threading her fingers into the hair at my nape. Mine go around her waist and pull her forward, turning her until her butt lands in my lap, as we share soft, half-open-mouth kisses.

My arms tighten around Sara's back and she wraps hers fully around my neck, bringing us as close as we can get. I deepen the kiss, sliding my tongue past Sara's lips. At the first touch, a small, almost-too-quiet-to-hear moan vibrates from her mouth into mine. I want to keep going, but that small sound brought my dick to life, and if I don't slow this down, in a minute, Sara will know it.

Pulling back a little, I slip my tongue out of her mouth but keep us pressed together. After a few drawn-out pecks, I pull back and look at her swollen lips, then into her dazed eyes. A wide smile crosses my face.

"Hey." Probably the dumbest thing I could say after a kiss that made me hard.

"Hi," she returns and beams at me. Her smile is beautiful and something I haven't seen much.

"I don't want to cut this short—trust me, not at all—but Gran-ma's kind of nosy, and considering most movies aren't this long, my guess is she'll be headed up your stairs soon."

She giggles. "I was going to make a joke about you having a curfew and your Gran-ma needing to come get you, but I know how Elaine is. Honestly I'm kind of surprised we haven't heard the door squeak open already."

"This is true. You know, she's been pushing to see this happen for a while. She started telling me about you before I even got the job here."

"Oh god, I'm not sure I wanna know what she said."

"Don't worry, it was all good, and you've more than proved she was right about everything." I push her hair out of her face and tuck it behind her ear. "What are your plans for tomorrow during the day?"

"I have an appointment tomorrow afternoon at four thirty, but before that, I'm free."

"How about we go walk around by the water? I haven't been down there in a long time, and Gran-ma said they've really built it up. We can get lunch."

"That sounds good."

"We can leave around noon so you don't get off your sleeping schedule, and I'll have you back by three."

"Perfect." She leans forward and presses her lips against mine again, then she pulls away smiling.

Sara moves off my lap, twisting so she's sitting facing forward next to me. Before I stand, I take her hand and use it to pull her up alongside me, then I cross the room to the door. I cup her face and place a few soft kisses on her lips.

"Good night, Sara," I say softly between kisses.

"Night."

I drop my hands and reach for the door handle. Pulling the door shut behind me, I listen for Sara to flip the lock before I head down the stairs. The door at the bottom squeaks open, and I head toward Gran-ma's— well, my—apartment. What I didn't expect was to see her sitting in the rocking chair right outside the door.

"Hey, what are you doing out here?" I ask as I go to lean against the rail in front of her.

"You didn't really think I was going to sleep?" she returns.

"No, but I also didn't think I'd find you sitting outside this late at night either."

"I'm glad I am, because now I know my job is done."

"What do you mean?"

"The look on your face as you walked through that door told me everything I needed to know."

"Gran-ma! Don't go jumping to conclusions. We just watched a movie." I roll my eyes.

"I'm sure that was all, honey. Did you kiss her good night?" she asks with raised brows.

"That's none of your business."

"Confirmed. Now I'm going to bed. I'm exhausted." Gran-ma lifts from her chair and moves to the door without another word.

I watch her for a minute, then I follow her, locking up behind me. Gran-ma retreats to her room, and I head to mine, thinking about the way Sara's lips felt and the beautiful smile I put on her face.

Sara

After Izach leaves, I throw the locks, then lean my head against the wood to listen to him walk down the stairs. At the squeak of the outside door, I move into my room to change and cuddle up for some late-night reading. The sound of voices floats through my window above the porch, and I realize Elaine pounced as soon as he walked out. A small giggle escapes my lips when I hear her trying to get information out of Izach, but thankfully he doesn't give in and offers a whole lot of nothing. Elaine isn't stupid though, and she goes in for the kill, asking him if he kissed me good night. Izach, being the gentleman he is, doesn't kiss and tell, but obviously his answer gives Elaine what she needs. She sounds satisfied with the little she got, and I hear them go into the house.

After throwing on my light sleep shorts and a tank top, I head across the living room to the bathroom, looking at the futon as I go. I can still feel Izach's lips, how it felt to have his tongue in my mouth, dancing and caressing mine, and his strong arms wrapped around my body. The best part is, I didn't get the urge to use him and move on. I'm actually kind of excited and looking forward to seeing where this might lead.

Flipping on the light in the bathroom, I stand in front of the mirror. The first thing I see is the flush of color on my cheeks. Touching my skin, I feel the warmth being with Izach left behind. I smile, then shake my head. I don't want to get my hopes up too much. I haven't had a boyfriend since I was fifteen, since before Trent ruined my life. But I don't let the bad thoughts take over. I want to fall asleep thinking about Izach and the way I feel when I'm around him.

I brush my teeth, then wash my face before I hit the light and head back to my room. Lying in bed, I grab my book from the nightstand and dive into the only romance I've allowed myself to have until now—maybe.

CHAPTER 12

Izach

It's a quarter after eleven, and I'm not sure if Sara is awake yet. I told her we wouldn't leave until noon, but I want to make sure she's up and getting ready. Filling a travel mug with coffee, I take off toward her apartment, passing Gran-ma, who is sitting on the porch with a devilish smile. Taking the stairs two at a time, I reach Sara's door in a couple seconds and tap on the wood twice. I hear her steps getting closer to the door just before she pulls it open with a confused expression.

"Hey, I'm not ready yet." She leans against the open door, trying to hide her barely covered body.

"It's okay. I made coffee; thought you might like a cup." I hand her the travel mug, which she accepts with a smile.

"Thank you, I was actually just getting ready to make some... I would ask you in, but I'm still in my pajamas."

"It's okay, I just wanted to bring you the coffee. Come down when you're ready."

"Okay, give me, like, a half hour and I'll be down, then we can take off a little early."

"Sounds good. I think we'll get lunch before we walk around."

"Works for me. I'm starving."

"See you in a bit." I turn and head back down the stairs.

After pushing through the door, I head right to the rail and stretch my hands over my head, grabbing the trim around the ceiling. I know Gran-ma's staring at me—I can feel her eyes burning a hole in my back.

"What?" I say and look over my shoulder at her.

"I talked to your mom this morning. She's coming in tonight instead of tomorrow."

"Why?" I'm surprised and a little annoyed, because I feel as though this is a ploy to get Mom to meet Sara.

Gran-ma frowns at me. "Because she won't get to see you for a while and wants to spend some time with both of us before I leave."

"Are you sure that's the only reason?"

"I'm not sure what you're getting at, but yes, that's the only reason."

"Good. I don't want Sara to feel ambushed just because you want Mom to meet her. You're the one who told me she doesn't have a relationship with her parents."

"It's not an ambush, Izach. Your mom's coming anyway; she just wants to come a day early. Not a big deal. And Sara will be fine, she doesn't hate all parents because she doesn't have a relationship with hers. She knows how to act around adults. It's not like I called her mom and invited her over."

Sighing, I turn fully toward Gran-ma and notice the sincerity in her eyes. "Okay, as long as you didn't ask Mom to come early because of what's going on with Sara and me."

"Speaking of that, what's going on between the two of you?"

"Gran-ma," I warn.

"You opened the door to that one."

"And I'm closing it. I'm going out to lunch. Do you want me to get you something on the way back?" I ask.

"No, I'll be good. Saving room for dinner."

"Right. Uh, do you wanna make me a list so I can stop at the grocery store and get what we need for dinner?"

"Already done. The list in on the counter under your car keys."

"Okay." I push off the rail and head in the house, stopping for the list first.

After picking up the list and my keys, I grab myself a travel mug of coffee and head back outside to sit with Gran-ma and wait for Sara. Instead of sitting on the rail, I sit in the other rocking chair and move back and forth while I drink my coffee. I had been contemplating looking for a landscaping job for the summer, but after last night, I'm considering a night job. After about ten more minutes of rocking silently with Gran-ma, I hear Sara's feet on the steps.

As Sara steps through her door, I take the opportunity to look her over. She's wearing tiny black shorts with a white, flowy shirt, and her hair is up in a messy knot on top of her head. Her makeup is dark around her eyes, something I've never seen on her before. When she notices me looking at her, her eyes sweep down my body. I'm wearing green cargo shorts and a white T-shirt, my normal everyday uniform.

"Morning." She smiles at Gran-ma, then looks back at me.

"Morning, sweetheart, where are you two off to today?" Gran-ma asks Sara instead of me.

"Canalside—to walk around and get lunch."

"That'll be fun. Izach has a list of things we need from the grocery store for dinner, so make sure he doesn't forget to stop." Gran-ma gives me a quick look, then smiles at Sara

I roll my eyes. "I'm not going to forget. You ready?" I ask Sara.

"Whenever you are."

I can hear the excitement in her voice. Motioning for her to go ahead of me, I wait, then jump in beside her and place my hand at the small of her back. Throwing a glance over my shoulder as we walk down the stairs, I see Gran-ma's smile. When she catches my eyes, she gives me a wink. Shit, I think I just opened another can of worms.

On the ride downtown, I let Sara know we're going to hit 716, the new sports bar outside of the hockey area, for lunch. She's okay with that. Apparently she's heard good things about it but hasn't had the chance to check it out yet. I find a lot close enough to walk to Canalside and the restaurant, and it only costs ten dollars for the day. Sara cringes at the price, but I tell her it's nothing compared to parking in Charlotte.

Before I can get her door, she's up and out of the car, so I run round to meet her and take her hand. She gives me a confused little smile, so I give her hand a little squeeze. I'm trying my best to remember which way to walk to get to 716, but picturing a map and walking on streets are two different things. When I go to turn the wrong way, Sara tugs on my hand and pulls me in the right direction with a little laugh.

"It's this way." She nods in the right direction.

"I thought you've never been here?"

"I haven't, but I come to Canalside during the week sometimes to sit by the water and read."

"Oh, and here I'm trying to impress you by knowing my way around from memorizing a map! So much for that plan." I smile as her laughter bubbles up again.

"You don't need to impress me, Izach. You're sweet and nice. That's all that matters."

"Why do you think I'm sweet?" I ask.

"Because you open the car door for me, you're holding my hand as we walk, and you've never judged me."

"How do you know?"

"I can tell. When some people first see my tattoos, dark hair, and makeup, I know they're judging me. Most of them don't even try to hide it."

"I have tattoos too," I point out.

"It's different when a girl has a lot of tattoos. You know, the whole double standard thing? It's okay for guys but not for girls."

"Well, that's bullshit. It shouldn't matter if you express your individuality with tattoos or art hanging in your house."

She shrugs. "I wish it were that easy, but it's not. The good thing is, I don't give a shit what people think about me."

"Good. It doesn't matter what other people think—except me, of course."

She pulls me to a stop and puts her hands on her hips. "Oh yeah, and what do you think about me?"

"Hmm, that's a tough question." I rub my chin to exaggerate my thought process.

"Really?"

"I'm thinking about it!" I pause again, then I snag her hand and start walking again. "Okay, I've got it. I think you're beautiful, determined, independent, sweet, and smarter than you give yourself credit for."

"That's a lot of thought for the less than a week you've known me."

"Well, you also have a great ass, fantastic legs, and you make the most amazing sounds when I kiss you." I look over to see Sara gaping at me.

"I don't make noises when I kiss!" she shrieks and stops walking, tugging on my hand so I stop along with her.

"You do, and it's so sexy. I was so turned on by them, I thought you'd feel the boner through my shorts." A little embarrassed by what I shared, I pull on her hand to get her to walk again and turn us to cross the street.

"Now I'm going to be paranoid every time I kiss someone."

Guiding her over the curb to the door, I look at her with raised eyebrows. "I hope you're not kissing anyone but me."

"Oh, that sounded bad, didn't it?" She giggles a little, sounding kind of nervous. "I'm not kissing anyone but you currently, but still! Now that's all I'm going to think about."

"It's hot. Don't let it bother you."

Stopping at the hostess stand, we wait for someone to seat us. After telling the girl we need a table for two, I drop Sara's hand and move mine to the small of her back and guide her behind the hostess. The room we're walking through is huge and covered from wall to wall with TV screens in various sizes, each one playing a game or sports show. We make our way upstairs and are seated at a table next to the balcony. Below us is a long blue bar that runs the whole length of the room, with high-top tables and booths filling the area.

Settling in across from Sara, I pick up the menu and look over the beer selection. Sara's studying her menu too, but I can't tell what she's looking at. From the corner of my eye, I see our waitress approaching the table.

"Hi, guys! I'm Candi. I'll be your server today." She looks us both in the eyes before continuing. "Can I get you started with something to drink?"

Looking at Sara, I can see she's not ready. "I'll take a Blue Light." Why the hell not? I haven't had a single beer since I got here.

Sara looks at me with wide eyes, then smiles. "I'll have one as well."

"Great! Are you ready to order, or would you like a few more minutes?"

Sara looks from me to Candi. "Can we get just a couple more minutes?"

"Sure, I'll get your drinks and be right back."

"Thank you," Sara responds politely before Candi walks away. "Do you know what you want?"

"Yep, I'm going for the Beef on Weck. How about you?"

"Um, I think…" She taps her index finger against her lips. "I'm going to get the Bases Loaded Hot Dog."

"Mmm, that was my second choice. I love Buffalo hot dogs."

"They're the best, that's for sure." Sara closes her menu and sets it on the end of the table just as Candi hits the top step with our drinks in hand.

"You ready?" Candi asks excitedly as she sets the drinks in front of us.

We order, and Candi walks away, her blond hair bouncing as she walks—not that I'm watching her walk away. I catch Sara's eyes and smile. With one hand on my beer, I reach across the table and take her free hand. While we wait, I ask her about sports, and I'm not surprised to find out she's a huge hockey fan; I'm not sure I've ever met anyone who lives in Buffalo who doesn't like hockey. After teasing her about her team having a shitty couple of seasons, then finally admitting they're my team too, our food comes and the conversation dies down.

Sara

Trying not to stuff my face full of hot dog and make an ass out of myself, I take small bites and look around while I chew. The whole time, I'm thinking about how I just want to shove this amazingly delicious foot-long monstrosity into my mouth. I finally stop my eyes from wandering and look at the mess Izach's made not only of his sandwich but also of himself. There's no controlling the laugh that bubbles up my throat.

"What the hell did you do to that sandwich?" I ask between giggles.

"What? It's messy." He swipes the back of his hand across his mouth.

"I take it you like Beef on Weck?" I ask sarcastically.

"Yeah, and I haven't had one in a while. It's so good—another amazing thing about this area."

"We do have some good food."

"And beer. Speaking of which, do you want another?"

"Nah, I'll get some water. It's too hot out there to walk around with a belly full of food and beer."

He shrugs. "You're probably right. So what do you want to do after lunch?"

"I thought we were walking around?"

"We are, but they have paddle boats and kayaks. I thought we could do something like that too."

"Oh okay, um, how about a paddle boat? I just don't trust myself not to flip a kayak."

"Sounds good, but I don't think you'd flip the kayak."

"I tripped over the carpet in my apartment. Anything's possible." I look at Izach with the most serious face I can muster and see his lip twitching as though he's trying to contain his laughter. "You can laugh at me all you want . But, you've only experienced a small smidgen of the calamity known as Sara."

"It can't be that bad."

"Think what you want. Just don't be surprised when I trip over my shadow as we're walking." He full-on laughs as I add, "I'm sure you'll be laughing as you help me up too."

The conversations halts as the server walks back to our table. "How is everything?"

"Great, thank you," Izach says around a bite of sandwich.

"Is there anything I can get you? A couple more Blues?"

"Actually, can we get a couple of waters and maybe a couple boxes?" Izach asks with food still in his mouth.

"Sure, I'll be right back."

"You want to take this home with us?"

"Why not?"

135

"Because it's gonna get nasty in the car."

"Didn't think about that. We can just leave it, save the boxes for someone else."

Along with the boxes and the water, Candi sets the bill on the table and tells us to take our time. As Izach looks over the bill, I snag my purse from between my feet and take out my wallet. I watch for Izach's reaction as I pull out a twenty and toss it on the table. He doesn't say anything but tilts to the side, takes out his own wallet, and dumps another twenty on top of mine. I didn't think he would pay for everything, but I'm kind of surprised he didn't fight me on it.

Since we don't need any change, Izach tucks the bills in the folder and leaves it in the middle of the table. He stands and reaches for my hand, then walks us down the stairs and outside. Because lunch took longer than we thought and I have to be back in time to go to my appointment, we head right down to the paddle boats. We're a little disappointed when we find out the paddle boats can only go in the canal and not out into the river around the harbor front like the water bikes and the kayaks can, and that's how Izach manages to talk me into renting a kayak instead. Thankfully they have tandem kayaks, so if I go in, he's going with me.

While I'm hesitating about the whole thing, Izach pulls out his wallet and pays for the trip, which is much more than lunch. He looks at me, but I'm still staring at the hunk of plastic called a boat—I don't want to give him a hard time in front of the rental place—then he slips his wallet casually into his back pocket. The attendant hands Izach two life jackets, and Izach sticks one between his legs while he holds the other out for me to step into.

"Oh god, I'm really not sure about this. I mean, I'm not really looking forward to getting wet."

"You're not going to tip us over. They're sturdy. Look at how wide they are." Izach nods toward the boat.

"You don't understand—"

"Do you trust me?" he asks.

"Um, I guess so," I say, rubbing my hands down my cheeks.

"Okay, well, I'm not gonna let you tip us over, so calm down and enjoy it."

"Ugh, fine, but if I fall in that nasty water, I'm gonna be pissed that you talked me into this!" I step into the waiting life jacket and spin.

Izach makes sure it's on right, then he fastens the buckles at the front and uses them to pull me closer. He places a sweet kiss on my lips that distracts me from my fit. "Just trust me. I won't let anything happen to you."

I want to believe him, but how can he protect something that's already broken?

CHAPTER 13

Sara

True to his word, Izach keeps us afloat in the
kayak, and to celebrate, I buy us ice cream on the way
back to the car. For the second time today, I'm
standing in my shower, letting the water run down my
body and wash away all my sweat. Izach ended up
dropping me off, then running to the store because
we were running behind. I couldn't take the chance of
being late for Jacqui.

With my purse in hand, I lock the door, then
bounce down my stairs. Elaine is sitting in her usual
spot, filling in a crossword puzzle. She just smiles as I
walk past her. Elaine knows I go out three times a
week, although she doesn't know about Jacqui or
where I go. I always thought I would tell her more
about me before I lost the opportunity, but since
tonight's my last night with her, I realize that isn't
going to happen. Maybe I'll write her a letter telling
her everything I should have before she left. Maybe
she'll write me back and tell me everything will be
okay. For now, I just shake off the thought and head
to my car.

Walking through the waiting room door to
Jacqui's office, the first thing I see is Miss Personality
sitting behind the glass partition. Ignoring Jill as usual,
I sign in, take my usual seat, and pop my earbuds in
my ears, making sure the music is low enough that I

can hear Jill. I still annoy her by pretending I can't hear her though.

"Sara?" she calls through the opening in the glass, and I don't respond. "Sara?" She stands and sticks her head through the window, looking directly at me. "Dr. Rosen is ready. You can go through to her office."

Not bothering to reply, I head through the door to Jacqui's office. As I turn the corner, I see her leaning against the door frame, waiting for me.

"What's the occasion?" I ask.

She looks at me, appearing confused.

"You're usually ass up with your head in a filing cabinet when I come in."

Ignoring my comment, Jacqui gives me an appraising look. "You going to take those out of your ears, or are we going back to normal this week?"

"What'd you mean by going back to normal?"

"Friday you came in sans earbuds. It was kind of nice not fighting with you to take them out," she explains as I walk into the office and head right to the couch.

I throw myself on it. "I forgot them on Friday, so it's a good thing you sent Jill home early. I'm not sure I could have handled actually having to hear her."

"You're so mean." Jacqui says with a laugh. "What has Jill ever done to you?"

"She has an annoying voice, and she judges me." I answer seriously as I pull the earbuds out of my ears and wrap the cord around my phone.

"She does not. Why would you think that?"

"Expressive eyes. You don't see it because you're not fucked up."

Jacqui takes a deep breath and blows it out as she drops into her chair. "So it's going to be like this today. How did things go last night with Izach?"

"Way to beat around the bush. They were fine. We hung out and watched a movie. Maybe we kind of made out a little, but nothing below the belt or under our clothes."

"Were you hoping for more?"

"No, I'm not sure I'm happy it went as far as it did. I think I really like him. I don't want to ruin it by pulling my usual."

"Sara." Jacqui's stern voice makes me roll my head so I'm looking at her. "It's been a long time since you've done anything like that. Why do you think you'll revert back to those habits so easily?"

"Well, I went from sleeping around to cutting. Which would you rather I do?" I ask seriously, even though I probably sound like a loon or a bitch.

"Neither, and I think you can manage to have a relationship with a man without doing either of those things."

I just roll my head back so I'm looking at the ceiling.

"Okay, why don't you tell me what's going on? Are you really afraid of messing things up with Izach, or are you upset because Elaine is leaving in a couple days?"

Just hearing Jacqui say it brings tears to my eyes. "There's so much I thought I would tell her about me before I didn't have the chance anymore."

"Sara, she's only moving; she didn't die. I'm sure she'd love it if you called and talked to her or wrote her a letter. You still have time to share things with her. It just won't to be face-to-face."

141

"I know, but it won't be the same. She's not gonna be able to give me a hug and tell me everything will be okay."

"You still have a little bit of time. If you're ready, then tell her. If not, then write her a letter, and the next time she sees you, she'll give you a hug and tell you everything will be okay."

Lying there for a few minutes without saying anything, I think about whether or not I'm ready to tell Elaine who I am. "I don't know if I can do it just because she's leaving. Baring your soul to one of the people you consider family is a little much to do the day before they move across the country."

"You'll know when the time is right."

"I will." I settle my hands under my neck, propping myself up a little. "I think I'll get Elaine's new address and write to her. Who doesn't love getting a letter in the mail?"

"Are you feeling a little better about Elaine leaving?" Jacqui asks as I turn my head back toward her.

"A little. I'm still going to cry when I have to say good-bye, but I'm glad I'll still have the chance to let her in even though she's not living below me."

"Is it important for you to tell her about your past?" Jacqui asks as she shifts in the chair uncrossing her legs.

"Yeah, it is. She's the only one—well, other than you—who I've been able to trust. She took a chance on me when I'm not sure anyone else would have."

"She did, and I'm sure she loves you like one of her own. Elaine saw something in you the day you knocked on her door to rent her apartment. It's probably the same thing I've seen since the day I met you."

I smile. "What's that, Jacqui? My upbeat, bubbly personality?"

She leans forward to drive her point home. "No, your determination. You could have given up after everything that happened, but you didn't. You survived until you could get out, then you made your own way. That's bravery, even if you don't think it is."

"Well shit, if you don't stop with all this emo crap, I just might cry."

"Okay, smartass. Moving on. Why don't we go back to how your homework went?" I watch as Jacqui sits back again.

"Ugh." I lay my arms over my eyes. "You know, this is all your fault."

"It's not, but if it that's what you need to think, I can handle it. Now finish telling me what's going on with Izach?"

Lifting my arms, I peek at Jacqui as I answer her question. "We watched a movie the last night, and today he took me to Canalside for lunch and to walk around."

"Yeah? How was it?" She crosses her legs and settles in as if I'm going to tell her the greatest gossip ever.

"It was fun. We went kayaking around the harbor front and had ice cream."

"So why do you think whatever this is with him is going to turn out the same as the guys you used?"

"Because I don't want it to. But everything good that happens to me eventually turns to shit."

"That's not true. Nothing has turned to shit since you moved here."

I sigh. "Nothing good has happened since I moved here. I just exist."

"That's not true either. You came here without a place to live, no job, and no friends. You found an apartment, which led you to Elaine, then you got a job that you've kept for five years. I would say those are good things. Just because they're not super exciting things doesn't mean they aren't good."

Tucking my elbows under my sides I sit up a little and look right at Jacqui. "You forgot one thing."

"What's that?"

"You. I found you, and that's probably the best thing that's happened to me."

"Well shit, Sara, now you're going to make me cry!"

"Way to be professional!"

"Please," She snarks with a smile, then goes right back to business.

That's another thing I love about having Jacqui in my life. She knows when I need serious and when I don't.

"I really want it to go somewhere," I say. "He's so sweet and kind. I feel comfortable around him. Even though I was tongue-tied when I first met him, I still felt oddly calm and safe. It scares the hell out of me because if things progress between us, I'm eventually gonna have to tell him about Trent. I don't want to see that pity in his eyes."

"Hearing what you told me just now and the other day, I don't think you're going to see pity when you tell him. I think he'll be pissed for you."

"He offered to help me get my equivalency diploma," I say.

"Really? And how do you feel about that?"

"I think I'm gonna do it. Izach said he'd find out the information and help me study. Maybe I could go to college next fall."

"That's an amazing goal, Sara..."

"But...?"

"But even though I'm glad you've found Izach and you have feelings for him, I don't want you to rush into this. You need to get to know yourself again as you get to know him. Don't force it. Take your time."

Swinging my legs off the side of the leather couch, I sit up and face Jacqui. I need her to know I'm serious. "I'm not stupid. I know myself, and I know when I'm pushing things. I promise I'll be careful. I'm not going to let things get out of hand, and if I need you, I'll text or call you."

"I know you will, but our goal is for you to not rely on me being there all the time. I just want you to be mindful of things so you're not calling or texting me whenever things get a little out of hand. You're getting better. Before this past weekend, you had gotten to the point where you almost never texted me."

"I'm starting to feel like you're done with me," I say with a little bit of sarcasm.

"Now's not the time to be a smartass. You know what I'm talking about." She leans forward in her chair, brows raised, and her eyes burn a hole into me.

Rolling my eyes, I say, "I know, I was just trying to make a joke. I get it. I have my tools, and you're there as a last resort."

"Not a last resort, Sara. Just if you absolutely need me. You know we've been working toward getting you to handle things yourself, and you're doing so much better. Let's keep moving forward."

Jacqui's right. I used to call her every ten minutes when I first started seeing her. Of course, at that

145

point, I was afraid of every little sound and cutting with every tiny bit of emotion I felt. I'd lost control and didn't know how to get it back, and Jacqui helped me. Now I'm not afraid. I've learned to control my urge to cut with rubber bands, butterflies, and tattoos.

"Speaking of moving forward, I want to talk about me getting a new tattoo. It's not because I want to cut; I just want something to remind me of Elaine. I'm thinking a little bumblebee or something like that."

Jacqui nods. "Okay, I'm good with you getting more ink, I just want to make sure it's not for the wrong reasons. But why a bumblebee?"

"Because she's cute and likes sweets, but piss her off and she won't hesitate to jam her stinger right into your ass."

Jacqui laughs. "I guess I can see why you'd go that way."

"So don't be worried when you see a new tattoo on me in the near future."

"I won't." Jacqui's tone is final, and I know she's not bullshitting me.

For the rest of the session, we talk about my last dinner with Elaine, how I'm going to miss her, and when I should send her my first letter. By the time the elevator hits the ground floor, I'm ready to say good-bye to her. But I've decided it's not good-bye—it's just "see you soon."

Izach

After dropping Sara off at the house so she could get ready for her appointment, I run to the store and get the things on Gran-ma's list. As I pull into the

146

driveway, my backseat loaded with bags, I see two heads over the porch railing. I stop in my spot and cut the engine, but before I get my door all the way open, my mom is standing in my field of vision, waiting for me.

"Hi, Mom." I step away from the car and give her a hug.

"Hi, honey, it's good to see you. Can I help with the groceries?"

Stepping out of my mom's arms, I flip the driver's seat forward, grab a couple bags out of the back, and hand them to her before I duck back inside and loop the rest over my wrist. "Thanks. How was your flight?"

"Good. I think Dad and the girls wanted to come too, but since we're leaving here on Wednesday, there wasn't really a point."

"Why'd they want to come?" I shut the door and hit the locks with my free hand.

"They want to meet Sara. Gran-ma told me that you've kind of hit it off with her." She grins at me.

"Mom, she's not like other girls. You can't get all crazy with her just because of what Gran-ma said. By the way, what did Gran-ma say?"

"She told me you've been spending time with Sara. She thinks the two of you are meant to be together."

I shake my head. "Okay, right there, that sounds a little crazy. We've known each other less than a week. Yes, I like her, but I also don't want to scare her away."

"Scare who away?" Gran-ma asks as Mom and I reach the stairs.

"Sara," Mom answers.

"You're not going to scare her away," Gran-ma says. "I can see it when she looks at you. She likes you."

"I'm not denying that, and I like her too, but she's not like other girls. She needs to be eased into things. You saw her the first night I was here. She barely talked to me."

"She's shy. It just took her a couple days to open up. In the five years she's lived here, I've never seen her with a guy." Gran-ma gets out of her chair and holds the door for Mom and me to take the bags into the house.

"I get that, but I still don't want to push her," I call over my shoulder. "I think Mom being here today might do that."

"Please, she'll be fine. It's not like we're planning your wedding," Gran-ma says.

"Christ," I mumble as I set the bags on the counter then reach to take Mom's. She's got a huge smile. "What?"

"I've never seen you like this about a girl."

"I don't think I've ever felt like this about a girl," I admit. From the minute I saw Sara, I knew she was different from every girl I've ever met.

"See, Gran-ma knows best. Now do you want me to ease Sara into meeting your mom, or are you going to introduce them?"

"I can do it. I don't want her to feel like I ambushed her, so let me do it my way." I give Gran-ma a pointed look, and she holds up her hands in defeat.

"Fine, I can take a hint. Why don't you run outside and intercept her? She just pulled in the driveway."

Before the last word left Gran-ma's mouth, I was moving toward the door. Sara's car is next to mine, and she cuts off the engine as I hit the bottom step of the porch. She swings her door open and stands, giving me a smile.

"Hey, what's up?" She looks happy to see me but confused as to why I'm meeting her at her car.

"Um, so I wanted to tell you before you were hit with a surprise." I cage Sara against her car with one arm on the door and the other on the top of her beater.

"Okay?" She exaggerates.

"My mom's here. She got in a little while ago." I watch her eyes for her reaction.

Sounding surprised, Sara asks, "I thought she was coming tomorrow?"

"She was supposed to, but Gran-ma kind of told her that we've been spending time together. She wanted a chance to meet you, so she came a day early."

"You're worried about me meeting her?" Sara asks with her brow furrowed.

"No, I want you to meet her. I just don't want you to be uncomfortable because Gran-ma told her about us." I drag my foot across the pavement.

"It's a little weird considering I'm not sure what we are, but that's typical Elaine. I can handle meeting your mom if you want me to."

"Of course I want you to. My mom's amazing, and you're going to love her." I'm relieved that she's not freaked out by Gran-ma's craziness. I snag Sara's lips for a quick kiss, then pull away, smiling at her; she smiles back. I step away and grab Sara's hand.

By the time we reach the porch, Mom and Gran-ma have come out of the house and each taken a rocking chair.

Stopping between them, I hop up on the railing and pull Sara in between my legs. "Mom, this is Sara. Sara, my mom, Erin Matthews."

Sara steps away from me to shake my mom's hand.

"Sara, it's so lovely to meet you. Mom's told me so much about you."

"It's nice to meet you too." Sara quickly retreats back to me.

"Erin, how about we go get dinner started?" Gran-ma cuts in. "Izach, can you start the grill for us?"

"Sure," I answer and watch them disappear into the house.

Sara turns in my arms. My hands were at her waist, but they move across her front and settle on her hips.

"I didn't know your last name was Matthews," she says with her head tilted to the side.

"Yeah, when Gran-ma introduced us, she apparently didn't think last names were important. I don't know yours either."

"It's Collins. What else didn't we get to when we met?"

"Um, well, I have three sisters, one older and two younger. Elyse is the oldest, then me, Emma, and Liza is the baby. She's fifteen."

"How old is Elyse?"

"She's thirty—Mom and Dad's surprise college baby." I chuckle as I remember calling Elyse the mistake of the family. Although my parents would

150

never call her that, it was an easy way to piss her off when we were younger. "How about you?"

"I have two brothers, both older: Matt and Noah." She sighs, then quietly adds, "I don't talk to them."

I touch her cheek. "You don't have to tell me about it. Not now. When you're ready."

"Okay."

"Why don't we go fire up the grill?"

She nods, so I move off the rail and wrap my arm around her shoulder to guide her toward the side of the house and the grill.

CHAPTER 14

Sara

My stomach's about to burst. Not only did I scarf down a steak, I also devoured roasted potatoes and corn. I'm to the point of unbuttoning my pants so I can breathe. I look over at Izach, who's working on the second mound of food he put on his plate, while Elaine and Erin talk about plans for their cross-country trip.

Nudging him with my elbow, I say, "I think I need to go lie down before I explode."

"You're full?" he asks between bites.

"Um, yeah, did you see how much I ate?"

"Meh, it wasn't that much."

"Ignore him, Sara. My son is a bottomless pit. Always has been," Erin jumps into our conversation.

"I can see that."

"I'm going to sit outside if you want to join me?" she asks with sincerity on her face.

"Sure."

"Don't worry 'bout me. I'll stay here and help Gran-ma clean the plates." Izach motions to Elaine with his fork.

"I'll come back and help clean up," I say. "I just need to stretch out for a minute."

"We can get it. You go relax with Erin." Elaine shoos us away from the table as she starts to clear plates.

"It's okay, I want to help," I argue.

"Please just make an old lady happy and go sit outside. We'll be out in a few minutes."

Giving up, I follow Erin out of the house. She takes Elaine's normal seat while I go to mine. We rock in silence for a few minutes before I turn my head and see Erin looking at me.

"My mom really loves you, you know," she says. "She's talked about you for years, but no matter how many times we came to visit, she never introduced us."

"I never knew you came. I mean, I knew when Elaine had company, but it was usually on the weekends when I was working."

"Right, she told me you work overnights at The Diner. So you were probably sleeping when we were here."

"Sometimes I was. Sometimes I was just relaxing before I had to go in."

Erin leans her head back against the chair but keeps her face toward me. "You could have met Izach years ago. He used to come visit Mom on the weekends when he didn't have too much work."

"Really? She never told me. Elaine's never really talked about any of you with me. She's always kind of skated around the whole family thing."

"She must have known the time wasn't right. She did the same thing with Eric—Izach's dad—and I. Mom's friend Charlene passed away when we were little, leaving behind her husband and son. Every Sunday, Mom made dinner and took it to them, but she never asked us to go with her. After I graduated from high school, just before I was leaving for college, she asked me to go." Erin looked out at the road. "Eric is Charlene's son. He was leaving to start his junior year the same day I was starting my freshman year. It was Mom's plan to wait until we were ready, then bring us together. She kind of has this way of knowing when the time is right."

"Really? Elaine introduced you to Izach's dad?"

"Yep, she knew we would end up together. On our wedding day, she told that story at our reception, and I don't think there was a dry eye in the room." Erin looks at me with her head leaned back against the chair.

"Huh, I've heard her mention timing before, but I never really paid attention."

"When I talked to her on the phone earlier, I asked her why she'd never introduced you to Izach before, and she told me the time just wasn't right." My eyes bug out of my head, and Erin must notice because she says, "I'm not trying to freak you out, Sara. I just want you to know why she does what she does."

"Oh," is the only thing I can get out.

"Izach likes you. I can tell by the way he looks at you."

"I like him too."

"I know. I can see it in the way you look at him. I'm glad she waited for the time to be right. I think you're good for each other."

"How do you know?"

"Just a feeling I have. It's a mom thing."

I stiffen. My mother never had "mom feelings." If she had, she would probably still be a part of my life.

Erin sighs. "She's going to miss you a lot, so make sure you stay in touch."

"I will. I'm planning on writing to her."

"That's wonderful! She'll love that."

"What will I love?" Elaine's voice booms as she pushes through the door with Izach behind her. I stand so she can sit down, and I hop up next to Izach on the railing.

"Nothing, Mom, stop being so nosy," Erin says.

"I'm not nosy! If I was nosy, don't you think I would be moving to Charlotte instead of Phoenix?"

"Why are you moving across the country when your family is Charlotte?" I've been curious about that since she told me where she was moving.

"My dad's dad lives there," Izach says. "Gran-ma said once Gran-pa died, she was going to move to Phoenix to be near him, because they'd both be alone. That was a little over five years ago."

Snapping my head toward Elaine, I ask, "Please tell me you didn't stay here because of me?"

"No, it just wasn't the right time. Now it is."

Elaine and her freakin' timing. She should have moved around the time I took the upstairs apartment, but she didn't. I want to press the issue with her now, but I think I just figured out what my first letter is going to be about.

She stands from her rocker and looks right at me. "Have you digested enough?"

"I think so. Why?"

"My darling grandson bought a cake to celebrate having the place to himself, and it happens to be my favorite."

"You did not?" I turn and give Izach the evil eye.

"It says 'Have fun in the Sun, Gran-ma, so no, it's not to celebrate getting the house to myself." He gives Elaine a look at she opens the door.

156

"Same thing." She smiles, then disappears into the apartment, leaving Erin and me giggling at a scowling Izach.

"Ya know, I'm starting to think she doesn't want to move just so she can give me shit on daily basis," Izach says.

"Oh honey," Erin says between giggles, "she'll call you and do that."

"I'm going to go help Elaine with the cake," I announce and hop off the rail.

As I walk by Izach, he grabs my arm and jerks me into him. Surprised, I give him a look just before he kisses me.

"What was that for?" I ask.

"Just because."

Izach

My eyes wander over to my mom after the door closes behind Sara. There's no hiding the smile on Mom's face, and I think her eyes are twinkling, if that's possible. I sigh and kick one leg over the rail so I'm straddling it, then I lean back against the support beam. Glancing back over at Mom, I notice she's not just looking at me—she's studying me.

"What?" I ask.

"I can't believe how much you remind me of your dad. It's crazy. He used to do the same thing when I left the room."

"What're you trying to say, Mom? That we're going to have an Elyse soon?" I tease.

"Ya know, your sister's not here to defend herself, so leave her out of it. And I hope not. Your

157

dad and I were together for a few years before I got pregnant, so please take your time and get to know each other before that happens."

"You sound so sure of us."

"Maybe I've acquired your gran-ma's powers." She winks at me.

There's no hiding my eye roll. "Please, Gran-ma doesn't have powers and neither do you."

"We'll see," she manages to get in before Sara slams into the door, knocking around the plates and silverware in her hands.

Before I have the chance to jump up, Sara has the door open and she's laughing about her clumsiness. She hands Mom and me a plate and fork as Gran-ma pushes through the door with the cake, sliced and ready to be dished out.

We sit and pick on each other for the rest of the evening. Mom shares war stories about growing up with Gran-ma, and Gran-ma defends herself. It's so easy to hang out with them and Sara. Even when I pulled Sara in to sit between my legs, neither my mom nor Gran-ma made anything of it.

Gran-ma was the first to get up and complain about getting tired. "Sara, before you start work tomorrow, we'll have one last dinner together at The Diner."

Trying not to be too obvious, Mom claims she's tired too and follows Gran-ma after about five minutes, leaving Sara and me on the rail, holding each other.

With my lips at her ear, I ask, "Do you want to watch another movie?"

"Sure. Did you return the other one?"

"Nope. We'll have to run to the store. We either can get another movie or you can always rummage through my DVD collection and see if there's anything you want to watch?"

Her head moves up and down against the side of my face. "Okay."

Sara

We stood in front of the vending machine, trying to pick a movie, for way too long. Nothing stood out for either of us. Taking a break, Izach runs into the store to get some pop and snacks for us. Just about as soon as he walks away, I decide on a movie. It's a brand-new romantic drama I've wanted to see since before it came out in the theatre. I stuff the DVD case in my purse and head in to find Izach.

"Did you find something?" he asks before I see him standing at the self-checkout.

"Yeah, I got one. You done?"

"Yep, I got us some drinks and popcorn." He slips away from the register, then grabs my hand.

Back in my apartment, I make the microwave popcorn while Izach sets up the DVD player. This doesn't feel as weird as it did the other day, so when I head into the living room, I don't think twice about sitting right next to Izach. He pulls me into him, so I have to kick my legs out to the side across the futon. He puts his legs up on the coffee table and hits the play button.

Only a few minutes in, the first make-out scene takes over the screen, and the fingers Izach was running up and down my arm stop. I'm trying so hard to watch the movie and ignore what he's doing, but I feel his body tense next to me. I turn a little so my back is against his side, and I pull his hand over my shoulder so it's resting across my chest. He takes a deep breath when the scene moves on, and his fingers rub the skin just below my neck. I know that isn't the only make-out scene—I'm very familiar with this type of movie—but what I didn't realize was the effect they would have on us while sitting so close together.

Pushing my arm into the cushion, I sit up, and Izach's arm falls behind me. I turn to look at him. "Hey, I wasn't… I mean, I didn't…" I can't find the words I'm looking for. "This movie, it wasn't to try to make us uncomfortable." Looking into his eyes, I'm not sure he gets what I'm trying to say. "I mean, I knew there were some sex scenes, but I didn't think…"

"I'm not uncomfortable. Well, maybe I'm a little uncomfortable, but it has nothing to do with the content of the movie."

"Why are you uncomfortable then?" I ask, looking at him through my lashes.

"Uh, how can I say this without sounding like a perv… you're lying across my body with my arm wrapped around your chest. I can feel you breathing, and when the movie gets a little hot, I feel your reaction, which is making me react, but not to the movie—to you."

"That's what I thought… but that wasn't my intention."

"I know. But your intention doesn't change the fact that I'm attracted to you and you have an effect on me. I just don't want things to go too fast because I

160

like you, a lot, and I don't want to push you too far before you're ready."

I blush. "I'm not a nun. I've been with a guy before. I know how this works."

"Trust me, the way you kiss me, I know you're not a nun." He slaps his hand across his eyes. "Shit, that didn't come out right. I don't mean I know you've been with guys. I just can tell you're not—shit!"

Giggling, I pull his hand away from his face. "I know what you mean, and no, I'm not inexperienced, but I'm also not overly experienced, if you know what I mean."

"I do."

"So what's the problem?"

"I'm trying to take things slow because I've never felt this way before, and I don't want you to think I'm some asshole." He tries to cover his eyes again, but I hold his wrist.

"I don't, and what you just said makes me like you more."

"Really? Because I totally just blew my dude status," he says.

"You didn't."

I decide to grow a pair, and lean in, closing the distance between my lips and his. When they touch, it's for just a second to let him know I'm feeling the same thing. Pulling back, I smile at Izach, then I return to my previous position and wait for his arm to come back around me, but he doesn't move. I sit back up.

"What?" I ask, looking at his stunned face.

"I don't think we should finish this movie."

"Why?"

"Why? Because that little kiss moved mountains for me, and if we keep watching this, I won't be able to keep my hands off of you."

I grin. "I guess I'll take my chances then. I've been waiting to see this since it came out at the theaters."

"Sara," he warns.

"I'm serious, I really want to see it!" I said with a straight face. "And I might not mind if you get a little handsy."

That was all it took. Within a second, Izach was off the futon and I was on my back with him looming over me. He crashed his lips down on mine, and I smiled against his lips before opening for him. It took no coaxing for our tongues to dance together, and the first little sound slipped up my throat. I froze. Holy shit, I do make sounds!

Izach pulls back quickly and looks at me.

"Gah, I do make noises!"

He lowers his head and kisses me once, twice, then pulls away again. "It's hot, trust me," is all he says before descending again.

This time when I make a little noise, I don't stop. I run my hands from his sides, up his back, into his hair. Without disconnecting from my mouth, Izach wraps his arms around my middle, and while he moves to sit on the futon, he pulls me up so I'm directly in front of him. Having so much space between our bodies feels weird, so I keep moving forward, getting onto my knees to crawl into his lap. Immediately I feel how Izach is reacting to our make-out session.

As my fingers twist in his hair, I feel Izach's fingers going up and down my sides. He stops at the hem of my shirt and hesitates, but doesn't breach the fabric. Getting brave, I pull my hands from his hair and reach between our bodies to grab the bottom of his shirt. I yank it up until it gets stuck under his arms.

He pulls away slowly, looking into my eyes. "Sara." His voice is barely a whisper. "We don't have to. I'm good with what we're doing."

"I know, but I want—I want to feel you beneath my hands."

Without another word, he takes his hands off my body and pulls at his shirt until it's freed from my grip and over his head. I hear the soft whoosh of the fabric hitting the floor somewhere behind me. My hands are back at Izach's side and move of their own accord. His chest, unmarked by tattoos, is perfectly sculpted with strong muscles rolling into a defined six pack. I run my fingers from his waist up to his pecs, where my hands separate and go to his shoulders. The whole time I'm moving, I feel Izach's eyes watching me in the flickering TV light. He doesn't move or say anything, letting me explore his body.

At the top of his right shoulder, I trace the outline of a black tattoo that swirls over to just above his collarbone. I put my lips on his skin, just below where my fingers are moving. Izach moves his head back a little, making room for me to kiss my way up his neck. When I reach the spot just below his chin, I sit back on his thighs.

"Hi," I say shyly, not sure what to say after I just sucked my way up his neck.

"Hi." He looks very aroused. "You having fun?"

"Maybe," I answer before biting my lip.

"Do you think I can have some fun?" He raises a brow with his question.

Nodding, I kiss him quickly, then pull away when he tries to take it further. I grab the bottom of my shirt and lift it over my head, then I toss it somewhere over my shoulder. Izach doesn't move to touch me, so I grab one of his hands and put it on my stomach, just above my pierced belly button. Slowly he draws a line to my side, where I have a cherry tree tattoo with very few pink blossoms. My breath catches in my throat as his index finger traces the trunk of the tree up to the branch that curves around my ribs just under my bra. The whole time, his eyes follow his fingers. I'm not sure if he sees them, but I know he can't miss feeling the little scars that line my body under the ink. No matter how faint they are, you can still feel them. In the heat of the moment, I didn't think about the scars or what having Izach touch them would do to me. What they might do to him?

When I was still living at home, I had to choose creative places to cut. Sometimes it was between my legs, other times it was the lower part of my stomach, but mostly it was my right side. Under the ink of the tattoo are hundreds of little lines put there by a razor blade. When I was ready, I covered them with a cherry tree in blossom, because it means renewal and this is my new life. This is me starting over.

As Izach's fingers move across my stomach, I can't tell if he's reacting to the scars or if he's just ignoring them. His fingers move up to cup my chin and lift my face so I'm looking at him.

"I know you felt them—"

He says, "You don't have to tell me, Sara. They change nothing."

"Maybe we should stop," I say with a sigh and try to turn my head away from Izach.

"If that's what you want?" He dips his eyes so they're level with mine.

"I think I want to put my shirt back on."

I move to get off of Izach's lap, but he stops me by shifting me to his side. He leans forward and snags my shirt from beside the coffee table. Balling it up, he holds the neck hole open, pulls it over my head, then lets go so I can put my arms through the holes. Bending again, he grabs his shirt.

"No, don't put it on," I say.

He looks confused when I stand and flip off the TV. Grabbing his hand, I pull Izach into my bedroom and stop right inside the door. I leave him for only a second to turn on the light. As the room fills with the soft glow from the lamp, I take Izach's hand again and pull him to the edge of the bed as I sit down.

"Lie with me for a while?" I ask softly.

"You sure?"

I love how he checks to make sure I'm really okay. I slide to the other side of the bed, making room for him to join me.

Lying on my side, I watch Izach's body, arms covered in tattoos, slide across my white sheets. He lies flat on his back, turning only his head to look at me, then gives me a small smile. I roll over so the front of my body is pressed up against his and my head is resting on his shoulder. Izach wraps his arm around my body, tucking me in tighter, and rests his hand against my lower back. I trace little circles on his chest and listen to his breathing until it evens out and I know he's fallen asleep.

CHAPTER 15

Izach

Rubbing my eyes, I crack them open a little and take in the morning sun streaming through the open blinds. Sara is curled into my left side with her leg thrown over mine, her arm wrapped tightly around my waist, and the top half of her body covering my chest. The soft puffs of her breath blow my chest hair.

Moving my right hand, I sweep away the black-and-blond hair that's fallen over her face as she sleeps. Her eyes are closed tightly, and her mouth is open just a little. Her lashes are fanned out across the tops of her cheeks. It's the most at peace I've seen her since we met.

Without moving too much, I wiggle my left arm under her body until I can curl it around her waist, pulling Sara closer. She snuggles into me as her eyelids flutter a little but don't open. I watch her, thinking about the soft bumps I felt on her side under her cherry tree. I know she has secrets she's not ready to share, but I hope that one day she'll tell me what haunts her, what keeps her away from her family, and why she felt the need to run away from everything she knew. For right now, I'm just glad she didn't push me away after she started to freak out. Instead, she let me hold her all night, keeping her safe. I don't think she's moved more than a muscle since we lay down.

Turning my head, I look at the alarm clock on the nightstand and see that it's only a little after eight in the morning. My mom took my bed so I was supposed to be on the couch for the night. That means when Gran-ma woke up at the ass crack of dawn, the first thing she saw was the empty couch. I'm sure she'll be ecstatic Sara and I spent the night together—that is, after I explain that we only slept next to each other.

Rubbing my hand in small circles against the exposed flesh of Sara's lower back, where her shirt rode up, I try to wake her enough to let her know I'm getting up. She wiggles a little, as though what I'm doing tickles, but still doesn't look as though she's anywhere near waking up. I know she has to work tonight, so I want to make sure she sleeps enough, but I have to do damage control with Mom and Gran-ma.

"Sara?" I whisper as I continue to touch her skin. "Hey, I'm gonna head downstairs."

A soft moan escapes her lips just before she nods against my skin.

Slowly I pull my arm out from under her and slide to the right, slipping her onto the pillow I was using. When I'm free, she turns into the pillow, curling herself into the mattress. I place a soft kiss on her forehead, then head into the living room to retrieve my shirt. I feel bad that she probably isn't awake enough to know I said good-bye, so I grab the small note pad on her coffee table and scribble a quick note.

Sara ~ Didn't want to wake you. Headed downstairs to have coffee with Mom and Gran-ma. See you later. ~ Izach

Slipping back into her room, I set the note under her phone on the nightstand, where I know she'll see it. I open her apartment door quietly and flip the lock before I pull it closed just as softly. When I get halfway down the stairs, I hear Mom and Gran-ma's voices talking about me sleeping upstairs, and I know I'm in for an earful. I take a deep breath, take the last few steps to the door, and push through it slowly so it doesn't squeak.

"Morning," I say, looking at Mom then Gran-ma.

"Morning, sweetheart, there's coffee ready if you want." Gran-ma gives me an I'm-going-to-be-a-great-grandma-soon smile, but Mom looks worried.

"Okay, I'll grab a cup after I brush my teeth. Be back out in a few minutes." I pass them, not waiting to hear if they have anything else to say.

Heading right to the bathroom, I take care of business, then brush my teeth. When I get to my room to change out of the clothes I was wearing yesterday, the first thing I notice is that Mom has unpacked my bags and put my clothes in the dresser, which I'll be moving to Gran-ma's room once she leaves. Mom also hung my coats on the rack behind the door. I roll my eyes. Mom cleans unnecessarily when she's nervous about something, and that something is most likely Sara and me spending the night together. I shake it off and get dressed in clean cargo shorts and a white T-shirt.

Standing at the counter, I pull the biggest coffee cup Gran-ma has from the cupboard and fill it to the top with coffee, leaving just enough room for a splash of milk and a teaspoon of sugar. I might have filled it a little too much, because when I pick the mug up, the liquid energy sloshes over the sides. I take a quick sip to make sure I can walk to the porch without coffee spilling all over the place.

Walking slowly, I cross the room to the front door, then swing it open, halting Mom and Gran-ma's soft conversation. I cross the porch and hop up on the rail between the two of them so I can see both of their faces. Gran-ma still has a small smile while Mom is sporting the concerned look.

"Izach…" Mom starts, but I cut her off.

"Nothing happened, Mom."

Her raised brow makes it clear she doesn't believe me.

"Seriously, we watched a movie, then went to bed. Yes, I slept in her bed, but nothing happened. I'm not stupid. I really like Sara, so I'm not going to mess things up by going too fast."

"I'm glad to hear that." The worry drains from Mom's face. "I like Sara too, and I think the two of you could really have something, so I also don't want you to screw things up."

"Thanks for the vote of confidence," I shoot back as Gran-ma chuckles. "What're you laughing at over there? I saw the smile you gave me when I came out the door."

"What smile? Can't I just be happy to see my grandson?"

"You had this you're-going-to-make-me-a-great-grandma smile, and I want you to know you're really jumping the gun on that one. We're taking things slowly, getting to know one another, so don't try to push it, old lady!"

"Who're you calling old? I'll have you know I still have the reflexes of a jungle cat," she teases.

"That's right, I forgot you moonlight as a puma. My bad."

"What a cranky smart mouth you are this morning, and to think I was defending you when your mother jumped to conclusions!"

170

I smile into my coffee. "I'm not really cranky. I'm just giving you a hard time while I can without having to call you. I just don't get the same effect over the phone."

"Thanks for preparing me. Now I know what the rest of my days are going to be like."

"Aww, Gran-ma, I'm gonna miss you so much." I hop off the rail, nearly landing in her lap, and place a sloppy kiss on her cheek.

"Mom, that's just his way of saying he loves us. You should have heard the things he said to me the day before he left to move up here," Mom chimes in as I go back to my spot.

"Really, it wasn't that bad."

"You pointed out that my trips to the salon will increase because you won't be home to keep your sisters in line. Then when you said good-bye to Elyse, you started singing 'My Favorite Mistake,' which I had to deal with."

"Ha, that was funny."

She shakes her head. "Your sister is so paranoid about being a mistake. She was a wreck."

"Well, she kind of was," Gran-ma throws in.

"Mom! She wasn't a mistake. She just wasn't planned—a happy surprise."

"In other words, a happy mistake," Gran-ma reiterates, trying to conceal her chuckle while I burst out laughing.

"Ugh, the two of you. If I'm going to deal with this all day, I need more coffee." Mom gets up from the rocker and shoots us each a dirty look.

After the door shuts behind her, I look at Gran-ma, who's now smiling, "Maybe we should drop the Elyse-is-a-mistake thing. I think hearing the truth kind of pisses her off." I nod toward the house.

"Maybe you're right, and your sister is my first and favorite grandchild."

My mouth drops open in shock, "Gran-ma! I'm your favorite. I'm your only grandson."

"Well…" She waits too long to speak again. "I'm just kidding. I love all of my grandbabies equally." She holds a closed fist against her heart for emphasis.

"On that note, I'm going to jump in the shower before I stink up these clean clothes." I hop off the rail, taking my semi-full coffee cup with me.

"I'll let Sara know where you are if she comes down."

Shooting her a smile, I say, "Thanks."

Sara

Rolling to my side, I crack my eyes open and look at the alarm clock. 12:34—I slept longer than I thought. Kicking the blankets away, I swing my legs over the side of the bed and force myself into an upright position. I don't think I've ever slept that long without interruption. Waking up without feeling tired is such a strange feeling. At some point, I felt Izach get up, but I couldn't bring myself to move. I was so comfortable.

I stretch my arms over my head to get rid of the tightness in my muscles. Looking at the nightstand, I see a small piece of notebook paper sticking out from under my phone. Giddy that Izach left me a note, I slide the paper out and read his scribbled handwriting. He's so thoughtful, but I wish he wouldn't have let me sleep so long. It just shortens the last day I get to spend with Elaine. At that thought, I propel myself off the bed and head right to the bathroom.

Turning on the shower, I let the room fill with steam before I undress and step under the spray. I quickly wash my hair, then slather it with conditioner. As I rub my soapy hands across my body, I think about Izach's hands on my skin. His touch was so gentle, tracing my cherry tree despite my freak-out. I'm so glad he let it go and didn't push for more, not that I expected anything different from Izach. He hasn't pushed me at all, which is so attractive.

After rinsing the conditioner out of my hair, I kill the shower and squeeze the excess water from my hair. I step out and grab my towel. Not bothering to run it over my body, I wrap it around my chest, then head back to my room to find something to wear. After picking up a pair of shorts and tank top from my laundry basket, I dress fast so I can get downstairs and spend as much time with Elaine as possible.

I sound like a herd of elephants coming down the stairs, and I can only imagine the sound has alerted whoever is on the porch, along with half the neighborhood, that I'm coming. Going too fast, I slam into the door and bounce back, my ass hitting the lip of the third step.

Making a fist and biting my finger, I try not to scream, but I can't hold it in. "Fuck, shit, oh my god." I start to pant. I'm not even sure I can stand up, and I'm pretty sure I just broke my butt. Then come the tears.

It only takes half a minute for Elaine's head to appear in the window of the storm door. "Sara?" She pulls the door open. "What happened?"

Biting my lip, I try to contain the sob that wants to escape. "I fell." I take a deep breath through the pain. "I think I might have broken my ass."

Elaine's eyes widen just before she lets out a belly laugh. "I'm sure you didn't break your ass." She extends her hand to me. "Here, let me help you up, and we'll have a look."

"You're not looking at my ass!" I shriek as I grab Elaine's hand. I attempt to use her support to stand, but Elaine ends up falling forward and catching herself on my shoulders. "Maybe this isn't a good idea. Why don't you go get Izach or Erin?"

Before Elaine can right herself and turn back to the door, Erin's head fills the window. Her neck snaps back a little as if she's trying to figure out what the hell we're doing. "Mom? Sara? What's going on?"

"Sara took a little spill, and I tried to help her up. Clearly it didn't work."

"Okay, let's get you guys up." Erin takes a hold of Elaine's forearm and helps her move back and out the door before coming back for me. "You okay, sweetie? Did you hurt yourself?"

"I think I broke my ass." I laugh as more tears drip down my cheeks. The way my body is jostling from laughing hurts my butt.

"Oh boy, that may make standing on your feet at work all night a little difficult."

"Sara? What's going on?" Izach steps around Elaine, who has backed all the way out the door but is still looking at Erin and me.

"Sara took a fall. I was trying to help her up, then I fell forward and now your mom's helping her up," Elaine explains as Erin helps me stand by putting her hands under my arms and pulling me up.

Sighing as the pressure and pain subside a little, I step forward, grabbing Erin's upper arms for support. "It's better now."

She continues to guide me over the threshold and out the door.

"I think I'm good. It's not hurting as much now," I say, and Erin drops her hands.

"You sure? Let me at least help you to the chair."

"I don't think I want to sit down. Let me walk it off for a minute."

"Maybe we should take her to urgent care. The way she hit the stair, she might have broken her tail bone," Elaine says from where she moved to the other side of the porch.

"No, I'm fine, I swear. Plus if I did break my tail bone, they wouldn't do anything but give me a hemorrhoid pillow, which I won't use. Just let me walk it off," I repeat.

Izach takes his mom's place at my front and bends to look me in the eyes. "Let's go walk it off." He grabs my right hand and turns toward the stairs.

As we pass, Erin runs her hand down my arm and squeezes my forearm while Elaine stands back and gives me a weak smile. Despite my ass being sore, having them care about me kind of makes me feel good. I give them both a small smile, then slowly walk down the stairs.

Once we're on flat ground and a few feet from the porch, Izach drops my hand and wraps his arm around my shoulder, tucking me into his side. "So what happened?"

"I fell. I was running down the stairs and hit the door thinking it would just magically open, but it didn't, and I bounced backward, landing ass-first on the lip of one of the steps. My butt hurts," I whine a little.

"Maybe we should get you some ice, or I could rub your butt for you?"

"As tempting as that sounds, I don't think you rubbing it will do anything, though the ice might. But it's starting to feel better just from walking around."

We make it to the end of the driveway and turn left, walking away from the house.

"You gonna be okay to work tonight?"

"Yeah, I'm on my feet all night. If anything, my butt's just bruised, so sitting might be a little uncomfortable."

"It's Tuesday though. Will you really be that busy?"

"Probably not, but I can stock and fill to keep myself going. The morning shift will be thrilled."

We pass the neighbors' house and I stop, making Izach stop with me. He looks down at me at the same time I push up on my tiptoes and meet his lips for a quick kiss.

"What's that for?" He smiles at me. "Not that I mind you kissing me."

"For caring. I just wanted to thank you."

"You don't need to thank me for caring about you. I couldn't imagine someone not caring once they've met you."

I mutter, "You'd be surprised," but let it go. Louder, I say, "So what's the plan for the day? I mean, I know we're going to The Diner for dinner before my shift, but what are you all thinking of doing before that?"

We walk again, heading toward the corner only a couple houses down.

"I don't know. I think the plan is just to hang out. Mom's going to work on packing up the rest of Gran-ma's things."

"I never asked— why are they driving?"

"Gran-ma doesn't want to give up her car."

"That's kind of funny, considering I don't think I've seen Elaine drive it in over a year. Does the car even start?" I ask, slipping out of his hold and looking into his eyes before we turn back toward the house.

Izach takes my hand instead of tucking me back into his body. "That's a good question. I wasn't aware she didn't drive anymore. I mean, since I got here, I've been doing her running around, but I just thought she was trying to get me acquainted with the area. I'm gonna have to check the car and maybe go for an oil change. You want to come with me?"

"No, I really want to spend a little time with Elaine alone. Do you think your mom will mind?"

"I'm sure she won't. Plus she's going to be busy packing. Gran-ma hasn't done shit!"

"That doesn't surprise me. When Elaine told me she was moving, I didn't think she meant in a week. I thought she would take at least a month to get things in order." We stop at the end of the driveway, and I look up to see Elaine sitting in her usual spot, working on a crossword.

"Yeah, well, that's Gran-ma for you. Timing is everything," Izach says as we start up the driveway toward the porch.

At the bottom step, Izach stops and drops a quick kiss on my lips before he goes toward the garage. I head up the stairs and sit in the other rocker, positioning my foot under my butt so my tail bone doesn't rest on the chair. For a few minutes, I listen to her pen scratch across the page of her book as she fills in the words of her puzzle. Looking around, I think of all the time we've spent on this porch, doing the same thing, and feel tears sting my eyes.

"If you're going to sit over there and cry, I'm going to have to ask you to go inside," she says without looking up.

"I'm not crying," I snap and pray the tears I'm holding back don't slide down my cheeks.

"Then why is your nose all red?"

"Allergies. How do you know my nose is red anyway? Your head's been in that book since before I sat down."

"Sweetie, not only am I a mother, I'm also a grandmother. We see everything, even when we're not looking."

"Speaking of your daughter, why aren't you helping her pack?

"I've packed a little, but Erin offered, so I'm letting her do the rest. It's not that much—just photo frames and other small things. I'm leaving the furniture for Izach. He can do what he wants with it. I'm pretty sure the two of you will be having a yard sale soon." She chuckles. "So my dear..."

"So..." I mimicked.

"I'm not good at this whole good-bye thing."

"Neither am I, obviously. Why don't we just call it a 'see you soon' thing instead?" I ask with a grin.

"I hope you and Izach plan to come see me. I probably won't come back here, no offense." She gives me a hopeful look.

"None taken, but why? You've lived here your whole life."

"Other than Izach and you, I have nothing else here. You're both young, so it'd be better for you to come visit me, don't you think?"

I smile. "I would love to go to Arizona. Seeing the Grand Canyon is in the top five on my bucket list."

"Maybe this winter, when it's thirty below here, you can come warm yourself up by visiting me?"

"I'll have to start saving now to make it happen, but consider this my reservation!" I reach over to shake Elaine's hand, and she chuckles but takes my hand anyway.

"Now what did you really want to talk about?" she asks after dropping my hand.

"What'd you mean? I wanted to spend some time together, just the two of us, before I have to go to work."

"How's your butt feel?"

"It's a little sore, but I'm fine."

"Good, because we're about to have a long talk." She looks at me over her glasses with a brow raised.

"Um, okay, should I be scared? Because I'm kind of scared."

"Please, I'm just going to give you some words of advice—starting with Izach."

"Izach's a name, not advice," I say.

"Don't be a smartass, you know what I mean. Don't push him away, even if you don't think you're ready to share everything with him. He'll wait for you to be ready. That boy is so taken by you, I'm sure it won't be long until he admits he's head-over-heels in love." My eyes go wide, but Elaine keeps going. "Don't lie to yourself; I see it when you look at him too. You'll catch flies with that thing hanging open like that. Next thing—you're such a smart girl, Sara, and I know Izach talked to you about getting your equivalency diploma. I think you need to follow through with that. You're not a waitress-for-life kind of girl, okay?"

"I'm going to. I think I might want to go to school to be a counselor or something along those lines. I'm not really sure yet, but I know I want to go."

179

"That sounds perfect for you. Just make sure you keep me posted on how things are going, and I'm not only talking about with school." She winks.

"Elaine," I warn, "I'm not the kind of girl who kisses and tells. Besides, Izach is your grandson, and that's a little weird."

"I didn't ask for a play-by-play. I just want to know how things are going between the two of you. For heaven's sake, girl, get your head out of the gutter!"

Elaine's look of disgust was so hilarious I couldn't hold back my laugher. "I'm sorry, I didn't mean to take it that way," I say between giggles. "It's just I don't really have anyone but you and Jacqui, and I've never really done this whole 'talk with my girlfriends about a guy' thing."

"Oh, Sara, as much as I love you and would love to have you talk to me, your sex life, especially with my grandson, is completely off-limits. But thank you for thinking of me as a girlfriend. You keep me young."

"You're welcome, and I promise I'll keep things PG." I get up out of my rocking chair and give Elaine a hug.

"What's this for?" she asks over my shoulder as my arms wrap around her neck.

"For loving me. Until you said that, I didn't think I had anyone in this world who loved me. It means a lot to me to hear that from you."

"Of course I love you, sweetheart." I sniffle, and she says, "Don't start crying on me again."

"I can't help it. I'm going to miss you so much." The tears start to fall as my shoulders shake.

Tossing her crossword book on the porch, Elaine wraps her arms tightly around my middle, making it impossible for me to stand. I kneel on the concrete in front of her and hold tight. At the sound of my first hiccuping sob, Elaine rubs small circles on my back. It's been so long since someone has comforted me like this, I never want to let her go.

"It's okay, sweetie, you can call me anytime. I'll always be here for you, I promise. I wouldn't let you walk away without a fight."

I nod against Elaine's shoulder. I know she isn't that person. She isn't like my family. Elaine would believe me; she would support me. She proved it when she let me move into her apartment.

"I'm so glad I found you," I say. "I don't know if I would have made it if you hadn't given me a chance."

"You came to me at the right time, Sara. It's all about timing."

The sound of the door to my right slamming makes me lift my head from Elaine's shoulder. I look quickly toward where the noise came from, but no one's there, so I look back at Elaine. Fresh tears are rolling down her wrinkled cheeks.

She loosens her grip on my back and brings her hand around to wipe my face. "You may not be my one of my granddaughters, but that's how I see you. I know there's a lot you haven't told me, and that's okay"—she pushes the loose hair away from my face—"but if you're ready and want to tell me, I'll listen."

"Someday I want to tell you what brought me to your door step, but not today."

This time Elaine nods. The next squeak of the door makes both of us turn to see Izach coming out of the house. He doesn't stop—he just keeps going down the stairs and around the corner of the house. He's giving me my time alone with Elaine.

181

My heart grows bigger. This family has managed to bust their way into my heart—Elaine years ago, and now Izach and Erin. I hope I get to meet the rest of their family, because I'm sure they'll squeeze right in there too.

Izach

I head to the garage with a huge smile. After I kissed Sara at the bottom of the porch steps, I looked up and caught the giant smile painted across Gran-ma's face. She's so happy that things are progressing with Sara and me, and so am I. She's amazing, despite the issues Gran-ma told me about and the few I've discovered myself, one of which I didn't even mention to Sara. When I was holding her last night, she jumped and her whole body tensed. I knew something was really wrong when she tried to push me away and said "No." But after I realized she was still sleeping, I pulled her in tighter and whispered that she was okay until the tension left her. That dream confirmed that something horrible has happened to her. I just hope she lets me in enough to trust me to help her get through it.

Pushing the garage door up, I take a good look at Gran-ma's car and notice about an inch of dust covering it. "Shit."

I approach the barely driven early 2000s Cadillac CTS. Stupidly, I didn't bring the keys with me, but I try the door anyway and find it unlocked. I dip into the hot box and pop the hood. The first thing I do is check the oil. It looks good, but god only knows how long it's been since it was last changed. After giving the rest of the fluids a once-over, I run back to the house to get the keys.

When I round the corner, just before I stomp up the stairs, I stop dead in my tracks. Sara is kneeling in front of Gran-ma, and I can tell they're both crying. I quietly sneak up the steps and duck into the house, letting the door slam behind me. So much for being quiet.

"Hey, honey, what are you up to?" Mom calls from Gran-ma's bedroom.

"I'm taking a look at that beast of a car in the garage."

"What's wrong with it?" She sounds concerned—considering she's going to drive it across the country, she should be concerned—as she walks out of the bedroom.

"Apparently Gran-ma hasn't driven it in a year, or maybe longer."

"Seriously?"

"That's what Sara said."

"How the hell has she been getting her groceries and going to her doctor's appointments?" Now Mom sounds worried.

"I'm sure she has the groceries delivered or asks Sara to pick things up for her. As for her doctor, let's hope she's getting a ride from someone."

"Shit, now I'm going to have to talk to her about this, and it'll probably piss her off."

"Whoa, Mom, little ears in the room!" I joke. My parents have always tried to avoid swearing in front of us.

"Please, Izach, I've heard your mouth. It's a wonder you got a job teaching children."

"Hey now, they're not really children, they're teenagers, and I can guarantee their mouths are much worse than mine."

"Whatever, let's get back on track. What's wrong with the car?" Mom asks, putting her hands on her hips.

"Not sure yet. I was just coming in to get the keys. I think I'll run it over to the quick oil change place and see if they'll give it a good once-over for me."

"Good idea. I don't want that thing blowing up on me halfway across the country."

"It looks like it's in good condition. Probably just needs a tune up," I say as I snag the keys from Gran-ma's junk cupboard and look over at mom.

"Okay, do you need any money?"

"Nah, I can get it. When I get back, I'll help you get the rest of this shit packed up."

"After I'm done in the bedroom, I'm stopping. We'll tackle the kitchen and out here when we get back from dinner," Mom says and turns to go back to the bedroom.

"Sounds good. I'll call you if there's anything wrong with the car."

Mom groans. "Please do. Thanks, honey."

I turn on my heel and head back toward the door. I can see from the window that Sara and Gran-ma are still having their moment, so I sneak out as fast as I can, but both of them look at me before I can bounce down the stairs two at a time. Spinning the key ring around my finger, I think about what's going on between the two of them, but I won't ask. If Sara or Gran-ma want to tell me, they will.

Not bothering to close the hood of the car, I slip behind the steering wheel and give the key a crank. The car starts with a wheezing sound, but after a minute or so, it sounds strong. I get out and close the hood. Leaving it running, I run to my car and back it down the driveway, creating a decent amount of space between the neighbor's fence and Sara's car. I hope I'll have enough room to get Gran-ma's out, but no matter how far I go, I can't make room. Looks as though I have to park my baby on the street.

Running back to the garage, I look over and see Gran-ma and Sara giving me a funny look, so I wave. Sara will explain what I'm doing. I'd love for her to come with me, but I know she wants this time with Gran-ma.

Jumping back in the car, I throw it in reverse and back down the driveway. As I pass the porch, I wave to Sara and Gran-ma. Sara waves back while Gran-ma gives me a weird look.

CHAPTER 16

Sara

Looking at myself in the mirror, I groan. The last thing I want to do is go out to dinner wearing my work uniform. I wish I could have found someone to switch shifts with me tonight, but even when I have more notice, getting coverage is like pulling teeth. I'm usually the one they come to for a schedule switch, so I'm more than owed, but I couldn't do it with one day's notice. I pull my hair up and brush the sides flat before tying an elastic band around my ponytail. I dig through my makeup bag for my eyeliner and mascara.

After making myself half up, I slide my feet into my nasty work shoes, then head out. At the bottom of the stairs, I see Izach's head through the glass of my storm door. When he notices me coming, he pulls the squeaking piece of shit open so I can join them. Erin is sitting in my usual spot, and she looks beautiful in a cute summer dress with light makeup. Elaine is sitting opposite her, wearing the same thing she's had on all day. Despite seeing him first, I didn't take a good look at what Izach has on. He's also changed, and is wearing dark-wash jeans with a green-and-white striped polo shirt.

When I step into his side, the scent of his cologne fills my nose. I can't place what he smells like, but whatever it is, I like it. He hangs his arm over my shoulder and pulls me into his side, placing a soft kiss on my temple. I look at him and give him a smile, which he returns.

Clapping, Elaine said, "All right, let's get this show on the road. I'm hungry." She pushes off the arms of the chair and stands.

"Why are you hungry? You've been sitting out here doing crosswords all day while Izach and I have been getting you ready to move," Erin asks Elaine but doesn't move a muscle.

"I've been visiting with Sara all day. We're not going to have that chance again," Elaine shoots back.

"I make you hungry?" I jump in, trying to defuse the tension between mother and daughter.

"Well, no, but the whole crying thing took a lot out of me. Now I need to reenergize."

"Christ." Izach pushes off the porch rail, taking me with him. "Let's just go. Sara starts work at eight so we don't have a lot of time."

Without another word, Elaine reaches for the post next to the stairs, then follows the railing down the steps. Erin follows Izach and me down the stairs. Elaine is waiting for us to join her, looking at her car in the driveway and Izach's on the street.

"Mom, you want to drive with Gran-ma in her car? You can follow Sara and me," Izach says.

"Izach, I have to take my own car," I say.

"We're taking your car. I'll ride home with Mom and Gran-ma."

"That's fine, honey. Do you have the keys?"

"Yeah." Izach reaches into his pocket, pulls out the key ring, and hands it to his mom. "We'll see you there."

He guides me to my beater. Automatically I go toward the driver's door, Izach walking right along with me. I thought he was going to try to talk me into letting him drive, but he stops and pulls my door open for me. Once I'm folded inside, he shuts it, then walks around the back of the car to the passenger side. He gets in and buckles up before I stick my key in the ignition and crank the beast to life.

"My car's a piece of shit," I say apologetically.

"Not gonna lie, based on what the outside looks like, I'm kind of surprised it still runs as good as it does. I think you have more duct tape on this thing than actual car parts."

"Duct tape is cheaper than taking it to the shop when something falls off," I say as I back down the driveway. "I've been saving to get something newer, but I don't have enough put away yet."

"When you're ready, let me know and I'll go looking with you."

"You'd do that?" I ask, surprised.

"Of course. I don't want some sleazy car salesman taking advantage of you. I know my cars. I can get you into something affordable that you'll look good driving."

"You trying to say I don't look good driving the beast?"

"You're probably the only thing that looks good in this car." Izach reaches over to turn on the radio.

"It doesn't work. Hasn't since I bought it. It's not worth it for me to get a new radio put in because I don't plan on keeping this much longer."

"So you drive around in silence?"

I shake my head. "No, I usually wear my earbuds, but I'm not going to be rude and put them in with you in the car."

"Well, thank you, I appreciate that you'd rather talk to me."

I look over and smile at Izach, who's already smiling at me. He leans over and kisses me softly but quickly, and I turn my head back to the road.

The diner parking lot is nearly empty when I pull in. Instead of parking near Erin and Elaine, I drive behind the building and park with the rest of the employees. I don't wait to see if Izach'll open my door—I just jump out, pushing the lock button down before I shut the door. Izach stands, and I notice him looking around the lot.

"It's not very well lit back here," he points out.

"I know. That's why we have one of the cooks walk us out to our cars if it's still dark when we leave. They're pretty good about making sure we're safe, because a lot of drunks hang around here after the bars close."

"Good to know. If you had told me you're walking out to your car alone in the dark, I'd be forced to pick you up so I'd know you were safe," Izach says as he meets me at the back of my car and takes my hand.

"That's a little dramatic, don't you think?"

"Not at all. I can't do anything about the other waitresses, but I can make sure you're safe."

We let the subject go as we walk over to Elaine and Erin waiting for us on the sidewalk. I take the lead, opening the door and stepping aside to let them pass through. Izach puts his hand above mine to hold the door for me, so I duck under his arm and head in with him right behind me.

"I'm just going to go throw my stuff in the back. Sit wherever you want." I motion toward the open booths before moving toward the counter.

"Hey, Sara, decided to come in the front door today?" Miguel yells through the pickup window.

"Don't get used to it. I'm having dinner with some friends before my shift," I shoot back.

After dropping my purse in my locker, I head back through the swinging door to the booth Elaine, Erin, and Izach have chosen. Before my ass even hits the empty vinyl seat next to Izach, Cheryl is at the table to take drink orders. She notices Izach's arm around my shoulders and gives me a huge smile.

"Hello, Sara's friends! I'm Cheryl, and I'll be your server tonight." She gives everyone a beaming smile. "What can I get you to drink?"

After ordering water, I ask, "Aren't you working overnight with me?"

"Yeah, they called me in because Rachel had to go get one of the kids. Apparently daycare isn't fond of taking care of sick children. I came in a couple hours early to cover for her."

"Oh okay, are you staying until four then or cutting out early?" I ask. Even though it's Tuesday, I'm a little worried because we never know what kind of crowd will come waltzing in when the bars close.

"If it's dead, I might, but I wasn't planning on it. I'm gonna go get your drinks. The specials for tonight are in the center flap of the menu. Be right back!"

"What should we get, Sara?" Elaine asks.

"You've been here before. You have to have a favorite?"

"I do, but I want to give something else a try. What's your favorite?"

"Um, I usually get a hamburger of some sort. Working here as long as I have, nothing tastes good anymore."

Elaine lets out a little laugh. "I can imagine. Well then, I think I'm going with breakfast for dinner. Can never go wrong with that."

"Me too," Erin says. "What are you thinking, honey?" she asks Izach.

"I think I'm going to get the Buffalo chicken sandwich with gravy fries."

"Sounds good!" Cheryl says, walking up and standing at the end of the table with our drinks on her tray. She passes out the drinks, then takes the rest of our orders before heading back to the counter.

Izach leans in and asks close to my ear, "She seems nice. Do you work with her often?"

"Yeah, I usually work with her a few times a week. There're three other girls who work mostly overnights. They're the ones who ask me to change shifts all the time, and they're definitely not as nice as Cheryl."

"Since they owe you, do you think you can get one of them to work the Fourth of July for you?"

"I can try. It's a Saturday, right?"

"Yeah, I'm gonna need you for the whole day," he says, stroking my cheek.

"I can ask Cheryl. She doesn't usually work Saturdays, and she doesn't have a family to make plans with. She's here more than the rest of us actually. The others won't go for it though."

"Cheryl gave you a giant smile when she saw us together. I think she might be willing if you told her I have plans for us."

"I'm sure she will." I turn back toward Elaine and Erin across from us, ending the conversation. I'll check with Cheryl later about changing.

Since the diner isn't busy, Miguel takes no time at all to whip up our food. I'm kind of glad I'll have a few

191

more minutes to spend talking with them before I have to duck away. For the most part, Elaine keeps the conversation flowing throughout our meal, directing almost all her questions to me, asking about my job and what kind of weirdos I have to deal with after they finish a night of drinking. I have so many stories, one dinner isn't enough time to tell a quarter of them.

After I take my last bite of food, I glance at my watch and notice I only have another half hour before I have to be the one serving the guests. It's my last half hour to spend with Elaine. Before I can lift my head, the sting of tears burns my eyes. I was supposed to get this all out earlier. I know Elaine doesn't want me crying in the middle of dinner, especially the last one I'll spend with her for who knows how long. I have to take a deep breath to get a hold of myself before I look at her again. When our eyes meet, she smiles at me, but it's a sad smile. She knows what I was just doing.

"You guys ready for the check?" Cheryl asks, appearing at my side.

"You can put it on my tab—"

"No, she cannot! This is my last chance to take you out, and I'm paying," Elaine scolds me with wide, crazy eyes.

"Okay, you can pay."

"Thank you. Now if you wouldn't mind, bring me the bill," she says to Cheryl, who's biting her lip to stop herself from laughing. Elaine looks over at Izach. "Why don't you go start the car? Make sure the air's turned up high so it won't be so hot when I get in."

"Sure, Gran-ma." Izach holds out his hand to his mom for the keys. "Come with me?" he asks, leaning close to my ear again.

"Sure, I still have a little time before my shift starts." I slide out of the booth.

Once he's standing, Izach takes my hand, and we walk to the front door. He pushes it open and steps aside so I can cross the threshold beside him. He directs me to the passenger seat of Elaine's car, then opens the door so I can slide in. Slipping behind the wheel, Izach starts Elaine's car, then cranks on the air conditioning.

"So… how's your butt? You going to be okay to work all night?"

"Yeah I'll be fine. It's a little sore, but running around all night I'll barely notice it."

"How about after saying bye to Gran-ma?"

"I hope so. If not, it'll be a very long night." I lean my head back against the seat and blow out a breath. "I wish I had a normal job, one where I didn't have to worry about finding someone to cover for me. Then I could have taken the day off, and if I need to break down, I could just go to my apartment. Now I have to suck it up and work all night."

He takes my hand. "I know, but you'll see her again. So it's not good-bye. It's see ya later."

"True. She did invite me to come see her this winter, to get out of the cold." Movement at the diner door catches my eyes. "I probably should bite the bullet and say good-bye now, so I have time to get cleaned up before my shift if I cry."

Izach lifts the back of my hand to his lips and holds it against them before he flips it and kisses my palm. "See you in the morning?"

"Yeah." My voice is soft and already filled with emotion.

As I reach for the door handle, Izach lets go of my other hand. I pop the door open and swing myself out. Erin is standing there, waiting to take my place.

Reaching out with her arms spread wide, Erin wraps her hands around my shoulders and pulls me in for a hug. "Sara, it was wonderful to finally meet you. You and Izach take care of each other, okay?"

"We will," I answer with a shaky voice.

She motions to Elaine standing near the trunk of the car. "I'll give you two a minute to say good-bye."

"Elaine…" I feel tears welling in my eyes.

"No crying, we got all that out earlier."

We step toward each other, and I wrap my arms around her first.

"Remember what I said earlier. Call and give me updates, not just on how things are going with my boy but also about work, your life, and hopefully soon, school."

Nodding against her shoulder, I manage a quiet, "Okay."

"I love you, sweetie. Take care of yourself. Let that star buried deep inside you shine bright. I sense good things in your future."

"I love you too." I pull back, and thank god, none of the tears have leaked down my cheeks. "Have a safe trip. Call me and let me know you made it."

"I will, sweetie. Have a good night at work. Maybe you could call me and tell me about the drunk idiots that come in?"

"I will." A little laugh escapes me as I let go of Elaine. "I'm gonna miss you." I back away, getting ready to take off toward the diner.

"I'll miss you too." Elaine grabs the handle and swings the door wide, then she carefully folds herself in as I walk backward toward the diner, watching her.

Once she's tucked inside, I turn and walk normally. I stop at the door and wait for them to pull out. As they pass, I throw them a wave, get three in return, and then I head into work.

Izach

We get home from dinner, and I go right into the house with Mom to finish packing the rest of Gran-ma's shit. Gran-ma, of course, takes her usual spot on the porch with her crossword book. Mom and I still have to get everything in the car and situated so they can travel comfortably, so we have a busy night to say the least.

Standing in front of Gran-ma's junk cupboard, I pull things out and pile them into a box. "I feel bad for Sara," I say just loud enough for Mom to hear me. "I guess I didn't realize how close she and Gran-ma are before today."

"I think they have an unspoken relationship. According to Gran-ma, they've always seemed to get each other. Gran-ma said that Sara would sit with her on the porch while she did her puzzles, but they never really talked. I guess Sara's a big reader. She'd just sit there and read, but they kept each other company," Mom says as she packs up photo frames from the wall.

"What about in the winter? Did Sara come down here and hang out?"

"Not that I know of, but I never asked." Mom stops what she's doing and turns toward me. "I think you two are good for each other."

"She's different. I don't know what it is, but it's there and I've felt it since the first minute I met her."

"I know, honey, I can see it when you look at her. Hell, I can see it when you talk about her. Just make sure you're careful."

"Oh god, you're not gonna give me the talk, are you? Because you're about six years too late."

"No, I'm not talking about sex, but you be careful with that too. I just want to make sure neither of you get hurt. The other night, Gran-ma told me she's never seen Sara with anyone, let alone a boyfriend, so ease into things with her. There's no need to rush it."

"I know, Mom. I told you, I'm taking things slow. Actually, I have this thing planned for us on the Fourth of July, so I'm hoping she gets the day off. I wanna make sure she knows I'm serious about us going somewhere, but for now, I'm not pushing it."

"That's all I want to hear. You mean the world to me. You're my little boy, and I don't want to see you get hurt." She turns back to her packing.

"Thanks." I go back to filing the box I'm working on too.

Somewhere around nine, Gran-ma strolls into the house, passes Mom and me, heads to her room, and shuts the door without a word. I look at Mom and shrug as she does the same.

By the time the car is loaded—with enough room for Mom and Gran-ma to be comfortable—it's well past midnight. I shut and lock the car doors, then practically crawl back to the house. I sent Mom to bed around ten since she'll need plenty of sleep if they're going to make any kind of dent in their drive tomorrow.

I lie down on the couch, and my thoughts drift to Sara and how her night's going. I hope she isn't too upset about saying good-bye to Gran-ma. Closing my eyes, I fall asleep while thinking about my plans for the Fourth and hoping she gets her friend to switch with her.

CHAPTER 17

Sara

It's been a little over two weeks since Elaine and Erin left for Arizona. As promised, Elaine called me when they arrived safely. The night I had to say good-bye to her in the parking lot was hard, and working a full shift knowing I wouldn't see her the following day nearly had me in tears all night. Elaine and I had never talked all that much when we spent time together, but we did keep each other company. We would sit on the porch, and she'd do her crosswords while I read or played some game on my phone. Since she left, Izach has been filling the void. We sit outside until its dark, then we either go up to my apartment or into his and watch TV. I don't think I've ever watched so much TV in my life—I'd rather read—but getting to spend time snuggled up on the couch with him is worth it.

Since the night we spent together, things haven't gone any further than heated make-out sessions while we watch TV. Izach is trying to go slow for me, so I don't freak out, but I'm ready for more, and I'm not quite sure how to tell him. He's planned something for this Saturday, which I had to get the whole day off for and make sure I found time to dye my faded hair a nice brown. I'm hoping whatever he has planned takes things a little further between us. In the meantime, I'm going to get Jacqui's opinion and see if she thinks I should just talk to him about it or wait and see. Up until this point, all she and I have discussed about my relationship with Izach is how well we're getting to know each other. So if nothing happens this weekend, I'll have to ask her for dating advice on Monday since she's taking Friday off. This is the exact reason I tell her she cannot take a day off.

Sara

Instead of getting ready for my Friday appointment—Jacqui's day off— and work like I usually do, I'm spending extra time with Izach. After spending the day hanging out, either on the porch or in the yard—he weeded the gardens while I lay in the sun—we headed to his apartment to find something to make for dinner.

"What about barbecue chicken?" Izach asks with his head buried in the freezer.

"Do we have enough time? I have to be at work at seven thirty, and it's five now."

"Sure, I'll put it in the microwave to defrost while I go start the grill." He pulls the chicken out of the freezer, immediately ripping open the package.

"Okay, I guess I can make some beans or corn to go with it."

"There're beans in the fridge. I stopped at the veggie stand the other night after I went to the store, so they're fresh."

Being so domestic with Izach feels natural, as though we've been doing it for a lot longer than a couple of weeks. I've always tried to eat dinner before I go into work so I can avoid eating shitty diner food, but now that I have Izach to sit down with, I find that

I'm less likely to just say forget it. Fridays tend to be more difficult though, since I have my appointment, so I guess Jacqui's day off kind of worked for my benefit.

Izach grills the chicken while I get everything ready inside, then we sit down and eat together. Before I know it, I have to run upstairs and get ready for work. It's the day before a holiday, so I know tonight will be crazy—the idiots don't only come out during a full moon. The good thing is time flies when I'm busy, so four o'clock should roll around faster than it normally does. I just hope I can sleep enough after work. I'm so excited to see what Izach has planned for us tomorrow.

Izach

It's only ten in the morning, and I can't sit still. I'm trying to be patient and let Sara sleep long enough so she can make it through the day I've planned and the fireworks tonight without having to take a nap. I didn't hear her come in last night—I barely ever hear her come in since I moved to the master bedroom—but I know she was working until four, so she had to have gotten home sometime around four thirty.

This morning, to try to kill time, I got up, got ready, and headed to the store for the things we'd need. I came home and packed the cooler, grabbed a change of clothes and a couple hoodies, and packed my car. Now I'm sitting on the porch, drinking my second cup of coffee and waiting. I keep going over the things Sara needs to get ready before we go. I hope I can convince her to do it without having to give anything away.

It's just before noon when I hear the slam of her door, then the pounding of her feet on stairs.

"Sara's up," I say with a smile. The squeak of her storm door has me tossing the crossword book on the porch and looking over my shoulder at Sara. "Good morning."

"Morning," she says groggily, then leans against the rail in front of me. "I tried to get up earlier, but I was beat. We were swamped right up until I left last night. They actually wanted me to stay a little longer, but I told them I couldn't. I'm pretty sure I won't get the tips from the tables I left behind."

"A lot of crazy drunk people?" I stand from the rocking chair, close the distance between us, and wrap my arms around her waist while hers go around mine.

"Yeah, they were a little out of control too. I think I'm gonna need a new uniform. Around two, a group of fucking adults pretty much had a food fight. Of course I had to jump in and threaten them with the cops to get it to stop, but not before I got pelted with ketchup, gravy, and whatever else was on their plates."

"Sounds like a shit night."

Sara nods, then looks up at my face with a smile.

I lean in and place a soft kiss on her lips. "Don't worry, what I have planned today will make you forget all about it."

"I'm looking forward to it. I just came down to grab a cup of coffee from you, then I'm going back up to take a shower and get ready. Anything in particular I should put on or bring with me?"

She gave me my opening. "Yeah, I think you might need a change of clothes, just in case."

Sara looks at me with a raised brow. "I'm not sure I'm okay with having to be prepared with a change of clothes. Just what do you have planned today? Am I gonna get messy?"

"No, you won't get messy. You're gonna have to trust me. I promise you'll love it." I step back and give her room to slip past me.

"Okay," she exaggerates sarcastically. "Let me go get my liquid energy so we can get going."

"No rush. I didn't plan on leaving until one, one thirty anyway, so you have time to get ready," I say to Sara's back, but she turns and shoots a beaming smile at me.

A few minutes later, holding the biggest coffee cup I own, Sara crosses the porch. I've picked up the crossword book and started working on a puzzle about Valentine's Day. All the words have to do with dates and love, so even though it's the middle of summer, the puzzle kind of goes along with my theme for the day.

Just as I knew she would be, Sara's ready to go and coming back down the stairs a little after one. Before she bursts through the door, I stand so I can take her things and put them in the car, but I stop in my tracks when I see her. She's wearing her hair down and wavy. Sometime last week, she dyed it, making it look more golden brown than the dingy black/blond it was when I first met her. She has on a red, white, and blue tie-dyed tank top with short jean shorts. Her outfit is festive but not over the top.

After she stops in front of me, I slip the strap of her backpack off her shoulder and fling it over mine. "I'm going to throw this in the car."

"Okay, do I have time for another small cup of coffee?"

"Yeah, there's a little left in there. Put it in a travel mug if you want. Can you hit the power button when you're done?" I back away, then turn to head down the steps.

"Yep, then we can take off and I can see what you're up to."

I throw her a smile over my shoulder. It's true I've been planning this for a long time, but I did so because I wanted to make sure we had enough time to get to know each other. I want Sara to be comfortable taking things further, and today is the day I hope our relationship turns into more. But first I need to make our relationship official, and I want that to be memorable for her.

After tossing her bag in the trunk, I turn to go back to the house, but see Sara heading up the driveway toward me.

"I locked the door. Please tell me you have your keys?" she asks.

I jiggle my pocket, and the sound of my keys bouncing around fills the air. "I do. We good to go?"

"I'm ready whenever you are, even though I have no idea where we're going."

"You know, if I really wanted to surprise you, I could blindfold you," I say as she follows me to the passenger door.

"Please don't. I'm not a fan of blindfolds."

"Don't worry, you're safe."

She leans up on her tiptoes and gives me a quick kiss before she slides into the car.

After shutting the door behind her, I take off around the back, then slip into my seat. "No questions. You'll be able to figure out where we're going once we get on the highway."

"Don't worry, I won't ruin your surprise." Sara cranks up the stereo after I start the car. "Consider this my way of staying quiet," she yells over the music.

Shaking my head, I chuckle and throw the car in reverse. Once I make my way to the entrance to the highway, I take the ramp going north and glance at Sara to see if she's figured out where we're going. She's looking out the window, taking in everything and singing along with the music. We go around the city and come up on the Grand Island Bridge. She has to know where we're going now, but I don't want to ask if she's figured it out.

After taking the second bridge, I get off at the exit for the casino and Niagara Falls. Circling the parkway, I follow the traffic into downtown Niagara Falls. I opt to park in the state lot closer to the park instead of trying to find something cheaper. This way I won't have to drag the cooler too far or take long to bring it back later.

"I haven't been here since I was little, before my aunt moved to Florida. We came as a family and walked across the bridge to go have dinner in Canada. I was probably nine or ten," Sara says after I cut the engine, surprising me with the information. Since the night she told me about her brothers, she hasn't talked about her family at all.

"Same here. We came up to visit Gran-ma when I was around the same age, all of us, and spent the day walking around. We didn't go to Canada though."

"We'll have to walk over there sometime. There's a lot more to do. Do you have your passport or enhanced license?" Sara asks as we pop our doors open at the same time.

"I have a passport," I answer over the roof of the car.

Sara lifts her face, eyes closed, and breathes in deeply. "Good, next time I'll plan the day, and we'll go over there and check things out." She drops her head and watches me duck back in the car and grab my bag. "Do you need me to get anything?"

"Yeah, can you carry this? I have to get the cooler from the trunk."

"Sure." She meets me at the back of the car, takes the bag, and slings it over her right shoulder.

Noticing her eyes start to wander again, I bring them back to me. "Not going to ask me what's in the cooler?"

"I'm hoping it's food, since I haven't eaten anything today."

"You're right, and while we're having our picnic, I'll tell you what's planned for today."

Sara falls in step next to me as we walk across the lot to the winding park pathways. I watch Sara taking in all of the different people around us. It looks as if every culture of the world is rushing around, all of them talking in different languages. As we get closer to the rushing water, we're cut off by a little boy and girl running away from their father as he yells at them in what I imagine is Chinese. When the father finally scoops one up in each arm, still yelling at them, Sara looks at me and giggles.

Jerking my head to the left, I lead her away from the hordes of people to find an area with a nice clearing. I probably should have taken today's holiday into consideration and realized there would be a million tourists walking around. I'm glad I got the park pass thing for us to do the Maid of the Mist and the Cave of the Winds. It even has tour times so we don't have to wait in line.

"How about here?" Sara asks, breaking into my thoughts. "It's nice and sunny but kind of off the path."

"Looks good to me."

I drop the cooler, take my bag from Sara's shoulder, and pull out the blanket. I shake it and try to make the fabric land perfectly, but it folds over every time. After the third time, Sara starts laughing.

"Ya know, you could help."

"I could, but it's more entertaining to watch you, and ya know, you could ask for help."

"Beautiful Sara, would you mind helping me spread the blanket?" I give her a sad puppy dog look, complete with my lip sticking out.

"Put your lip away, I'll help you." She takes the corners opposite mine. "The faster we get this spread, the faster you can feed me."

"Thank you. Now sit, so I can get this hunger of yours under control." I kneel on the corner of the blanket.

After flipping the lid of the cooler, I pull out containers and two bottles of Pepsi. Sara kneels, then shifts to the side with her legs tucked partially under her. She doesn't reach for any of the food but watches me. After I drop the last item, I reach for my backpack and grab the paper plates and plastic utensils I stowed in there this morning.

"So this one has bread, and this one has turkey, ham, and salami. I only brought mayo. I probably should have asked if you like it."

"I eat mayo. What's in this one?" Sara points at the largest container.

"That's loaded potato salad, and it's amazing. I tasted it at the store."

"Mmm, that sounds good."

"Go ahead and dig in. We have about an hour and a half to eat."

Sara tears into the bread, handing me two slices before putting two on her plate. While she goes for the mayo next, I pull the lids off of everything else. After she's done, I work on my own sandwich, only to be distracted by her groan of approval when she takes the first bite.

"Oh my god, that's good! I was so hungry," she says, holding her sandwich close to her mouth.

"I can see that."

"Are you trying to say I'm a pig?"

"Not at all, but you kind of groaned really loud when you took a bite." I bite into my own sandwich.

Our friendly banter continues throughout lunch. When we're done eating, we take care of cleaning up and throwing everything back in the cooler. I'll clean it out when we get home, but for right now, I just want to take a minute to relax and enjoy the fact that Sara doesn't have to rush off to work or an appointment.

She breaks the silence. "I love people-watching. I think this is the perfect place for it. At some point today, every culture will pass by us."

"Me too," I say without any thought, noticing a ray of sun peeking through the trees and bouncing off Sara's hair, making it look as though she has a golden halo.

"Uh, Izach?"

"Yeah?"

"You're looking at me."

"I know. I like watching you." I scoot across the blanket and position myself behind Sara, caging her in with my legs and wrapping my arms around her.

208

"Although I might like this more." I run my nose up the outside of her ear.

Leaning her head back on my shoulder, Sara turns her lips toward me and I gladly take them. I start with a soft kiss, but I can't control it. The longer my lips are pressed against hers, the more I want into her mouth. I don't give a shit that we're in a public park crawling with people. It's as if the world around us has faded away, and the only thing left is the two of us. I tilt her chin toward me, then run my tongue along the seam of her lips. When she opens for me right away, I know she's feeling what I am. My tongue enters her mouth to tangle with hers and explore the depths of her mouth.

It's only a minute before her hands are off the blanket and I'm supporting most of her weight along with mine. She reaches up awkwardly and does her best to pull my face closer. Easing off a little, I pull back, but she follows my movement. When I detach our lips, I kiss her a couple times before putting some distance between our faces.

"As much as I'd like to keep doing that, I don't want to get arrested for being indecent in a public park."

A flush of pink touches her cheeks before she nods.

"Why don't we get this shit back to the car and walk around a little bit before we do the Maid of the Mist and Cave of the Winds?" I ask.

"Okay." Sara puts her hands on the blanket and pushes herself forward, then she turns to look at me. "I've never done either of those things."

"Really?"

"Nope, not even when I was here before. I can't remember why. Maybe it was too busy."

"I guess I should be honored that I get to be there for your first time." I wiggle my eyebrows at her.

"Yeah, you get to pop my Niagara Falls cherry!" she throws right back at me, which is another thing I love about her.

"Let's go so we can get to business. I can't wait to get you in one of those sexy blue ponchos." I bend my knees and jump to my feet before grabbing her hand to help her up.

"Ooo, now you're getting my blood boiling." She gives me a sexy grin as she crashes into my chest.

With a swat to her ass, I let Sara go to fold the blanket and stuff it back in my bag while I get the cooler. We follow the same path back to the car, and a couple people follow us, hoping for our spot. I'm sorry to disappoint them, but I've got plans with my girl. After stowing our things, we head toward Old Falls Street just to check it out.

I hadn't planned on coming over here, so I didn't check online to see what they had. As we walk farther down the street, things get livelier. They have life-sized board games with pieces you have to pick up and carry to move. At the end of the street is a stage with a band already playing. They apparently don't mess around when it comes to celebrating a holiday.

Leaning into me to avoid people, Sara pushes up on her toes to say in my ear, "We have to come back some time. I wanna play giant checkers."

"Me too. I didn't know this was here, or we would have come sooner." I take the opportunity she presented and give her a kiss. "Ready to hit the Maid of the Mist?"

"Yep!"

Sara

The Maid of the Mist ride is incredible! The boat ride is so smooth— not that I didn't think it would be after watching it like ten times before feeling comfortable enough to get on. Izach pushes me right to the railing so I'll be close as possible to the falls, then he cages me in with his arms. The mist coming off the rushing water soaks us through the completely useless ponchos. As we pass by the American Falls to the Horseshoe, I squeeze Izach's arm and nod toward the rainbows forming where the water hits the rocks. I can't get over the beauty right in front of me, and it's hard for me to comprehend that this is practically in our backyard. I'm giddy and grateful that he planned this for us.

After making it back to dry land and ditching the pointless blue ponchos, we move to the observation deck on the tower.

"I can't believe how beautiful it is here." I sigh and sag into Izach's body when he pins me against the rail again.

"Hmm, it's nice."

Rearing my head back, I look at him out the corner of my eye. "What do you mean, 'It's nice'? It's amazing, one of the natural wonders of the world."

"It's got nothing on you, Sara. As far as I'm concerned, my arms are wrapped around the only natural wonder in the world," Izach says seriously, which makes me want to laugh and melt into a puddle at the same time.

211

"You're nuts, but thank you." I roll my head back and tuck it under his chin.

"I only speak the truth, beautiful." He places his lips softly on my head. "I hate to cut this short, but we have someplace to be." Izach steps back and tucks me into his side.

As we cross the foot bridge to Goat Island, I can't help but look over the side at the raging rapids below us. The movement of the water is so captivating. If Izach didn't have his arms wrapped around my shoulder, I may have stood there for the rest of the day. But he keeps us moving until the Cave of the Winds comes into sight. This is the reason why Izach made me bring a change of clothes. We saw it from the Maid of the Mist, so I know we'll be able to practically walk under the water.

After we're suited up in more blue ponchos, Izach takes my hand and moves us along with the flow of people to the elevators. Surprisingly, I'm not as nervous about walking under Niagara Falls as I was about getting on a boat that didn't get nearly as close. It might be adrenaline, but I'm so pumped right now. I've already thanked Cheryl a hundred times for switching shifts, but after this, I'm going to have to thank her a million more times. When the elevator doors open, we wait for the car to empty before filling it with our group.

"You're totally not freaking out right now," Izach notices.

"Nope, I'm pretty excited for this. It's kind of dangerous!"

"Oh shit, you're an adrenaline junkie. Why didn't I see this before?" He shakes my hands, emphasizing his observation.

"Please, I am so not. Didn't you see me before we got on the Maid of the Mist, or how about the kayaks?"

"I don't think they were dangerous enough for you." Izach pulls us onto the elevator right before the doors close, and we start to go down. I make an eek face at him, and he says, "Don't tell me you're starting to freak?"

"No, I'm good. I'm ready for this!" I say. So ready that I didn't pay attention to one word coming out of the speaker giving instructions.

The doors open, and people flood out of the car. I guess we weren't the only ones not paying attention. Although, looking at our companions, I'm not sure any of them understand a lick of English. Following the small group, we step under a sign that lets us know we've arrived. Izach pulls me toward the outside of the group so we can walk right along the railing, closest to the water. We take stairs up to the hurricane deck and get absolutely drenched. The water is so close, I can almost reach out and touch it.

"Oh my god this is so awesome!" I yell to Izach. Being close to rushing water, I can't hear a damn thing, not even myself.

Instead of screaming back at me, Izach just gives me a thumbs-up and a giant smile. Stepping up to the rail on the hurricane deck, Izach cages me in again. He leans into my back and holds me tight. I savor the moment, so happy to be here with him. Despite his tight hold, I manage to turn in his arms to look up at him. He smiles, then kisses me, a deep, sexy, "thank god I'm soaked, so my panties don't ignite" kiss. He doesn't bother with leading up to it and thrusts his tongue right into my mouth, most likely feeding off my excitement.

Too soon, he breaks away with a couple more quick kisses. Backing away from me, Izach grabs my hand again and leads me back down the way we came, and we take time to actually look around us. The water bouncing off the giant rocks as the sun catches the droplets makes several small rainbows all around us. They're so close I just want to reach out and touch one. Too soon, the tour is over and we're heading back to the elevator with the other drenched tourists.

"Now I know why we needed extra clothes," I say, ripping the paper-thin poncho from my soaked body.

"Do you want to go change, or do you want to walk around and dry off?"

"Meh, it's hot and there's a little bit of a breeze. We'll dry."

"Okay, but if you need to change before we go to dinner, we can stop back at the car and grab our clothes." Izach takes the balled-up plastic from my hands.

"Where're we going for dinner?"

"Hard Rock. I'm giving you the total experience." He does his little eyebrow wiggle again. He's so cute it's sexy.

"I can see that. I like it!"

Spending the rest of the afternoon walking around Goat Island, Three Sisters Island, and Luna Island definitely dries out our clothes, but we quite possibly make them wet all over again—with sweat. It's so freaking hot, and I'm going to regret not bringing sunscreen with me. I can already tell my cheeks and nose are burnt to a crisp.

As we walk around the islands, Izach holds my hand and points out different birds and animals to me. I can't help squealing when we see a couple baby raccoons wrestling. They're so cute, rolling around in the middle of a flower bed. It's like a scene right out of a Disney movie. Izach laughs as he pulls me toward Three Sisters Islands.

We walk across two amazing old stone bridges and end up standing with our toes nearly in the water. I step away from Izach onto a rock overlooking the river. Closing my eyes, I pull in a long breath and blow it out slowly, basking in the sun as the breeze cools my skin. Strong arms wrap around me, and I turn my head to see that Izach has stepped onto a rock behind me.

"Can I assume you're enjoying yourself?" he whispers in my ear.

"Yes, it's been a long time since I've felt so relaxed and free. I love it here," I say, rubbing my cheek against the side of his face.

"Then we'll have to come back again."

"Promise?"

"I promise."

We stand like that for a few more minutes, just enjoying the sounds of the birds and the water running in front of us. I almost fight him when Izach says it's a quarter after five and we have to head back to the car to get ready for dinner. As we were walking, Izach called ahead to put our names on the wait list. At that point, there was an hour before we'd be seated, so we kept walking around.

When we're a few feet away from the car, he pulls out the keys and unlocks the doors. I dive in the backseat and let the dark-tinted windows cover me while I change. Izach shakes his head, then does the same thing in the front seat, the air conditioning vents blowing directly on him.

By the time we finish dinner, the sun's almost gone from the sky and the amount of people around the area has increased tenfold. Cutting through the crowds, we head back over to Goat Island to watch the fireworks over the falls. Just before we reach the rail above Prospect Point, to the right of the Horseshoe Falls, the first boom sounds. Colored lights beam against the water from Canada, and bright colors fill the night sky. I stand back-to-front with Izach, his arms around my waist.

A few minutes into the show, Izach leans down, putting his lips to my ear. "Sara?"

Turning my head toward his, I answer, "Yeah?"

"I want you... will you be my girlfriend?"

Tensing a little with surprise, I wiggle away and turn away from the spectacular sight to face him. "Did you just ask me to be your girlfriend?" I tease him a little.

"Yeah, I did. So you gonna answer my question?" he fires back.

"Yeah..."

"Yeah? Yeah, you're going to answer me, or yeah, you'll be my girlfriend?" He looks slightly confused.

"Yeah, I'll be your girlfriend." I lift up on my toes to kiss him.

With his arms tightening around me, Izach pulls me as close as humanly possible. Getting a little daring, I slip my hands into his back pockets as our kiss deepens. In one pocket, my hand comes into contact with his wallet, and in the other, my fingers brush against a small square packet. Grasping what I can only imagine is a condom, I pull it out of his pocket as I pull away from his lips.

Holding the small foil packet between us, I ask sarcastically, "What's goin' on here—wishful thinking?"

Izach looks like a deer in the headlights. I'm pretty sure he's not picking up on my sarcasm.

"Um, no. I mean, I guess, I was hoping, but if you're not ready... I didn't mean for you to find that."

I can't help but laugh.

His face becomes completely serious. "Are you fucking with me?"

As seductively as I can, I press against him and put my lips right below his ear. "Not yet, but I'm glad to see you're prepared." When I pull back, Izach's eyes are even bigger than before.

"Would it be bad if we skip the rest of the fireworks so I can get you home and make that happen?"

"I mean, maybe we can head toward the car, but not too fast. I want to see the rest of the fireworks."

Turning me in his arms, Izach walks backward through the crowd, blindly dodging people as we move. I can't help but laugh. He's trying to so hard to make this day/night everything I could want, and he's succeeded. Because of that, and the fact that I want the same thing he does, I free myself from his hold, grabbing his hand. Until he catches on, I have to pull him, moving left and right through the crowd, toward the car. As soon as he realizes what I'm up to, he just about breaks into a run, nearly knocking over families as he goes. He only slows down when he realizes he's nearly tugging my arm from its socket.

We manage to make it back to the parking lot in record time, and before the show is over. Izach makes sure I'm tucked into my seat before he sprints to the driver's side, drops into his seat, and cranks the engine. A little happy dance is going on in my head, and my panties, as we pull out of the lot and head home.

CHAPTER 18

Izach

My palms are sweaty the whole ride home. So much so that when I was trying to open the front door, I kept losing my grip. I'm not nervous—well, I'm kind of nervous. I just want to make sure Sara's good with this. She says she wants it, but she also wanted what we did a couple weeks ago. Hopefully this time will be different since we've given each other a commitment of sorts. We're officially together, and I'm so freakin' happy she's finally mine.

Standing behind me at the door, Sara seems calm as ever. When I drop my keys a second time, she snatches them up before I can even bend over. Taking my place in front of the door, she slips the key in the lock, shooting me a smile over her shoulder as she pushes inside. I might have to clear up why I'm such a spaz. I don't want her to think I don't want her, because there's nothing I want more.

After tossing the keys on the counter, Sara stalks back to me. "Izach…" She breathes out. "I promise you I'm okay. Don't worry that we're going too fast. I want this more than anything, and I only want it with you."

It's as if she read my mind. I place my palms on each side of her face. "That's all I needed to hear."

I kiss her softly before pulling back and lacing our fingers. I walk us into my bedroom, turning the dimmer on the overhead fixture so just enough light graces the room. "Our first time is going to be slow. I want to take my time and show you what you mean to me."

A shiver rolls through her body.

"I know we've talked about this, but I want to make sure you're with me every step of the way, so before I do anything, I'm going to wait for your cue. Are you with me?" I ask.

She squeezes my muscles. "I'm with you."

"Good," I breathe as my head descends to hers.

When our lips connect, Sara's hands slide up my arms and around my neck. She goes for the short hair at the bottom of my neck, twisting and pulling it as I devour her mouth. My hands roam the lower half of her body, running around her waist, up to her underarms, then down over the swell of her ass. Our tongues move together as little sounds of pleasure slip out of Sara. On my third pass down her back, I grip the bottom of her shirt and pull our mouths apart.

Looking deep into her eyes, I lift the fabric away from her skin but stop when I get to her bra. I watch, waiting for the sign to continue. Sara dips her chin then lifts her arms, so I pull the shirt up and off before tossing it aside. She goes for my shirt, but I step away.

"It's about you, not me." I cup her cheeks, then touch my lips to hers softly. I pull back to gauge her reaction.

"I want to feel your skin." She pulls at the material again, and this time, I don't stop her. She steps back, putting a little space between our bodies.

Lifting my arms, I let Sara remove my shirt. She stops once she gets my arms trapped against my head, then she leans forward and places her lips on my chest above my heart. I can't stay still—that small gesture is enough to rock my world. Bending my elbows, I grab the opening at my neck and force the shirt up and over my head, then toss it over Sara's shoulder.

Following my shirt, Sara's hands move up. Her body falls forward, flush with mine. I take the opportunity to reach around her back for the clasp of her bra. Slipping the hooks open one by one, I feel the fabric become loose and sag against my body. I rub my fingers up and down her exposed back, relishing how soft it feels against my calloused hands. She sighs, seeming to enjoy the attention.

"I could stay like this forever, in your arms, with you rubbing my back. It feels so good," Sara says, nuzzling her face into my neck.

"I can keep doing this all night if you want."

She lifts her face and looks at me. "I'm curious to see what's next." She winks.

Dipping my head, I capture her mouth, separating her lips and thrusting my tongue deep within her mouth. I force Sara backward until she bumps into the bed while I continue to worship her mouth. She doesn't show any signs of slowing things down but tangles her tongue with mine with just as much hunger.

Sitting, Sara pulls her lips away from mine, and I almost fall forward on top of her. She shrugs, pushing her perfect tits together, so the straps of her bra slip halfway down her arms. The cups gap away, giving me a sneak peek of her hardened nipples. Her hands move to the button fly of my cargo shorts, and she manages to get the top one free before I capture her wrists.

"This is about you," I say again.

"Trust me, seeing what you have in there will still be about me, I promise."

"Not yet." I run my palms up her arms to the bend in her elbows. I pinch her bra straps, but before I slip them down, I look at Sara to check her reaction and make sure we're still on the same path.

Sara's looking up at me through her lashes, her eyes hooded and mouth slightly open. With my fingers still holding the thin straps, she leans back, exposing herself with my help. Sara keeps going until her elbows hit the bed behind her. Her feet, which were on the floor between mine, lift as she moves toward the middle of the bed.

The sound of a thud between my legs makes me look down, and I see Sara toeing off her shoes. Her shorts and panties are the last pieces of clothing separating me from her whole body. Wanting to see the whole picture, I bend over her lower half and run my hands from her knees to the middle of her waist. I pop the button on her shorts and lower the zipper. Slowly sliding my hands over her pelvis to her hips, I hook my thumbs through a belt loop on each side and pull the denim down.

When her shorts get caught on the swell of her ass, Sara bends her knees, putting her bare feet on the mattress. She thrusts her hips off the bed, giving me more than enough room to continue my descent. Dropping her ass back to the mattress, she lifts her feet so I can pull the shorts free.

I swing Sara's ankles to my right shoulder, then place a kiss on a small, black heart tattoo just below her calf. My eyes roam down her long legs to her panties, then I burst out laughing. "How did I not notice you had Batman underwear on?"

"Not sure how you missed something so badass."

"Considering what they cover, I'm not sure how I overlooked that either." I wiggle my eyebrows at her.

Sara

Hearing Izach's reaction to my underwear takes away some of my nerves. I know I've been playing a good role and making him think I'm not nervous, but I am. It's been five years since I've had sex, and back then, I used it as a coping mechanism. I was in high school and didn't give a shit about those guys—they were just easy. Izach is different. I really like him, and I think I might be falling for him. I want this to be different. I want to feel something.

He still has my ankles on his shoulder, and he's just looking at me. I'm not really sure why, but the way his eyes are roaming my body makes me feel amazing. He always looks at me as if I'm the only girl in the world, but now he's looking at me as if he wants to take a bite out of me. If he does, I'll let him. Touching his lips to my tattoo again, he runs his hands down my calves, stops at my knees, then goes back to my ankles.

"What are you thinking?" I ask. I'm still nervous about messing this up, and I can't really read Izach.

"I'm thinking how beautiful you are naked."

"But I'm not naked. I still have my Batman undies on."

"I guess we'll have to fix that." He separates my legs, putting my feet on the bed on each side of his thighs.

Leaning forward, Izach bypasses my panties, coming up over my body. I feel the mattress dip down

223

where he puts his knee on the bed. With an elbow at each side of my head, he lays his weight on me. Not wanting to lose control, I wrap my arms around his lower back, drawing lines across his taut skin with my fingers. He puts his lips just a whisper above mine, not touching, but I feel his breath against my swollen flesh. His eyes search mine. I don't know if he wants me to tell him to keep going or just show him, but I decide to show him.

Lifting my head off the bed, I put my mouth against his, and within seconds, he pushes his tongue in and moves it with mine. My head lowers back to the bed with the pressure of his kiss. Sliding my hands up his back, I try to reach his hair, but I'm trapped by his arms. Sensing my need, Izach lifts his body off me just enough for me to pull my arm free and get them around his neck.

Izach rips his lips from mine and kisses a trail to my ear, then he takes my lobe between his lips and gives it a little nip. To give him more room, I turn my head. The touch of his tongue, then the gaze of his teeth against my neck makes me writhe beneath him.

"Izach…" I breathe.

Sucking and nipping at my heated skin, he follows the line of my neck to where it meets my chest. My fingers move up into his mess of hair, twisting and tangling it as he moves lower on my chest. Stopping in the middle of my sternum, Izach smiles at me before moving on to tease my already-hard-enough-to-cut-glass nipples. He pulls the left into his mouth and sucks hard, letting it go with a pop, then he rolls his tongue around the hardened nub. My back arches off the bed, and I can't contain the groan that slips from my lips.

Shifting his weight, Izach brings his hand down to my waist, then runs it up my side to knead my sensitive globe as his mouth travels across my chest to my right nipple. Putting his palms on the bed again, he lifts himself to fully cover me. There's no coaxing a kiss from him this time—his mouth takes mine and steals my breath. Our tongues tangle, fighting to get our fill.

When he rips away from our kiss, Izach and I are both panting heavily. His face hovers over mine before disappearing from my field of vision. I feel the touch of his soft lips on my stomach, just above my belly button. Then at my side, where the cherry tree is. Looking down, I watch him slide his feet to the floor.

Catching my gaze, he stops. "You okay?"

"Yeah," I say softly.

Sitting up, I slide to the end of the bed. I don't give him the opportunity to stop me as I go for the rest of the buttons on his shorts. Gripping the waistband and the elastic of his boxers below, I tug the material down his legs. Running my palms against the outsides of his legs, I lift my head until I come face-to-face with his very hard cock. Gripping the base of his shaft, I lean forward and pull the tip into my mouth. Rolling my eyes up, I see Izach's head fall back, then I hear his low groan. Grabbing Izach's ass hard, I pull in as much of his length as I can, letting his head bump the back of my throat before I slowly slide it out while applying pressure to the underside of his cock, feeling the ridges and veins rub against the roof of my mouth and tongue.

Lost in what I'm doing, I don't pay attention to what Izach is doing. I close my eyes to savor the sounds of pleasure I'm causing him. So when his hands meet my armpits and pull me up, I'm a little shocked.

The last inch of his cock is plucked from my mouth with a pop.

"Hi!" I say, looking into his hooded eyes once we're nose to nose.

"Not going to complain about what you were doing, but I did say this was all about you." He steps forward, making me drop to my ass on the bed.

"Trust me, that was very enjoyable for me." I wink as Izach lifts one leg, then the other out of his pants.

"I'm glad it was, but I promise this will be much better for you." He leans over my body until I'm flat against the mattress.

Starting with my nose, Izach places soft kisses all the way down my body to the top of my Batman panties, not showing one spot more attention than any other. Lifting his head, Izach grips my waist, pushes me to the center of the bed, then slides his hands down to the top of my undies. Hooking three fingers around the elastic band, he pulls them toward him. The fabric moves and wiggles over the curve of my ass—I lift up on an elbow to watch—then down my thighs and right off my feet. His eyes meet mine as he twirls the black-and-yellow panties around his index finger, letting them spin off and fly across the room.

The giggle that bubbles up my throat is quickly extinguished when I see the predatory look in Izach's eyes. For a second, I'm a little scared, then I remember he's Izach and he'll never hurt me. A shiver that has nothing to do with the moment of fear and everything to do with the promises this gorgeous man has made runs through my body.

Putting a knee between mine, Izach bends forward, keeping his eyes on mine the entire time. He grabs my knees, kneading the skin, and slowly pushes them apart. When he seems satisfied with the amount of space he's created, his palms move to the insides of my legs, continuing their ascent toward my aching center.

Dipping his head, Izach touches his tongue to my throbbing bundle of nerves, and I nearly rocket off the bed. Pushing against his forearms with my thighs, I try to squeeze my legs closed, but he won't let me. The second swipe has me wiggling and writhing even more. I grab the blankets and twist my fingers in them. Lowering a little, Izach runs his tongue through the juices spilling from my depths. Circling my nub again, he takes it into his mouth, applying the right amount of pressure to make my eyes roll back.

"Oh my god, Izach." I pant. "Please, I need you to…" The words get lost as he sucks hard.

My back arches off the bed as he releases his hold, then he slides his tongue up and around my clit. Going right back in, Izach sucks hard, and I'm lost. My breaths come out ragged as I push myself into his mouth.

"Oh, yes… uh god…" I manage to get out as my orgasm explodes out of me.

The loss of Izach's weight against my legs has me lifting up again, looking toward the side of the bed. I see Izach bend and rustle through his jeans. He pulls the condom from his back pocket, then tosses the packet next to my hip before he leans over the bed, putting his knees between mine. With his left hand next to my head, Izach drops his lips to mine and kisses me deeply. As our tongues tangle, the fingers of his right hand run through the fluids between my legs, then a strong finger pushes inside me. The pressure sends my eyes flying open. I feel him curling the end of his finger with each stroke.

Lifting his mouth from mine, Izach continues to move his finger in and out of me. "You okay?"

"Yeah." I feel my lids lowering as his palm rubs against my core. I whimper when he picks up speed and puts a little more pressure on his hand.

Taking my sounds of pleasure as a green light, he adds another finger to the mix, curling them inside me. My muscles tighten again, and the sensation telling me to close my legs takes over. Dropping his hips to block my movement, Izach lowers his head and captures my second orgasm with his kiss.

As my muscles settle, Izach pulls his hand from between my legs and sits back on his shins. I follow his movements with my eyes as he grabs the condom and rips the package open with his teeth. He rings the head of his cock, then rolls the latex down his hard shaft. I can't stop my tongue from sweeping along my bottom lip as he sheathes himself. Moving back over me, Izach puts an arm on each side of my head. I feel his hardness bobbing at my entrance, waiting to push inside.

"I want you to guide me inside you. Connect me to you, Sara," he whispers just a breath away from my lips.

Arching my neck off the bed, I take his lips as I reach between us, hold his condom-covered erection, and guide it to my center. My other hand moves to his taut ass, putting a little pressure on him as I line us up. When Izach's head dips in, I let go of his shaft and put both hands on his butt. Squeezing his flesh, I lift my hips as he pushes in. Inch by inch, he slowly enters me until he's buried.

Izach pulls his lips away from mine and looks me in the eyes before he pulls out just as slowly, then he repeats the movements. Wanting him to go faster, I dig what nails I have into the muscles of his backside, coaxing him by lifting my hips with his movements. As he goes faster, I slide my hands up his chiseled back, feeling each muscle work. At his shoulders, I grab tight, pull my legs off the bed, and wrap them around the backs of his thighs, making each thrust go deeper.

"Sara…" he breathes, placing his sweat-slicked forehead against mine. "God you feel so good."

He picks up the pace a little more, slamming into me, then retreating. My inner walls tighten fast, sucking and squeezing his growing cock with each press.

"Izach… I can't… oh god, I'm going to…" I can't even finish before another orgasm rips through my body. Arching my back, I tighten my legs around him as my fingers dig into the backs of his arms.

"Stay with me, Sara," he demands.

His movements pick up, pounding him into me as he starts to reach his own climax. Izach groans with one pulverizing thrust. His body goes rigid above mine as spasms roll through him, and he buries his face in my neck. A few quakes thrust him in and out quickly before Izach collapses on top of me.

"Holy shit, that was… amazing." He's breathing heavily.

"It sure was." I sound dreamy as I tighten my legs around him and move my arms around his shoulders.

Lifting his head from my neck, Izach looks deep into my eyes, then he dips his head, capturing my lips in a bruising kiss. When he lifts his head again, both of us are breathing hard. Pushing with his arms, Izach rolls to the side, then slides to the end of the bed to stand. I watch him disappear through the door and come back within seconds. He moves to the head of the bed and pulls down the covers, while I turn so that my head is at the pillows. After I'm situated under the blankets, he crawls in beside me, stretching his arm out so I can roll into him.

I play with his spattering of chest hair for a while until my eyelids start to feel heavy, and I lose myself in sleep. When the sun streaking through the blinds wakes me, I decide to return the favor and wake Izach, making it all about him.

CHAPTER 19

Sara

Sitting in the waiting room, I wait for Jacqui to get her crap together so I can go in and spill my guts, and I reevaluate my snarkiness. Poor Jill has gotten way too soft over the past few weeks—she even smiled at me today. Jill has never smiled at me, not in the five years I've been coming here. I must be off my game. Probably has something to do with all the good in my life, something I haven't had since I started seeing Jacqui.

"Sara?" Jill calls through the glass partition.

I look over to acknowledge her but don't bother removing my earbuds or replying.

"She's ready for you," Jill says.

Standing from the nasty plastic chair, I head to the door closing off the office from the waiting room and bust through it. Jacqui's leaning against the frame of her open door. Giving her the most sarcastic smile I can muster, I pass her and head right to my spot on her couch. I pull my earbuds out of my ears and wrap the cord around my phone.

"Please tell me that smile was meant to be sarcastic?" Jacqui asks as her greeting.

"Nice to see you too. I'm well, thanks for asking."

"All right, so we're going with complete smartass today."

"Meh, I feel like I've been off my game, so I need to step things up. Don't take it personally."

"How can I not when you're directing it at me?" she asks, raising her brows and holding her iPad against the arm of her chair.

"Please, Jacqui, you know I love ya and would never be mean to you. I usually get it all out of my system with Jill, but for some reason, I keep forgetting I don't really like her. I blame Izach for making my life seem somewhat happy."

"Oh yeah? I think that's the first time in five years I've heard you say that word. Are you going to share?"

"Well... since you've practically dragged it out of me, I suppose I can tell you that we're official. He's my boyfriend and I'm his girlfriend, and we might have had sex on Saturday night." I give her a strained smile, then wait for her reaction.

"Okay, I'm happy you're together officially, but—"

"Shit, here comes the but," I interrupt, shaking my head.

"But don't you think having sex so soon after becoming official is a little fast?"

"We've been dancing around it for a while now, so no, I don't think it was too fast. Why do you?"

"Because I know your past, Sara. You've used sex as a coping mechanism for your emotional pain, and I want to make sure that's not what you're doing with Izach."

"I thought about that. Remember a while ago when I told you about our little make-out session, when I freaked?"

"Yeah."

"Well, that night, I tried to push things, and I think it was because I was falling back into old habits. But now, it's different. I really care about him, and it seems right. Not like I'm doing it for the wrong reasons."

"So tell me about it?" Jacqui moves her iPad to her lap and leans her arm on the chair while she holds her chin.

"Looking for all the dirty details?" I wiggle my eyebrows at her.

"No, I want to know why it's different. What's changed?"

Rolling my head back into the couch, I look at the ceiling before I answer. "Everything! I was so sad about Elaine leaving, which is why I tried to push things before." I look over, and Jacqui rolls her free hand for me to continue. "When we were messing around and he touched my scars, he didn't judge me or ask for an explanation. He just ran his fingers over them and told me I could talk about when and if I was ready. That's when I knew he was different and why I didn't push him away." I bite my lip and turn my head toward Jacqui. "I think he might be my one."

She heaves a deep breath. "I'm not trying to hold you back or stop you from finding happiness, but I want you to think about this before you dive in headfirst. I know I told you this before, but I want you to take things slow and make sure you know one another before you invest your heart."

I see the concern in Jacqui's eyes. "I think it's a little too late for that. I'm totally falling for him, and I think I have been since the night I met him. Is that weird?" I turn my head toward the ceiling again.

"No, a lot of people believe in love at first sight. I don't want to say relationships built like that don't last, but it's hard to create something based on first impressions alone. I don't want you to get your heart broken or suffer any setbacks."

Blowing out a sigh, I snap up and throw my feet to the floor so I can face Jacqui. "I know, and trust me, I don't want him to break my heart either. But I don't think he will."

"What makes you say that?"

"Because I'll probably break his." I drop my head and cover my face with my hands.

"And why do you think that?"

"Come on, Jacqui, you know. Why would anyone want to be with someone who's ruined?"

She taps her iPad. "You're not ruined, and the time you spend getting to know each other now will show him that. But down the road, if this does go somewhere, you'll have to tell him the truth."

"I know, and that terrifies me. I don't know if I can handle the look on his face, whether its sympathy or disbelief. Either way, it's gonna suck."

"I'm sure Izach will feel sympathetic, but if he truly cares about you, he'll stand by you and be what you need. From what you've told me so far, I think that's the kind of guy he is."

"Yeah?"

"Yes, but I still don't want you rushing into this," she warns.

"Yes, Mom."

For the rest of the session, Jacqui asks her usual questions. Have I cut? Did I feel as though I wanted to? Have I felt overwhelmed, sad, or unusually crazy? Okay, maybe she doesn't say crazy, but that's what she means. As always, I answer with a no, but this time, like almost every time since I met Izach, I mean it.

Izach

It's been a week since Sara agreed to be my girlfriend. That might not mean anything to some guys, but to me, it means the world. She's so much more than I thought she would be when I first met her. She's smart, determined, absolutely beautiful, and extremely independent. Not that I didn't pick up on that right away.

We're both still getting used to being in a relationship. She's trying to give in and let me do things for her, and I'm trying not to do everything for her. We've had a few little arguments about it, but mostly we've laughed over how ridiculous we're being. Other than that, our routines have fallen in line very fast.

On the nights Sara works, I stay downstairs, because she doesn't want to wake me when she gets home. The nights she's off we rotate between our two apartments, staying in mine first, then hers, then back to mine. I like waking up with her arms wrapped around me or her lips wrapped around my dick. Two days this week, she woke me up by pulling me into her mouth, which of course led to us spending half the day in bed and taking turns showing each other different things that get us off. I now know Sara's a reverse cowgirl kind of girl. I've never felt any chick come as hard as she does when she's riding me backward. It's something a guy can get really used to.

Tonight, like every Friday, Sara has to work, so I'm going to drop by and surprise her after I go out with a couple buddies of mine from college. She left early to go to her appointment, which she hasn't told me about yet but promises she will soon. I know there're secrets behind her eyes, but I'm not pushing her. She'll tell me when she's ready. For now, we're having a good time, in and out of bed.

Taking my friends to meet her is kind of a big deal to me. Since she and I met, the only people we've been around together are my mom and Gran-ma, who calls to "check on how things are going" at least three times a week. I swear I've talked to her more times in the past month than I have in my whole life. But I'm glad Sara means so much to her. I'm not sure of how Sara will react to me showing up at The Diner with my friends though. I hope she's not only excited to see me but also to meet the guys. I guess time will tell.

After Sara leaves for her appointment and work, I wait on the porch and try to stomp out some of my nerves with one of Gran-ma's crosswords. I probably look like the biggest loser when they pull in the driveway.

"Hey, asshole!" Jake yells out the driver's side window. "What are you doing up there, knitting?" He squints at me as I rock back and forth in the chair.

"No, dickhead, I'm doing a crossword."

"Even better, you loser!" Andy yells as he pulls his giant frame out of the other side of the car. "You mind tucking your pussy back in your pants so we can go drink?"

"Wow, asshole, nice to see you too," I throw back.

"Don't asshole me. I have a chick to drink away. Let's get this show on the road." He bangs his hand on the top of the car.

"Um, hate to point this out, but six o'clock is a bit early to hit the bars. Why don't we have a drink here?"

"Sounds good to me. The faster we get this emo-dickhead drunk, the better off we'll all be," Jake says as he slams his door.

"That bad?" I ask as he climbs the stairs, Andy not too far behind him.

"I swear he almost started crying five times on the way here."

"Shut the fuck up. I did not!"

Jake turns around and points at Andy. "You did, and I get she cheated on you, but dude, you need to get over that shit."

"Didn't he just find out a couple days ago?" I ask.

"Yeah, but so? He's acting like a little bitch. She cheated. Get over it. Better yet, get under someone new. What about Ashley? Didn't Jamie say she moved to Buffalo?"

"I'm not sleeping with my ex's best friend." Andy walks past me to get in Jake's face. "And I'm done talking about that slut Jamie and her bitch friends."

"Okay..." I say. "How about I go get some beers?"

"Sounds good to me," Jake says at the same time Andy says, "Please."

Leaving the two Neanderthals on the porch, I head into the kitchen. I'm starting to reconsider telling them about Sara. Jake's a self-proclaimed man whore, and now that Andy is single, I know they'll both give me shit for tying myself down. Not that what they say will matter. I've done the whole playing the field

237

thing, and Sara's it for me, issues, secrets, whatever else I don't know about her, and all.

I grab three beers out of the fridge, then slam it shut. After popping the caps off, I toss them in the general direction of the garbage can. I hear one hit the floor but don't bother to go pick it up. I push through the door and find my chair stolen by Andy, the other still occupied by Jake. After handing them each a beer, I jump up on the railing across from them.

"So who's driving tonight?" I get the hard question out of the way, knowing none of us wants to forgo drinking to be responsible.

"This is a city. Can't we take a cab?" Jake asks.

"I guess. I don't really wanna pay for a cab…" I say.

"Stuff it, you're not driving. We're here to hang out for the weekend, and that means getting shit-faced together. Plus you and I both know we'll need to be trashed to stand listening to Assface whine about Jamie all night."

"Shut the fuck up! You don't know what it feels like," he says.

"You're right, and I don't plan on find out—at least not anytime soon. Which brings me to the most important question of the night: where can we find some hot poon?" Jake looks me in the eyes and points at me with his beer bottle.

Cringing, I decide to come clean. They're going to find out anyway. "Um, yeah, I have a girlfriend."

"Seriously? You just moved here. Why aren't you sampling?"

I'm surprised that question came from Andy. "First off, girls are not for sampling, and second, I don't want to. We're getting too old for that shit anyway."

"We are not old. What the fuck, you whipped already?" Jakes asks.

"Don't do it, Izach. Chicks are nothing but a fucking headache," Andy adds.

"Right? That's what I'm saying. Look at Andy. He's a freakin' mess." Jake sweeps his arm out toward Andy.

"Sara's different," I say. "She's not like the girls we met in college. You'll see. We're gonna grab food at The Diner later. That's where she works."

"Whatever. You two assholes ready to go?" Jake sets his empty bottle on the porch and stands. He reaches into his pocket and pulls out his cell, pushing the button on the side to bring it to life. "Need me to find a cab company?"

"Nah, we can walk to the bar on the corner, have a drink, then go from there." Tipping my beer bottle back, I suck down the rest of it, then set the bottle next to the bottles Jake and Andy abandoned.

We head down the block toward the dump on the corner. It's still too early to go out, especially if I want to meet up with Sara at the end of her shift, but I can't handle sitting on the porch and listening to my friends complain. I invited them over for a cookout tomorrow, but I'm seriously reconsidering after the bitchfest that just took place.

Sara

"Ugh, my god, is this shift ever going to end?" Cheryl whines as I pass her on my way to pick up an order.

"You're telling me. I don't know what's going on tonight, but I haven't had a minute to pee, let alone try to get something to eat."

"Party of three. Looks like you're up again." She points the empty plate in her hand toward the door, where Izach is standing with two guys.

"Yeah, I'll get that one." I fly past her, a plate full of food in each hand.

Stopping at the table next to the entrance, I set the food in front of my customers and ask them if they need anything else. When they respond with nos, I take the few additional steps to where Izach is waiting. Before I say anything, I pick three menus off the hostess stand and tuck them between my forearm and chest.

"Hey," I greet him with a little excitement and maybe some confusion. "What are you doing here?"

"We, uh, went out and had some drinks. They're hungry, and I wanna see you." He slurs half his words while his friends laugh behind him.

"Ah, so you're all drunk. Wonderful," I say sarcastically, biting my lower lip. "All right, follow me."

I move into my section, to a booth near the back that's farthest from the door and closest to the bathroom. After the boys sit, I put a menu down in front of each of them.

I look at one of his friends, then the other. "Hi, I'm Sara. I'll be your server tonight. Is there anything I can get you to drink?"

A gentle touch on my arm pulls my attention to Izach. "Hey, is this okay?"

"What do you mean?"

"That we're here while you're working?"

"It's fine. You need some water." I look at the guy sitting next to Izach. "What can I get you?" I ask when he looks at me with raised eyebrows.

"Uh, can I get a Dew?" he asks, and I nod.

If I wasn't at work, I would have said, "I don't know. Can you?" because he's Izach's friend. But since I'm not looking to lose my job tonight, I write down his order and move on to the guy sitting across from them. "How about you?"

"I'm Jake, since rude forgot to intra-duce us," he slurs, sounding like a complete ass.

"Nice to meet you. Do you want something to drink?" I've learned over the years that if I don't stop them, drunks will just keep going.

He pretends to study the menu, not even on the page listing the drinks. "Yah, I'll git a Coke."

"Pepsi all right?"

"Is fine."

"Okay, let me run and get your drinks. I'll be right back to take your orders."

Slamming my tray on the counter, I turn to the computer and type in their drink orders. Movement from behind the serving window catches my attention, and I look up to see Miguel giving me a look. He doesn't say anything, just shakes his head. I turn back to the screen and finish tapping in my order. As I finish, Cheryl comes up behind me and puts her hand on my back.

"You okay, chickie?" she asks before she switches places with me.

"I'm fine."

"You don't seem fine."

Letting out a long sigh, I come clean. "The table that I just sat…"

"Yeah?"

"That's my boyfriend and his drunk friends. I didn't know they were coming in. Shit, I'm not so sure I want to see him like this."

"You don't want him to drink?" she asks.

"No, it's not that. I just didn't think he'd ever come in here drunk, especially after all the stories I've told him about our drunk customers."

"Just treat them like any other customer and hope they accidentally empty their wallets when leaving you a tip." Cheryl smirks with one eyebrow raised.

"Right."

Grabbing six glasses from next to the fountain machine, I fill three with the boys' drinks and three with water, then I set them on my tray. As I approach the table Izach looks at me. I can tell he feels bad about ambushing me but doesn't want to say it in front of his friends. After setting down the drinks, I turn to leave, but I'm stopped by a hand around my wrist.

"Sara, these are my friends, Jake"—he motions to the idiot across from him—"and Andy." He nods at the half-passed-out lump next to him. "Guys, this is my girlfriend, Sara."

"So you gonna give us free food, Sar-rah?" the idiot asks.

"Um, no, this isn't my diner. I don't give things away for free." I shut him down.

"Stop being an ass, Jake." Izach gives my wrist a squeeze.

Ignoring it, I take their orders and head back to put them in, then I check on my other tables. Too soon, Miguel is yelling, "Order up, Sara." I grab the guys' food and deliver it to them without lingering at their table longer than I have to. As I move through the packed diner, I notice Izach's eyes follow me. Glancing at his friends, I see a heated argument developing, which usually means food's about to fly. I quickly drop the order I'm holding, then return to their table.

"Hey, guys, can I get you anything else?" I ask to interrupt the standoff between Jake and Andy.

They both look up and shake their heads before going back to whatever they were talking about.

I stay a minute, looking down at Izach. "How are you getting home?"

"Cab," he answers, still not sounding remotely sober.

"I'm out in ten minutes if you want me to take you. Are these two idiots staying with you?"

"No, they're staying at the Hampton Inn on Elmwood."

"Good, I'll call them a cab and take you home. You guys ready for the check?"

Izach nods.

After calling them a cab, I print out the bill and drop it on their table. I run around and check all of my tables, making sure they don't need anything else before I bring their bills to them. Looking out the window every few minutes, I watch for the cab. When I see it, I run to the door and call to the driver that they'll be right out, then I go wrangle the idiots. As I walk up to their table, Izach stands and helps Andy to his feet, then yells at Jake to get off his ass. The three of them head past me and go out the door.

Shrugging, I head back to their table to make sure they didn't stiff me, not that Izach could get away with it. I find a one hundred dollar bill tucked into the billfold. I tuck the leather case into my apron pocket, then I help Sam, our nighttime bus boy, clear the table.

After counting out my tips to split with Miguel and Sam, I head back out to the dining room with my purse slung over my shoulder. Izach is at the counter, holding himself with an elbow on the Formica and his palm cupped under his chin. Without a word, I grab his hand, help him to his feet, and direct us out the front door.

On the drive home, I hear the soft rumbles of a snore and look over to see Izach passed out in the passenger seat. I roll my eyes and contemplate leaving him in the car the rest of the night. But as soon as the beast squeals to a halt in the driveway, he's up and opening his door. I watch him walk straight to his front door without giving me a glance, as if he forgot I was with him. Deciding not to be a bitch, I follow him and make sure he gets to his room without breaking his neck. After I flip the lock on his door, I head upstairs to crash.

CHAPTER 20

Sara

The sensation of my bed dipping with someone's weight makes me roll over and crack my eyes open. Izach is sitting on the edge, bent over with his head in his hands. I blink hard a couple of times to get the sleep out of my eyes, then I roll over to face his back. He doesn't acknowledge the fact that I'm awake, and it's freaking me out a little.

Placing my left hand on his back, I break the silence. "Hey."

Still nothing.

"Izach, are you okay?"

He lifts his face from his hands and looks at me out of the corner of his eye. "I feel like such a jackass."

"Okay?"

"Last night, I wanted to come meet you at work so the four of us could spend the night together, but of course I had to get wasted with those dipshits. Now I feel like shit, and I woke up alone."

Biting my lip, I hold back my words. I kind of feel bad he feels like shit, but he did it to himself. His friends are jackasses but they're his friends, and I won't call them out to him without really knowing them. Even though I had to break up a potential food fight last night.

"I'm sorry, Sara. We shouldn't have gone to The Diner last night. Not after we got so wasted."

"Izach—"

"No, don't try to sugarcoat it. I think—well, I'm hoping—I put on a good front when we got there, but I was tanked. I shouldn't have done that to you, not after what you've told me about the drunk assholes you have to deal with. I'm sorry. I really am."

"Izach," I snap to get his attention. "It's not a big deal. I mean, I was a little blindsided when you came in, especially when I noticed how drunk you were, but I'm glad I could make sure you made it home safely."

"Yeah, but because I was so drunk you wouldn't stay with me." He turns his head fully to look at me.

"Well, I was kind of pissed this morning when we got home."

"Really? Did I do something stupid?"

"Um, possibly, but I probably overreacted. I was annoyed that you just got out of the car and walked into the house like you were alone. You didn't acknowledge I was with you or that I drove."

"You didn't overreact. That was an asshole thing for me to do." He puts his hand on the side of my face. "Thank you for making sure I got home and that I didn't pass out in the front yard."

"You're welcome. Now are you going to just sit there, or will you lie down so we can get a little more sleep?"

Without another word, Izach stands, pulls his shirt up and over his head, then reaches for the waist band of his jeans. From how wrinkled they are, I assume he didn't bother taking them off before he crashed last night. I slide to the other side of the bed when he puts a knee on the edge. Lifting the sheet, he slips in next to me, then hooks an arm around my waist and pulls me into his front.

After I'm comfortably tucked into his body, I tilt my head up to softly kiss him. He returns my kiss, then places several fast pecks against my lips. The fifth time he brushes his soft but very red lips against mine, I capture the back of his head with my hand and hold us together. What started as an innocent kiss turns into something more than I expected.

The soft touch of Izach's tongue on my bottom lip has me opening to him. With our mouths fused together and my hand in his hair, he rolls me to my back and pushes deeper. His hand, which was at my waist, pushes up my nightshirt, baring my awesome Hello Kitty underwear to the room. I can't wait to see his reaction to them, although it probably won't be quite the same as his reaction to my Batman undies. Reaching the underside of my boob, he rubs the skin my bra usually covers.

Pulling away from my lips, he gets right down to business. Putting a knee on the bed between my legs, he pushes himself off me, making me release the tufts of hair at the back of his neck. Once Izach is upright, he gently pulls me up to sitting. Bunching the bottom of my shirt, he tugs it up and over my head just as he did with his own.

"You're so beautiful," he whispers, then guides me back to the bed with a hand behind my neck.

Bypassing my lips, Izach buries his face in my neck, teasing my sensitive skin with the promise of what's to come. Moving lower, he follows the line of my collarbone to the base of my neck. Traveling farther down, Izach traces the crease of my cleavage with his tongue. I hiss when he latches onto one of my pebbled nipples, pulling it into my mouth hard. The sensations shooting through my body, straight to my center, have me arching my back off the bed. With a nip to my now-oversensitive skin, he pulls away and moves to the other side.

"Izach…" I breathe, and he lifts his face to look at me with hooded eyes. "I need to feel you inside me."

Lifting more of his weight off me, Izach bends to the side and reaches for his jeans. As he does, I grab my panties and wiggle them down as far as I can with one of his legs still between mine. I wait for him to grab the condom from his jeans pocket and watch as he fumbles trying to get his pants, then finally decides to get up. I take the opportunity to push the pink Hello Kitty undies the rest of the way down my legs and off my feet. Izach puts his knee back on the bed as I finish, his condom-covered erection bobbing in my face.

Lying back, I keep my eyes locked on his as he settles between my legs, pushing them apart with his hips. Izach settles his cock at my opening, waiting for me to reach down and guide him home, just like the first time we had sex. I line him up just right before he thrusts his hips and plunges into my depths. The initial sensation works through my body, and I wrap my legs around his lower back, elevating my hips just enough to allow him to move deeper. Picking up the pace and moving in and out of me as if he's keeping beat with a song, Izach claims my lips. The kiss is full of passion, tongues tangling, dancing in time with his movements. The heat resonating between our bodies creates a sheen of sweat across our skin.

Tearing his mouth away from mine, little gasps and groans emanate from him. The walls of my pussy contract with each pass of his pubic bone over my clit. I bite my lip as my orgasm takes over, my muscles quivering and shaking as he pumps his growing cock. I can't stop the groan that rumbles out of my chest as I hit my peak. Izach slams into me hard, working to get himself there with me. With one last thrust and a loud moan, he collapses on top of my spent body.

"Oh my god…" he pants, stealing the thought right from my brain.

"You can say that again," I chime in, and we both laugh.

Placing a quick kiss on my lips, Izach rolls off of me, then off of the bed. He disappears through my bedroom door into the living room and comes back a minute or two later, sans condom. With a smile he drops back to the bed, facing me. He leans forward and places another sweet but quick kiss on my lips.

Izach

After I'm assuming hours have passed, I jump at the sound of someone pounding up Sara's stairs. Turning my head, I see that she's still fast asleep and curled up next to me, no doubt worn out from our morning activities. I look toward the alarm clock on the nightstand next to Sara's bed and notice it's just after one. A loud knock at the apartment door makes Sara stir next to me.

"Izach?" she asks, voice laced with sleep.

"I'm here. Let me go see who it is." I swing my legs over the side of the bed and grab my jeans from the floor so I can pull them on as I walk across to the door.

Not bothering to check who it is or if the person can see Sara lying in bed, I tug the heavy door open. A woman with blond hair and blue eyes, just like Sara's, is standing on the other side. She stands ramrod straight, head held high, in a pink sweater set and jeans. Her purse is tucked tightly at her side.

"Um, can I help you?" I ask tentatively.

"I'm looking for Sara Collins. This is her apartment, isn't it?" she asks with certainty.

"It is. May I ask who you are?"

"She's my mother," Sara answers from behind me.

I look back to see disgust clearly written across her face. "Okay—"

"Sara, we need to talk," her mother interrupts me.

"First off, Mother, this is my home, and you interrupting my boyfriend is rude. Secondly, I have no desire to talk to you. How did you find me?"

I look between them as Sara spits words at her mother.

"It's about Trent."

My eyes go back to Sara. Her face is the color of an egg shell, and her breathing has picked up.

"Sara—" her mother says softly.

"No, I can't do this, not right now. You need to leave." Sara stomps forward, pushing me back from the door and taking my place.

She looks at Sara with pleading eyes. "I'm not leaving without telling you what's going on. This is important."

Lifting her hands to her face, Sara pushes her fingertips into her forehead, then runs her hands down her cheeks, stopping at her chin. "I need some time."

"I'll come back later, but I'm not going home until I tell you what's going on."

"Um, Sara?" I cut in, taking Sara's attention away from her mother. "Jake and Andy are coming over for a cookout later. They'll probably be here around four." Trying to give her the out I think she's looking for.

"Okay, um, we can't do this today." She looks back at her mother, who appears annoyed by my intrusion.

"We are doing this today. What I have to tell you is for your protection."

Combing her fingers through her hair, Sara relents. "Fine." She turns to me. "Izach, can you give us some time? I promise I'll explain everything to you, but I can't have you here for this."

"If you want me to go, I will, but if you need me, I'm here for you, no matter what. I'll go call Jake and Andy. They'll be in town for a couple more days. We can reschedule."

Nodding, Sara looks at me with sadness in her eyes. "Thank you, and I promise I'll explain later."

Stepping forward, I put my lips to hers, leaving them there until she responds, which takes a minute. I lift my head, then put my hand on her shoulder and run my palm down her arm to her hand. I give it a squeeze before I pull away and walk out past her mother. I'm not halfway down the stairs before I hear the door shut. Closing me out of whatever's going on in Sara's life.

When I reach the bottom of the stairs, I crash through the storm door and let it slam shut. I've never felt so helpless. I don't know whether I'm upset or angry—maybe a little of both. I know Sara has a lot of secrets, things that happened in her past. That was confirmed by her expression when she saw her mother and again when she went pale at the mention of that Trent guy's name.

Punching the brick post won't get me anywhere, so I head into my apartment to find my phone. I need to tell Jake and Andy the cookout is off. Maybe I'll ask them to come by after Sara goes to work, if she goes. Right now, I'm just hoping she trusts me enough to tell me what's going on. But before she does, I need to make sure she knows I'll stand by her no matter what. The ghosts of her past won't have an effect on our future, because I'm falling in love with her.

CHAPTER 21

Sara

"Your boyfriend seems nice. What does he do?"

I can hear the judgment in her voice. "Not that it's any of your business, but he's a teacher." I wait to see if she tries to backpedal. When she doesn't, I move on. "Tell me how you found me, then say what you came here to say."

"Sara, my god, I've missed you so much. I can't believe how you've grown. We've missed out on so much of your life because we were so stupid."

"Mother, please, this whole 'making amends' thing isn't going to happen, so get to the point." I put my hands on my hips.

Her deep sigh doesn't go unheard. I watch my mother cover her mouth as tears form in the corners of her eyes. She shakes her head as if she's clearing her thoughts, then she forges ahead. "It's Trent—"

"So you've said," I interrupt, maintaining my stance.

"He's been accused of raping four women. At first it was only one—"

"No, it was two, or did you forget what he did to ruin my life?" I yell, throwing my arms out to the side.

"No, I didn't forget." She waits for another outburst that I manage to hold back. "After the first

253

one came forward, three others followed. He's been arrested and arraigned, then Celia bailed him out."

"And..." I roll my hand for her to continue.

"He's gone."

"What do you mean, 'He's gone'? Did someone kill him?"

"No, I mean he took off," she says. "There's a statewide search for him, but they're fairly sure he's crossed state lines."

I suck in a deep breath and wrap my arms around my waist to hold myself together.

"We think he's coming here, to find you," she adds.

"What makes you think that? And what, you think he's going to find me because you did?" I ask even though I'm not sure I want to hear the answer.

"He, um, mentioned you to Celia the day she bailed him out, and it wasn't too hard to find you. A simple internet search was all it took."

"Wait, you searched my name on the internet and found me? It was that easy?"

"We had to pay for the search, but yes, after fifty dollars it was really easy to find you."

I cross my arms over my chest. "What makes you think Trent's coming here? Why would he after all this time?"

"He said it was your fault, that you started this."

"So he admitted what he did to me? That's why you believe me now?" I accuse.

"No, he didn't admit anything, but the fact that he brought you up after not mentioning you for the past eight years made your aunt wonder if what you said was true."

"And because of that you believe me?"

"Sara—"

"No! That man ruined my life. Before he raped me the first time, I was happy. I had things to look forward to. Eight years ago, I wanted to make something of myself—even go to the Olympics for swimming. Now I've found someone who makes me feel whole again, who's helping me find my way, and you come here and rip the rug out from under me. Thank you for your concern and the warning. I'll make sure I watch my back, but this doesn't change anything between us."

Tears are back in her eyes. "Sara, please hear me out—"

"It's about eight years too late for that." I move across the room and grab the door handle. Pulling it open, I say, "I'm sorry to cut this heartfelt reunion short, but I have to go relive the shitty past I haven't told my boyfriend about, and hope he doesn't run for the hills because of all my baggage." As the words came out of my mouth, I feel tears burning at my eyes.

"I'll go, but only because you're asking me to and I'm respecting that. I want to make things right between us. I know somewhere in your heart you do too. So when you're ready, I'll be waiting," she says.

Knowing nothing nice can come out of my mouth, I decide to keep it closed as I stand there, holding the door. Once my mother has cleared the threshold, I slam the door and throw my body against it. Crumbling to the floor, I let go of the tears I held back in front of her. They're not for her though—that ship sailed years ago. No, they're all for me. I was hoping to have more time before I had to tell Izach about my past, but there's no way I can put it off after this.

Unable to pull myself together, I crawl back into my bedroom, heading for my phone on the nightstand. I grab it, pushing the button on the side to bring it to life. With my back to my bed, I swipe the lock screen and go right for Jacqui's contact information. I put the phone to my ear and wait as it rings twice before she picks up.

"Sara?"

I hear confusion and worry in her voice. I don't respond.

"What happened?" she asks.

"My mother was just here." My voice wobbles, but I'm able to get the words out. "She told me Trent was arrested for rape."

"Oh my god!" she shrieks. "So is he in jail? Does this mean they believe what he did to you?"

"No, he's not in jail." I take a deep breath and pinch the bridge of my nose. "Apparently my stuck-in-denial aunt bailed him out, and he took off. My mother seems to think he might come after me."

"What makes her think that? Did he say he was coming for you?" Jacqui sounds a little panicked.

"I guess he mentioned me to Celia before he ran. Sadly, that's what it took for them to believe me."

"Oh, Sara, I'm so sorry."

"That's not the worst part." I clench my teeth together hard. "Izach was here when she showed up. I have to tell him."

"Sara, remember what I said to you. I think Izach will surprise you, but you can't go into the conversation believing he's going to judge you."

"I just don't know if I can handle him looking at me like I'm broken. I don't need him to feel sorry for me."

"I don't think he will, but you'll never know unless you rip off the Band-Aid. I'm here if you need me. I think you need to go have a conversation with him now. I'm guessing you didn't talk to your mom with him there?"

"No, I asked him to leave, and I think that hurt him. I'm going to have to fix that too." I drop my head back against the bed.

"You can do this. I know you can. Call me later if you can, but if not, at least text me so I know you're okay."

"I will… Jacqui?"

"Yeah?"

"Thank you for being here when I need you."

"Always, Sara."

"Bye." I end the call, not bothering to wait for her good-bye in return.

Izach

After coming downstairs, I decided it would be best for me to sit inside so I'd have at least a little more stopping me from sneaking upstairs and pressing my ear against the door like a stalker. But the sound of a door slamming makes me get up and look out the window. A second later, Sara's mom walks by the picture window, then down the steps. I watch her head to the car parked at the curb right in front of the house. Now that she's gone, I'm really not sure what to do. I want to go to Sara, but I don't want to push her to talk, especially if she's upset.

Deciding to give her a little time, I grab my phone and go sit in Gran-ma's chair. Scrolling through my contact list, I find the number I'm looking for and hit it with my thumb. Three rings later, I hear the voice I know can help me.

"Izach?"

"Yeah, Gran-ma, it's me."

"It's so good to hear from you, what's been going on?"

I lean my head back and rest it against the chair, pausing before I answer. "In the past five years, did Sara's mom, or any of her family, come visit her?"

"No, not that I know of. I mean, I wasn't there twenty-four hours a day, but I never saw anyone. Did her mom come to see her? Is Sara okay?" Gran-ma's voice is laced with concern.

"Yeah, her mom showed up a little while ago. She didn't stay long, and Sara made me leave while they talked. I'm a little worried about why she came here. She said something about it being for Sara's protection. Do you know why Sara would need protection?" I ask, rubbing my forehead.

"No, I'm sorry, honey, I don't. How did Sara react to seeing her mom?"

"She didn't want to talk to her. Well, until she mentioned the name Trent. That's when Sara asked me if I could give them a few minutes to talk."

"I wish I could tell you what that was about, but Sara never told me. I thought when I got her first letter she would give me a little something, but she's still locked up tight."

I sigh. "I'm a little freaked out from the look on her face when her mom said that name. I'm not sure if she was sick or scared. I kinda want to go check on her, but I don't want to push her, especially if her conversation with her mom went as bad as I think it might have." I rock the chair forward and lean my forearms on my knees.

"I can't tell you what to do. What does your gut say?" she asks.

"My gut tells me to give her a little space, that she'll come to me when she's ready, but at the same time, I'm scared she'll just close up and cut me out. She's supposed to go to work tonight, and I don't want her to go without telling me what's going on, but what if telling me just upsets her more?"

"Sounds like a shitty situation. I think you should give her some time, but don't let it go on too long. I know how much she means to you—I saw it from the very beginning—so you have to fight for her. Don't let her shut you out."

"Thanks, Gran-ma." I pause at the sound of footfalls on the stairs. "Actually, I think she's coming down, so I'm going to let you go."

"Okay, sweetheart. Call me if you need me, both of you. I love you."

"Love you too, Gran-ma. Bye."

"Bye, honey."

As I listen to her last two words, I turn my head and see Sara coming through the storm door. I check to make sure my phone disconnected, then I tuck it in my pocket.

"Hey." I get up and go to Sara, but she raises her hand to stop me from reaching her.

"This isn't going to be easy for me, but you deserve to know. I was going to tell you eventually, when I got the balls to, but apparently the universe has different plans for me, as usual. Do you mind coming upstairs? I can't sit out here and say what I need to say."

"Sure." I reach for her hand, but she pulls it away from me.

Turning back to the door, Sara pulls it open and heads up the stairs with me following her. She pushes her slightly ajar door open, steps through, and goes right to the futon. I watch her hug one of the throw pillows and squeeze it tight. My nerves are completely on edge. Not only am I worried about what she's going to tell me, but I'm terrified by the fact that she's already pulling away from me.

"Is it okay if I sit next to you?" I feel like I have to walk on eggshells right now.

"Yeah, you can sit next to me." Her voice sounds normal, not at all matching her actions.

Slowly I cross the room and drop onto the futon next to her. I leave a couple inches between us, pulling my leg up so I can face her. "Are you okay?" I have to hear it from her, although I already know the answer.

"Not really, but it's not because of my mother. It's because of what I have to tell you." She takes a deep breath and blows it out. "Izach, about my past, there's a reason today is the first time I've seen my mother in five years."

"I kind of figured there was a reason. You don't seem like the type of person who would cut someone off without one. What happened, Sara? You can tell me. Nothing you say is going to change the way I feel about you."

"You say that now, but I know better," she counters nervously.

"Why don't you try? I'm not other people. I care about you, and nothing will change that."

Taking another deep breath, she blows it out, then rests her chin on the throw pillow. "You know how I have appointments two or three times a week?"

"Yeah?"

"I'm in therapy. I probably don't need to go as much as I do, but Jacqui, my therapist, is the only one, outside my family and anonymous people from group therapy, who knows what I'm going to tell you. She's the only one I've really be able to open up to, so I go see her a lot, even though it's unnecessary. I couldn't even bring myself to tell Elaine." She buries her head for a second, then lifts it, her lips pulled between her teeth. She takes a deep breath through her nose. "My aunt Celia moved to Florida to when I was younger, and I always wanted to go visit her, but my parents wouldn't let me because she was busy and I was too young. For my fifteenth birthday, Mom and Dad surprised me with a plane ticket. I was so stoked to leave, I pretty much had everything packed that night even thought I wasn't leaving for months, until my summer break from training—"

"Training?"

"Yeah, I was a swimmer—a pretty fuckin' good one too. If I had stuck to it, I might have gone to the Olympics. But after Florida, a.k.a. best birthday present in the world," I add sarcastically. "I stopped trying."

"Sara, if I got a trip as my birthday present at fifteen, I would have thought it was amazing too."

"Well, if I knew then what I found out later, I wouldn't have been so excited. See, Aunt Celia lived with her boyfriend. They had been together a few years and started to talk about getting married. From the first word that passed through his mouth, I thought Trent was amazing. Not only was he cool, but

261

he was good-looking and funny. I used to think I wanted to find a guy just like him when I got older. I thought Celia was so fuckin' lucky."

"That's the name your mother mentioned," I state.

"Yeah, I'll get to that. So the plan was for me to stay for my whole break—a few weeks. Celia planned to take the last week I was there off, so we could have some quality time together, but she had to work for the first couple. She is, or was, a trauma nurse. While she was home, I spent time with her, and the rest of the time I hung out with Trent, which I thought was a pretty sweet deal." She clears her throat a couple times, then swallows. "I'm going to grab a bottle of water. You want one?"

"I'll get it. You stay here." I head into the kitchen to grab two waters from the fridge, then go back and hand Sara a bottle. "Here ya go."

"Thanks." She untwists the top and takes a long pull, drinking a quarter of the bottle. Gripping the bottle in front of the pillow, she launches right back into it. "The first week was great. We went to beach in the morning before Celia had to get ready for work, and after she left, I hung out by the pool, catching up on reading. The day it rained, we caught a movie before she left. At night, I had dinner with Trent, we hung out a bit, then I'd crash. I thought it was the perfect vacation—free of my parents, hanging out with two cool people, and pretty much doing what I wanted. But the following Sunday, Celia went to work early. She tried to pick up some extra hours because she was going to be off the following week." Sara stops and looks at me. "This is the hard part. I'll spare you the details, but you'll probably fill in the gaps."

"I'm not going to jump to any conclusions based on what you tell me. Share what you feel comfortable sharing."

"Okay," she says softly before taking a deep breath and looking at the pillow in her lap. "That Sunday, after Celia went to work, Trent and I spent the day at the beach and walking around a shopping center near their condo. When we got back, we had dinner and watched TV until I went to bed." She looks at me quickly, then back down. "It had to have been about an hour after I laid down when I heard the door to my room open and he sat on the edge of my bed. I thought something was wrong, but he assured me everything was fine and pushed me back down."

I clench my jaw, pretty much knowing what's coming next.

"Leaning over me, he kissed me. Of course I asked what he was doing—it's not like I'd never kissed a guy before, but he was my aunt's boyfriend. So nonchalantly, he said exactly what he was doing—kissing me. When I questioned him again, he told me I wanted it, that he'd seen it in my face all week. I denied it. The thought had never crossed my mind. Yeah, I thought he was hot, but I was a kid and he was an adult." Sara takes a deep breath and blows it out again.

I want to touch her, to give her some comfort, but I'm not sure how she'll react. I slide a little closer, then touch her right shoulder and leave my hand there. I watch Sara closely as she turns her head toward me, unshed tears in her eyes.

"I was a virgin, Izach. He took everything from me."

"He raped you?"

263

"Yeah, he raped me, and when I tried to fight him off, he hit me." A few tears slide down Sara's cheeks.

My heart's breaking for her, but I don't want her to see sympathy in my eyes. I know she doesn't want that.

"I attempted to find ways to stay away from the condo, to stay away from him, but at the end of the day, I had to go back. It happened four more times before I left to go home, and there wasn't a damn thing I could to about it. He had an excuse for every bruise I got, and my aunt believed him. My plan was to tell my mom and dad when I got home, but I didn't know my aunt had already shared my clutziness with them."

"What do you mean?"

"I mean whatever story Celia told my parents must have been very convincing."

"Your parents didn't believe you? That's why you left?"

"Ding, ding, ding." She shakes her head, then rubs the tears from her eyes. "I told them as soon as the car doors shut behind us, but they were skeptical. They called Celia and Trent to confront them about my story and were told I was making it up. My parents believed them over me, so for the next three years, I barely existed. I quit trying at swimming. I couldn't quit altogether because I needed a cover for my extracurricular activities—"

"What do you mean by that?" I ask.

"Let's just say Trent opened something inside me and he took the special out of it, so I used it to make myself feel better. Like I was wanted by someone. Clearly my parents didn't give a shit about the fact that their fifteen-year-old daughter had been raped."

Her anger starts to bubble up, and she clenches her fists. "I was so fucked up. The scars you felt on my side, they're a direct result of what happened. I couldn't handle all of the pain, so I started taking it out on my body. The physical pain made the inside pain feel more real."

"You're covering them now though."

"Yeah, it's kind of a therapy I'm giving myself, but it took a long time for me to be ready to cover them. The cherry tree means renewal. It kind of symbolizes me starting my life over. The butterflies are also a form of therapy, although tattooing them isn't really part of it. I can't help it though; I still crave the pain." She runs her fingers over the butterflies covering her left arm.

"What are you supposed to do with the butterflies?"

"Draw them on. It's part of this self-hurt program Jacqui told me about. She wanted me to try that instead of cutting, but it wasn't enough, so I put them on permanently. I'm still not ready to cover them all, but I'm getting there. Jacqui helps a lot, and so did Elaine."

"Gran-ma? How did she help? I thought you didn't tell her?"

She shakes her head. "I didn't, but she gave me a chance. I showed up on her doorstep looking for an apartment. I had already been turned away by two other people, but she was different. She invited me in, asked me some questions, then offered me the apartment. Even after I told her I didn't have a job yet and that I had dropped out of high school. I guess she saw something in me that she liked, or trusted. She's never told me why she did it."

"She told me it was the right time. You know Gran-ma and her timing thing."

"Yeah, well, it was the perfect time for me. If she hadn't taken that chance on me, I would have run out of money a lot sooner and probably ended up on the streets. I owe her my life. She saved me from so much, and I've never even told her that."

"I'm sure she understands. Gran-ma loves you, Sara." I squeeze her shoulder and slide a little closer so I can reach more of her back.

"I know, and I love her, but I think it's time for me to come clean, which is why I started writing her. Now that you know, it only seems fair to tell her too."

"It's not about being fair. It's about doing what's best for you, and trust me, it'll be okay if you never tell her. She'll love you anyway."

"I know, and that's one of the many reasons I love her." Sara leans toward me. I'm not sure if she even realizes she's doing it.

"So what's going on now? What did your mom tell you about this Trent guy?"

Sara sits up straighter. "Apparently he's been accused of rape by some other girls, so now my family believes me. He was arrested, but Celia bailed him out, and now he's on the run. My mother thinks he might come after me, but I don't think he will. It's been eight years, and I never went to the police."

"Wait, why didn't you go to the police?" Izach sounds confused and a little angry.

"My parents didn't believe me, they never would've taken me and by that point I didn't think the police would believe me either. I was only fifteen."

That's understandable, I guess I didn't think about it from fifteen year old Sara's point of view. "So, why does your mom think he'll come after you?"

"I guess he said something to Celia, or she said something to him, about me. Who knows? But I'm not really worried. If anything, he's probably headed to Mexico."

"I'm driving you to and from work until we know he's been caught," I state, unnerved by her lack of concern.

"Izach, he's not coming here, and if he did, he wouldn't be able to find me, it'd be too risky for him. Plus, nothing in this apartment is in my real name."

"What do you mean? How did your mom find you? Is Sara Collins not your real name?"

"No, it is, but when I moved in, because of my age, I couldn't get the utilities in my name, so they're all in Elaine's. We never changed it. My mom found me on some paid internet search site. I'm not sure which records are public, but I'm assuming it's something with my insurance. Trent's probably freaking out, and I'm sure he's not going to take the chance of using a credit card for an online search. It'd be too risky."

"I still don't want you driving yourself. You leave so early in the morning, and the lighting in that parking lot sucks."

"Izach, I'll be fine. I never walk to my car without one of the cooks. Even if I tried, they wouldn't let me."

I sigh. "I would feel better if I drove you, but if you promise me that you'll never go into the parking lot alone, then I guess I won't push the subject."

"I promise."

Sara

Izach's protective tone makes me smile. Not once during my whole sob story did he look at me as though he felt sorry for me. Instead he grabbed my shoulder and gave me the strength I needed to keep going. Telling Izach felt so different. I mean, the first time I told Jacqui, she looked at me as if I was broken and she felt bad. That turned into our first blowout and was the day Jacqui learned how to handle me— her words, not mine. Anytime I've had to share, I've prepared myself for the looks, for the sympathy. For god's sake, last group meeting I went to, those looks pushed me over the edge. I couldn't even finish the story.

I let my body fall into Izach's, and he runs his palm across my back, reaching my other shoulder. He could be feeling sorry for me or seeing me as broken, but he hides it well, and because of that, I'm going to let him be here for me. He's the first person I've encountered since I was fifteen years old who didn't completely freak out at my scars or tense up when he heard the truth, which is just another reason why I'm falling headfirst in love with him—not that I'll admit it without knowing how he feels first.

CHAPTER 22

Sara

Just over a week ago, I told Izach everything, and nothing's changed between us. His reaction is making me realize I probably could have given other people, like Elaine, a chance and let her know more about me while she was here. So I wrote her a letter, telling her the same thing I'd told her grandson. I thought it would be so much more difficult, but it wasn't.

After I finished telling Izach, we went back to our normal lives. I texted Jacqui, letting her know what I had done and would tell her how it went at my appointment. Then Izach and I hung out on the porch for a bit before I had to go to work. I actually felt really bad that he'd cancelled on Jake and Andy, but they ended up coming over on Monday. It was better then anyway, because I was off and able to get to know them without rushing to get ready for work.

All week, I was worried my mother would pop up again, either at the house or at work. I knew she was hoping for more than I gave her, but you can't undo the past. I did look up what she told me about Trent though, just to see how big of a deal it actually was. According to the news story, three women, all around my age, claimed that Trent had raped them repeatedly, over the course of a week, while they were nannying for him and Celia at their vacation home. Apparently the girl he attacked this year wasn't

269

fazed by his threats, and she also tracked down the other two girls. Nowhere in the article was my name mentioned—not even in the quotes from Celia. I assumed Trent was long gone, probably living in Mexico or even farther south. The article did mention that he had cleared out all of their bank accounts before he disappeared.

My last little bit of paranoia disappeared the night I checked under my car with Miguel standing a few feet away. He had a field day with that, asking me, "What the fuck are you doing, checking for a leak?" I was too embarrassed to admit I was a little nervous about Trent being on the loose. Miguel didn't have any idea who Trent was, and there was no way in hell I was telling him about my past. So instead I laughed it off and told him he was right, that I needed to check shit like that during the day. I haven't bothered to look since then.

This week, my schedule's a little different. Cheryl called in a favor, and since she took my Fourth of July shift, I swapped with her. Instead of working Wednesday, Friday, and Saturday, I'm working her Thursday and she took my Wednesday. After my Saturday shift, I have the next three days free, and I plan to make the most of them. Tomorrow morning, Izach and I are heading out of town to spend a couple days in Watkins Glenn before he starts work. I'm kind of excited to go since it's been over ten years since I was there last.

Before leaving for work tonight, I packed everything I would need for the next three days. I probably packed way more than I'll actually need, but you can never be too prepared. This is actually my fist trip since I was fifteen, so I'm a little out of practice when it comes to packing. When Izach saw how full my duffle bag is, his eyes bugged out of his head, then he saw my book bag is also stuffed full. He didn't bother saying anything, but I could tell he thought I was a total girl.

Right before I leave for work, I haul my bags downstairs for Izach to pack in his car. I don't get out of work until four and we're leaving at seven, so instead of having to load the car while I'm half asleep, I tried to be ahead of the game. My plan is to come home and crash for two and a half hours before Izach comes to wake me. Even though we've grown closer, we still stay in different apartments when I'm working. It's not fair for me to wake him up when I get home.

"Hey," I say as I drop my bags just outside Izach's front door. I can see him in the house, standing in front of the open refrigerator. "I'm going to leave my bags out here so you don't have to drag them back out when you pack the car." I open the door and head right to the kitchen island. Leaning on my elbows, I watch Izach move things around, looking for something to eat.

"Sounds good to me. Do you want something to eat before you head to work?"

"No, I think I'm going to go in now and have Miguel make me a steak-and-cheese sub for dinner. It's been a while, and I'm feeling the need to eat some crappy food."

"Sounds good. I should come too since there isn't shit to eat in here."

I came around the counter to look into his fridge. "Yeah, I think we might need to do some grocery shopping when we get back. My refrigerator looks even worse than yours."

"Well, that settles it. Let's head over to The Diner and get some junk food. I'll get us road-trip snacks and fill up the tank on my way home so we don't have to stop again in the morning."

"Sounds good to me! I'll meet you over there?"

"Yep, I'm just going to change my shirt." Izach slams the fridge door and turns to me. He holds my cheeks and lowers his lips over mine. The kiss is slow and a little more than a see-you-in-five-minutes kiss. When he finishes, he moves his hands from my face to my waist. .

Scrunching my face, I pull back slightly, but he holds tight. "You're such a dork."

"This might be slightly true, but you love me anyway."

He said it so casually, but hearing it come from his mouth, I know I have to acknowledge it. "You know, you're right."

"Right about what?" he asks, sounding confused.

"About me loving you. I do, you know."

"You love me?" He raises his brows with a big smile.

"That's what I just said."

"Hmm, not really. You kind of beat around the bush a little." He looks deep into my eyes.

I can't hold back the smile that's threatening to split my face. I love teasing him.

"Would you say the words if I admit something to you first?" he asks.

"I already know you talk in your sleep," I throw at him with a hint of sarcasm.

"I don't, and that's not what I'm talking about." He raises his brows and looks at me.

It seems we're at a stalemate. I think neither of us wants to say the actual words first, but Izach smirks before leaning down to place a soft, quick kiss on the tip of my nose.

He pulls back. "I love you, Sara."

My insides melt a little. "I love you too. I feel like I always have and this"—I look around us—"was always meant to happen."

He smiles and dips his head again, claiming my lips.

Breaking our connection, I speak against his mouth. "As much as I don't want to stop doing this, we have to get going if we want to eat before I work." I feel Izach's smile before he pulls away and lets me see it.

"Well, it's not my fault you're trying to suck all of my energy from me," he tosses over his shoulder as he heads toward his bedroom.

I shake my head. "Such a dork," I say too quietly for him to hear.

Sara

Sunday nights are usually fairly slow, but tonight has been absolutely crazy! I'm starting to think there's a full moon or something, but I've been so busy, I haven't had the chance to go look out the window. The only times Cheryl and I have actually spoken to each other were in passing, with our hands full of food. If the diner doesn't slow down soon, I'm probably going to get stuck here past four, and that doesn't work for me.

At around three fifteen, the flow of drunk and semi-drunk people seems to slow. I finally have a minute to fill all of the containers I placed on tables during our whole night rush. Standing at the back counter with a giant tub of salt in one hand, I fill shaker after shaker.

"Oh my god, what the fuck happened tonight?" Cheryl comes up next to me, setting down an armful of empties.

"I think there's a full moon or something. I'd tell you if I'd actually had a chance to look out the window," I say, picking up another shaker.

"Well, thank fuck it's almost over! And lucky you, you don't have to come back until Thursday."

"Yeah, after tonight, I'm really looking forward to it. Switching shifts seems to have worked out in both our favors." I fill the last of my shakers and push the small glass containers together so I can wrap an arm around them and take them back to the tables.

"I'm glad. I felt really bad about you having to work four days in a row without a break."

"Meh, sometimes it happens, but I'm getting something good out of it. I'm going to go drop these off, then I'll grab the napkin dispensers so we can start refilling them."

"Works for me. I'll be over as soon as I get this shit done."

Running around for the last forty-five minutes of our shift, Cheryl and I get everything done before the morning crew comes in. As usual, Miguel walks us out the back door and stops behind my car, which is parked next to Cheryl's. I call good night to both of them before slipping behind the wheel and cranking my sickly sounding engine. I give them another wave before leaving the parking lot and heading home.

Pulling into the driveway, I slam my car into park and hope to hell the loud engine didn't wake up Izach. A while ago, to make me feel better, he told me he doesn't usually hear me, but I'm pretty sure my car could wake him and half the neighborhood.

Throwing the door open, I kick my tired legs out and pull myself up by using the door frame. Keys still in hand, I head up the porch steps to my door. To my surprise, the lower door isn't locked. It's not the first time I forgot to lock it, but thankfully no one looking for a place to sleep has wandered into my stairwell. I take the stairs slowly, trying to be quiet, then I slip the key into my lock and shove open my apartment door.

Passing through, I notice something move to my left, then pain shoots across my head. Lights out.

Izach

The sound of Sara's beater pulling into the driveway wakes me, so I listen for her to make it up the stairs. I don't hear the usual sound of the door closing behind her, but I do hear a thud and a muffled male voice.

"What the fuck!" I sit up, wide awake, and reach for my phone on my nightstand as I jump out of bed. Gripping the phone I listen closely to see if I hear the voice again. When I do, I slide the screen awake and fumble to dial 9-1-1.

Tearing through the house, I nearly trip when the dispatcher's voice comes on the line. "9-1-1, where's your emergency?"

I rattle off Sara's address as I stumble to my door. "I think there's someone in my tenant's apartment. She came home from work, and when I usually hear the door slam, I heard a thud and a man's voice. She lives alone. There wouldn't be a man in her apartment unless it was me." As I cross the porch, I nearly fall on the chair outside Sara's door.

"I've put out the call. A police officer will be there shortly."

"Thank you," I say, then hit the end button.

As quietly as I can, I pull open Sara's storm door and slowly close it behind me. Thank god it doesn't squeak. Taking the steps one at a time, I hear the voice again. The guy is blaming Sara for something, but I can't quite make out what. Putting my hands on the landing, I peek around the corner into the apartment and see Sara lying in the middle of the room, tape over her mouth and her hands stretched over her head with duct tape around her wrists. Her head rolls toward me, and her eyes get wide when they focus on my face. The sound of steps getting closer has me ducking down. I listen carefully to try to figure out what he's doing.

Then his whisper fills the room. "You're such a little fucking bitch. You started this—teasing me, making me want you. I didn't want this. I wanted a quiet life with my Celia. But, no, her slut niece had to come and throw herself at me, give me a taste of something I couldn't live without. Now I'm fucked!"

I hear skin connect with skin and a muffled squeal form Sara. Leaning forward again, I see a guy, possibly in his early thirties, sitting on Sara's stomach. "Fuck," I mouth.

I have nothing with me to defend myself or Sara, other than my fists and the element of surprise. I stand and move to the landing, teetering on the top step while trying to stay out of sight. I look around the doorjamb. He's undoing Sara's top, stopping with every other button to rub his hands across her skin. Bile rises up my throat. I have to do something. I can't stand here and watch this asshole violate her. I pull back and take a deep breath. Looking in once more, I see that he's buried his face in her neck, giving me a perfect shot at his ribs.

Taking the opportunity, I rush into the apartment and swing my foot. It connects, and an oomph rips from his mouth as he falls onto his side, off of Sara. I grab her upper arm to pull her away from him. Unfortunately, he's not down as long as I would have liked him to be, and he's on me before I can get her up to her feet.

"Who the fuck are you?" he screams as he throws me into the open door.

My back hits the corner, and I nearly fall to the floor as pain spreads up and down my spine.

His hands go under my chin and around my neck, and he pushes me back against the door. "Oh, it's the boyfriend. I've seen you coming up here or pulling her into your place. She's a nice piece of ass, isn't she?"

I pull away from the grip he has on my neck, swinging my fist, and hit him right in the jaw.

"Fuck, you little prick!" He squeezes my throat tighter. "I guess I wasn't as quiet as I thought. No worries, Sara. I'll get rid of him so we can have some fun."

Trying to suck in as much air as I can, I wrap my hand around his wrists and squeeze. When he doesn't let up, I claw at his skin, but I'm losing strength. I'd knee him in the balls, but my legs are outside of his. I can't keep my eyes open any longer. Black closes over me.

CHAPTER 23

Sara

Rolling my head to the side, I feel pain shoot through my skull and down my neck. I try to raise my hand to my forehead, but the pinch of something in my hand has me stopping. I'm afraid to open my eyes, but I have no choice, so I crack them a little. Light just about blinds me. I snap my eyes shut and listen to what's going on around me, trying to figure out where the hell I am and what the fuck happened.

The last thing I remember was Izach getting slammed into the door.

"Oh my god, Izach!" I sit up, snapping my eyes open regardless of the pain. The curtain in front of me moves, then is pulled aside as a woman in scrubs walks toward me. "Where's Izach?"

"Miss Collins, I'm Lisa. If you wouldn't mind sitting back, I need to check your vitals. On a scale of one to ten, ten being the worst, what is your pain level?"

"Where's Izach?" I ignore her question.

She puts light pressure on my shoulder, guiding me back down onto the mattress. "I'll see if I can get you some information after I take care of you."

"I need to know if he's okay?" I feel tears welling up in my eyes.

"I understand, and I'll try my best," She answers sympathetically. "But, right now I need to know what your pain level is at."

"It's about a five, maybe six, I'm not sure." I say as I settle into the bed and lift my arm for her.

After writing down my answer she looks at my face before slipping a blood pressure cuff around my upper arm. "I'll go check with the officer when I'm done. They're going to want to talk to you anyway."

"Can I have my phone? I need to call Jacqui." I don't care if the nurse knows who I'm talking about.

"Sure, your purse is in your patient bag. Let me grab it for you."

"Thanks." When she hands me the plastic bag, I rip it open and dig around until I find my phone and pull it out to text Jacqui.

Me: At the ER. IzachAt hurt, they won Ize hands me the plastic bag, I

Jacqui: Are you okay? Is me the plas

Since she's on her way, I don't bother replying. I lean my head back against the pillows and close my eyes. After the tight hold of the blood pressure cuff releases, I hear Lisa moving around, then I hear the hooks sliding as the curtain closes. I'm not sure how much time passes or if I fell asleep, but the sound of someone next to me makes me jump and cower against the rail of the bed.

A police officer stands next to my bed. He's young, maybe a few years older than I am. "Miss Collins, I'm sorry to startle you, but the nurse said you were awake."

"I was, but I think I might have fallen asleep."

"You hit your head pretty hard when you fell." He grabs a small notepad out of his chest pocket. "I'm

Officer Montes. I need to ask you some questions about what happened this morning—"

"I need to know about Izach," I say, cutting him off.

"Mr. Matthews was unconscious when they brought him in. I haven't gotten an update yet, but I'll go check when we're done."

"I'm sorry, but I can't. I need to know if he's okay. Can you go check now? I promise I'll answer your questions when you get back."

"Miss Collins—"

"Please, I'm begging you. I need to know he's okay."

He looks at the ceiling, then back down at me. "I'll go ask, but I can't guarantee anything."

"Thank you," I say quietly as he pushes the curtain aside and walks out.

The sound of Jacqui's voice resonates through the room. I'm not sure if she's talking to a nurse, a doctor, or the cop, but I'm glad she's here. I hear her say thank you, then the curtain slides open.

She breathes my name, sounding relieved to see me. "Oh my god, I was freaking out, and when you didn't text me back…"

"I'm okay, but Izach… I don't know if he's okay or what's going on." Tears slide down my cheeks.

"I asked, but they won't tell me since he's not my patient or family."

"The cop who was here went to find out, but I'm so scared."

She takes a deep breath in, then blows it out, indicating that I should do the same. "He's in good hands, Sara. I'm sure he'll be okay." She sounds unsure though. "Tell me what happened?"

"Trent was in my apartment when I got home from work this morning. He hit me when I came through the door. When I came to, Izach was in the doorway. Trent was on top of me…" I cover my face as a sob breaks free.

"It's okay, take a minute." Jacqui pulls my hand from my face and holds it.

Breathing deeply a few times, I try to get the rest of the story out. "He was unbuttoning my shirt. Izach ran through the door and kicked him. He pulled me away from Trent, but he wasn't fast enough. Trent attacked him. He was choking him," I rasp as a fresh round of tears comes.

"Shh, it's okay, Sara. Izach was protecting you. He knew what he was doing, and I'm sure he's okay."

"I just need to know. I'm not even sure how long I've been here. I know nothing."

"It's been about four hours since you were brought in. I checked when I asked about your condition." She looks sympathetic as my eyes widen. "We'll find out how he is. Just lay back and try to relax."

A few minutes later, the curtain slides to the side and Officer Montes walks back into the room. "Miss Collins, Mr. Matthews is having some tests run. They weren't able to tell me much, but I'm sure you can check with the doctor when he comes in." He looks from me to Jacqui, who's sitting in the chair next to my bed.

"What kind of test?" I ask, trying to control myself.

"I'm not sure." He reaches into his pocket and pulls the small notepad back out. "Now, I need to ask you some questions about what happened."

I nod.

"Do you mind if we have a minute alone?" he asks, looking at Jacqui.

"Jacqui's my therapist. Can she stay?" I ask before Jacqui has a chance to respond.

"Sure, that's fine. When you came home this morning, did you notice anything out of the ordinary?"

"Yeah, my porch door was unlocked, but I didn't really think anything of it. I've forgotten to lock it before, but other than that, everything was normal."

"Okay, why don't you tell me what happened? I know you lost consciousness, but tell me as much as you remember."

Not looking at Officer Montes, I try to remember everything that happened. "When I got to my landing, I unlocked my door and pushed it open, but before I had a chance to shut it, I was hit in the head, hard. The next thing I remember is Izach looking through the door at me lying on the floor. My hands were taped above my head, and Trent was sitting on my chest. I was gonna try to hit him, but Izach ran in and kicked him in the chest, making him fall off me. Then Izach grabbed my arm and pulled me to my knees. That's when Trent pushed Izack into the door, and in a second, I could hear Izach choking." I feel a tear slide down my cheek. "I managed to get up, and I went to the kitchen looking for something to hit Trent with. I grabbed a frying pan, but when I got back, Izach was on the floor and Trent was coming at me." I look at Officer Montes taking notes. "The next thing I remember is waking up here."

"That's good, Miss Collins. What is your relationship to Trent O'Connell?"

283

"The last I knew, he was my aunt Celia's boyfriend, but apparently in the years I've been away, they got married."

"Did you know he was a fugitive?"

"My mother came last Sunday and told me he had been accused of rape and ran after my aunt bailed him out of jail. I haven't spoken to them or the rest of my family in over five years. Trent raped me when I was fifteen, and this morning he was saying it was my fault he couldn't control himself, that it was my fault he'd raped other girls."

"You never reported the rape?"

"I wanted to, but my parents didn't believe me. I waited until I turned eighteen, then I left." I lower my head again, pulling at the blanket covering my lap.

Officer Montes clears his throat again. "All right, Miss Collins, I think we're done for right now, but we'll have more questions you'll need to answer."

Confused, I look up and see a doctor standing behind Officer Montes. I didn't even hear him come in.

"I'm going to leave you my card," the officer says. "If you happen to remember anything else, please call me. If not, I'll talk to you again once you're released."

"What about Trent? Did you arrest him?"

"Mr. O'Connell is in police custody and will be taken to the holding center once he's medically cleared. It seems you and your boyfriend did a number on him," Officer Montes offers with a smirk.

"Thanks," I respond as he leaves.

"Miss Collins, I'm Dr. Firid, the emergency attending on duty today. I'd like to talk to you about your head injury," he states in a thick accent. "Is it okay to release information in front of your…"

"I'm Dr. Jacqueline Rosen, Sara's therapist," Jacqui responds.

"Dr. Rosen, nice to meet you."

"Likewise."

"You can talk around her," I say.

"Very well. Miss Collins, you have two contusions, one on the side of your head and one on the back. You suffered a grade-three concussion. The CAT scan ruled out any bleeding in your brain or swelling, but you're still likely to have some blurred vision, dizziness, possibly vomiting, and a fairly intense headache. We're going to keep you here in the ER for about another hour for observation. The recovery time for this kind of head injury can take anywhere from two to six months, and when you're discharged, we'll give you a prescription for some mild painkillers to help ease the pain. Do you have any questions?"

"Can you tell me anything about Izach?"

"Are you family?" he asks with raised brows.

"He's my fiancé," I lie, not daring to glance in Jacqui's direction.

Dr. Firid sucks in a deep breath before he answers me. "Mr. Matthews has been admitted for observation due to injuries to his trachea. Once you're released, one of the nurses will show you to his room."

"Are you discharging me now?" I ask, eager to see Izach.

"In about an hour, after we check your vitals again. I'll see to your discharge papers."

"Dr. Firid?" I say as he turns to leave. "Thank you."

"You're welcome, Miss Collins. Take care of yourself." He tips his head at Jacqui, then slips past the curtain.

"That's a pretty bad concussion, Sara. You're probably going to have symptoms for a while."

"I'll be fine as soon as I can see Izach."

Izach

A beep bouncing around in my head makes me crack open my eyes. It's so loud, and my head's killing me. When the light hits my eyes, the pain is even worse. I feel as though I'm going to barf. I bring one of my hands up against my forehead to block the light a little. Looking around, I can see I'm in a hospital room, but I have no idea how I got here. A soft snore at my right pulls my attention, and I see Sara sleeping on a chair, leaning forward with her head resting on her arms.

"Thank god." My voice comes out in a scratchy whisper. I hear a sound from the other side of the room and turn my head toward it too quickly. The nausea comes back.

"Mr. Matthews, I'm glad to see you're awake. I'm Ashleigh, your nurse," says a girl in scrubs, crossing the room with a rolling cart. "She's been in here since they discharged her a couple hours ago. We called your family not long after you were brought in, so we expect they'll be here shortly. I was told they needed to fly in."

"Yeah," I croak.

"It's best if you try not to talk. Just nod or shake your head. After I'm done here, I'll get Dr. Fatelli so she can explain your injuries. I know the police will need to talk to you, but we'll give you a little time before we call them." She straps a blood pressure cuff on my arm.

Watching the nurse, I don't notice Sara lift her head until she softly says my name as though she doesn't believe what she sees.

"He shouldn't talk. His trachea is very badly bruised, and he needs to rest it," Ashleigh says as she marks down the reading. "All right, let me go get the doctor for you."

"Izach, I'm so sorry." Sara's voice pulls me back to her.

When my eyes lock with hers, I want to tell her it's not her fault, but my throat hurts too badly, so I shake my head.

"No, this is all my fault. I should have taken my mother's warning more seriously. Asked her more questions about it."

I keep shaking my head and pull my hand from under hers so I can press my fingers against her lips.

Sara stops talking and looks at me, really looks at me, then her tears start. "Oh my god, he could have killed you. I thought he was going to when I heard you choking."

I catch a few of her tears when I put my hand against her face. She grabs it with both hands, turns her mouth to my palm, and kisses it.

I hear my mom call my name from the door, and I look over to see her and my dad coming toward me.

"Oh my god, look at his neck, Eric," Mom says to Dad as they step up beside the bed. "Oh, honey, are you in any pain?"

Shaking my head, I try to let Mom know I'm okay.

"Sara, honey, why aren't you in a bed?" Mom asks.

Sara turns away from me to look at her. "They discharged me a couple hours ago after they made sure my head was okay."

"They discharged you? Look at your face! Where's the doctor? We need to get you in a bed."

"Erin, I'm okay. My head hurts, and if I move too fast, I feel like I might throw up, but other than that, I feel fine. My friend Jacqui was here. She's been looking after me. She had to run out for a little bit, but she'll be back." She looks at me for a minute, then turns back to Mom and Dad. "They said his trachea is really bruised and he shouldn't talk. He has a grade-three concussion, the same thing I do."

"Please tell me this guy's in jail?" Dad pipes up.

I've been wondering about that too.

Sara says, "They've arrested him, but he's here because Izach and I hurt him while trying to fight back. Once he's cleared, they said they'd take him to the holding center."

My dad tenses, and I roll my eyes. "They better hope I don't find out what room he's in. I'll make him look worse than the both of you did."

The sound of someone wheeling a cart into the room makes all of us look at the door. The same nurse comes in, followed by a female doctor.

"You must be Mr. Matthews's parents?" The doctor asks as she gets closer. "I'm Dr. Fatelli. I've been taking care of your son since he was brought in this morning."

"Nice to meet you. I'm Erin, and this is Eric." Mom moves her hand between the two of them.

"Mrs. and Mr. Matthews, your son suffered severe trauma to his trachea. It's going to take some time for him to fully heal, but I don't believe there will be lasting damage. He also has a grade-three concussion, and after a CAT scan, we were able to rule out any brain bleed or swelling. His back was also badly bruised, but that too will heal. You son and his fiancée are both very lucky their injuries weren't more severe."

I see my mom and dad's eyes bug out at the same time mine go wide.

"Since you're here," the doctor continues, oblivious to our surprise, "I'm comfortable discharging your son. You'll just need to keep a close eye on him— actually on both of them—for a few days."

"Thank you, Dr. Fatelli. We'll make sure that Izach and Sara are both looked after," Mom says.

"Good. Ashleigh's going to take his vitals again while I get his discharge paperwork ready. Do you have any questions for me?"

"No, just thank you for taking such good care of him." My mom reaches out her hand to shake Dr. Fatelli's.

"My pleasure." She moves to the end of the bed and touches my blanket-covered foot. "Mr. Matthews, I recommend you rest your voice as much as possible. You don't want to do any further damage by straining to talk."

I nod, agreeing to stay silent.

"Good. Just give me a little bit, and we'll have you out of here." She squeezes my foot, then turns to leave the room.

I feel as if there's an elephant in the room while Ashleigh takes my vitals. No one speaks until she's finished jotting down information on my chart and has wheeled her cart out the door.

My mom sighs, and I look at her. "I can't believe this happened, but I'm so glad both of you are okay. I don't mean to question you, especially after you've suffered a traumatic experience, but do the two of you have something to tell us?" She raises an eyebrow and looks between Sara and me.

Sara smiles and shakes her head. "They wouldn't let me see him unless I was family, so I lied. You didn't miss an important announcement."

"Okay—not that I wouldn't be happy if you were engaged." Mom winks at me. "But it's a little soon for that."

Sara

Hearing the relief in Erin's voice makes me so sad. If it wasn't for me, she wouldn't be visiting her son in a hospital.

"I'll be back in a minute." I kiss Izach on the cheek before I walk away from the bed and out the door.

Just down the hall is a small empty waiting room, so I duck inside and pull my phone out of my pocket. I'm not sure if their number is still the same or why I even want to call them, but I need to tell my mother she was right. Bringing up the keypad, I push in my childhood phone number, then lift the phone to my ear.

After the third ring, I hear my father say, "Hello?"

"Da—dad?" I stumble over the word. It's so weird to hear his voice after so long.

"Sara, is that you?"

"Yeah, Dad, it's me." I fold myself into one of the chairs, keeping my arms bent and resting on my knees.

"What's going on? Are you okay?" He sounds slightly panicked, which kind of surprises me.

"I'm okay, and so is Izach. I'm not sure what Mom told you, but he's my boyfriend." I take a deep breath. "Trent broke into my apartment and attacked me today. He hurt Izach when he tried to help me, but we're both going to be okay."

"Are you at home?"

"No, I'm still at the hospital. Izach's getting discharged soon, then we should be on our way home. I just wanted to call and let you know what happened."

"We're coming, Sara. As soon as I get off the phone with you, I'm calling your mother and we're coming."

"No, Dad, please don't come. I'm fine. We're fine"

"I need to see that you're fine. I need to let you go so I can call mom. We'll see you in a little over an hour."

"I don't want you to come, please. I'll call again soon. I just wanted to let you know what happened before you heard it somewhere else." I hear complete silence. Just as I pull the phone away from my face to see if the call is still connected, I hear his voice.

"Sara?"

"Yeah, Dad?"

"Thank you for calling to let us know you're okay."

"You're welcome." I disconnect before he can say anything else. I'm not sure I could handle hearing it.

I should call Jacqui to let her know what's going on, but I send her a text instead, asking if she could meet me at my apartment in a half hour. She says sure and asks if we have a ride home, so I tell her Izach's parents are here. I try to get up from the chair as slowly as I can, but I still get dizzy and have to grab the wall.

When I get back to Izach's room, he's sitting up and wearing a pair of scrub pants and a shirt. He looks at me and smiles. I can't help but think that this is my fault, yet instead of being mad, he's smiling at me.

"Ready to go?" Erin asks, coming out of the private bathroom.

"Yeah, I'm ready." I cross the room to help Izach off the bed.

Once he's standing, I wrap my arm around his waist as his goes around my shoulders. We walk through the hospital halls and right out the front door without letting go of each other.

Sara

During the week after Trent attacked us, Izach and I had to meet with the police and give official statements, then we had to talk to the district attorney. He explained the charges against Trent, here as well as in Florida, and how things would play out. The whole thing was a little over my head, but I got the gist of it—Trent's going to jail for a long time. Just knowing that lifts a giant fucking weight off my shoulders.

Since I don't want to leave the house, or Izach, Jacqui comes over for our sessions. She actually checks in on a daily basis, just to see how the symptoms from my concussion are. Today, she wants us to talk in my apartment, instead of using Izach's spare bedroom, where Erin and Eric are staying.

Sitting in a rocking chair, I wait for Jacqui to walk down the driveway.

"Hey," I say when she gets to the bottom of the porch stairs.

"Hey, yourself. You ready to head upstairs?"

Biting my lip, I nod.

"Good, let's go."

I stand from the rocking chair, then pull open the storm door. "You know, Jacqui, I'm really starting to like these home visits—"

"Don't get used to them. They're only for this week," she says before I can be a smartass.

"I was just going to say it's more comfortable than your stuffy office." I step through the door first and take the stairs as slowly as I can.

"Sure, you were," she shoots back, climbing the stairs behind me. "Take your time, Sara. I know this is hard for you, but it's necessary."

"I know. I'm okay, just give me a minute." I stop a couple steps from the top as an image of Izach peering around the door at me flashes in my mind.

"Take a deep breath through your nose and blow it out your mouth," Jacqui instructs. "That's it. Now take one step at a time. You're almost there."

Doing what she says, I make it to the landing, then put my hand on the door handle. I know Eric and Erin came up and cleaned the day we got home from the hospital, so I won't find anything out of place, but I'm still nervous about seeing any remnants of Trent in my space.

"You can do this," Jacqui encourages as I turn the handle and push the door open.

Taking a few steps in, I wait for Jacqui to be right behind me before I go any farther.

Once I feel her at my back, I cross the room toward the futon while looking around. I'm not sure my apartment has ever been this clean. Looking toward my room, I don't see any clothes spilling out of my hamper. Turning the other way, I don't see any towels on the bathroom floor. Erin really went to town in here.

"How are you doing?" Jacqui pulls my attention back to her.

"I'm okay, just noticing how clean it is up here. Izach's parents came up to clean the mess from Trent and get some clothes for me, but I didn't expect to see this place spotless. It even smells clean."

Jacqui laughs as she rounds the coffee table and drops onto the futon. "It does smell clean. I should ask Erin what she uses."

"Are you trying to be funny to distract me?"

"Maybe. Did it work?"

"A little. It just feels weird to be up here. I'm not afraid Trent's going to come back, but I feel like he's invaded my safe place. It's not safe anymore."

"I know. Did you and Izach happen to talk about changing anything in the house? To help get rid of the memories from that night?"

"He wants to get rid of the apartment and make it a single-family home, and I think I'm okay with that. As long as it looks different, I think I'll be okay."

"That's a lot of work. Are you planning on doing it yourselves?"

"I talked to my parents again actually. My dad's a contractor. He said he'd draw something up for us, once he comes to check the place out."

"Wow, I didn't know you'd talked to them at all?" she says as a question.

"Yeah, well, after I shot my dad down in the hospital, I didn't want them to just show up here. I figured calling again would keep them home."

"I'm proud of you. I know it'll take a long time and you'll never get back the relationship you once had with them, but I'm glad you're giving them a chance."

"I'm not so sure I can really give them a chance, but if my dad's willing to help us out with the house, I might as well take him up on the offer. It'll save us money."

"Sara…" Jacqui warns.

"What? I didn't outright say we were using them."

She frowns at me. "I guess letting your dad help you is a step. You can decide how much you'll let him in once things start. What about your mom? Did you talk to her?"

"Yeah… it didn't go as well as talking with Dad, probably because she doesn't have anything to offer, but she did apologize a million times before I told her I had to go."

"She probably feels responsible, Sara, not just for the attack but for everything."

I stare at my hands. "She doesn't need to. I realized recently that if things hadn't happened the way they did, I wouldn't have Izach."

"Maybe, or maybe you would have met him under different circumstances."

"I guess we'll never know." I shrug.

"What about your brothers?"

"I haven't talked to them. Mom said she told them everything when the truth about Trent came out, and neither of them have talked to her or Dad since. I guess they're mad, probably at me too."

"Why do you think that?"

"Because I never told them about it, then I ran away without a word."

"That's understandable, but you won't know how they feel unless you talk to them." Jacqui sucks in a sharp breath. "So you've been up here for almost an hour. How do you feel?"

"Okay, I guess."

"Good. We'll try this again tomorrow and see if it goes better. But in the meantime, how about some homework?'

I can't stop my eyes from rolling. "Seriously?"

"Yes, seriously. Tomorrow, or maybe later tonight, why don't you and Izach come up here together? It probably won't be easy for him either, but I think if you give each other support, you can deal with things together."

"Yeah, I guess we can do that."

"Good. Now I have to head to group. Walk me out?" Jacqui asks as she stands.

"Yep, right behind ya."

Izach

Rocking back and forth, I sit on the porch and wait for Sara and Jacqui to come downstairs. They've been up there for just about an hour, so I know they'll come down soon. I came outside when Mom left to take Dad to the airport. He wanted to stay longer but had to get back to work and the girls, who have been calling every day. They're starting to drive me nuts. I'm not sure I've ever talked to any of them this much. The sound of footsteps takes my mind off of my sisters, and I turn my head just in time to see Jacqui push the storm door open.

"Hey, Jacqui," I croak. My voice still sounds like shit, but it's getting better.

"Hi, Izach, how are you feeling?"

"A little better every day."

"That's good," she says as Sara steps onto the porch behind her. "You sound better."

"I'm getting there, as long as I don't overuse my voice."

"I'm sure Sara loves that—you can't really give her a hard time about anything."

"He never gives me a hard time. He loves me." Sara steps behind my chair and leans down to wrap her arms around my neck.

"Once your voice is better, start giving her a little bit of a hard time. She could use it." Jacqui winks at me.

"Don't you have to get to group?" Sara asks from above my head.

"No need to get bent out of shape. I was just kidding."

"I know, but I like giving you shit."

"Oh, I'm well aware. Anyway, I'll see you two tomorrow. Sara, don't forget about your homework."

"Yes, sir." Sara moves one of her hands, and I see her salute Jacqui.

"Such a smartass. See ya later," Jacqui calls as she steps off the porch.

"Homework?" I rasp.

"Yeah, she wants us to go upstairs together so we can face things."

"It's a good idea."

"Yeah, Jacqui seems to be full of those. It's why I started talking to you that day when you were weeding," Sara says in a dreamy voice.

"Really?"

"Yep. You, my love, were homework, and clearly I got an A on that assignment." She swings around, landing right in my lap, and returns her arms to around my neck.

"Hmm, I'd go with A plus." I wrap my arms around her middle and bring her closer so I can place my lips over hers.

EPILOGUE

Sara

"Izach, what the hell is taking you so long? We're going to be late!" I yell through the front door from the porch.

"I'm coming! Her flight doesn't even get in for another fifteen minutes, then it takes time for them to get everyone off the plane."

"I know, but I want to make sure we're standing there waiting when she walks around the corner."

"Sara, you don't know which way she's coming from. She might not even have to walk around a corner," Izach yells back.

He's right. There's only one direction that has a corner blocking who's coming in at the Buffalo airport.

"I don't give a shit! I want to be there no matter which direction she comes from." I'm still yelling as he pushes open the storm door. "Finally!"

"Let's go, I don't wanna be late," he says, rushing by me after he pulls the door closed.

"You're such a smartass!"

"I've learned from the best," he fires back as we walk down the driveway to his Charger.

We get in at the same time and nearly knock heads. I rush to buckle my seatbelt as Izach cranks the engine, then does his belt. After putting the car in drive, he takes my hand and pulls out of the driveway.

Looking up at our house, I smile at how different it looks. Last year, when my dad offered to draw up some plans for us, I took him up on the offer. It was for completely selfish reasons, but I'm glad I did it. Things aren't fixed between my parents and me, but they're getting better. We're talking, and my dad and Izach's dad came to help Izach convert the two units of our house into one. It took a long time and a lot of work, but changing the house to something else was the best thing for all of us. It helped get rid of the nightmare Trent brought into our lives and gave us a space to start over in.

Izach also helped me get my high school equivalency diploma over the past year. Falling back into studying wasn't as hard as I thought, and I passed with flying colors. Now I'm getting ready to start community college in a couple of weeks. My major will be social work, because I just don't think I could hack it as a psychologist. But I still want to help people, so I think this will be a good fit.

In June, Izach finished his first year of teaching and can't wait to go back in September. I, on the other hand, am no longer at The Diner. I left not long after the incident with Trent because I wanted to change to a day shift and they couldn't accommodate me. So now I'm working at a hipster coffee shop, as Izach calls it. I mostly work during the day, and I never have to work past nine at night.

"Where are you going?" I shriek. "Short-term parking is over there." I point at the other lane.

"Okay, hold on. I'll make sure we get to the right place." Izach cuts across to the lane with the sign marked Short-Term Parking.

Pulling up to the barrier, he reaches out of his window and takes a ticket. We park at the bottom of the ramp so it won't be too difficult to get back to the car while towing suitcases. Izach actually manages to snag a front row spot with a direct path to the crosswalk. After he cuts the engine, he jumps out, crosses behind the car to get my door, and helps me out.

Checking my watch, I notice the flight landed just about five minutes ago, so we shouldn't have to wait long. We make it to the seating area right before Elaine walks around the corner. A giant smile covers her face when she sees us, and I can't help but smile back.

"Sara, Izach!" she practically yells. "Oh my god, I'm so glad to see you." She wraps an arm around each of our necks. "I've missed you so much."

"Hi, Gran-ma." Izach pulls back a little to kiss her cheek.

"Elaine." I wrap my free hand around her side and squeeze her. "How was your flight?"

"Who the hell cares how my flight was? I want to know how you're doing. And the house—what does the house look like?"

"We're fine, and the house is amazing. Izach, Eric, and Dad did a great job. We can't wait for you to see it."

"Speaking of Eric, Izach, are your parents coming in?"

"Yeah, they'll be here tomorrow. Sara and I wanted to spend a day with you alone before anyone else came."

"Well, I feel special. How about we go get my bag so we can check out your house?"

"Sounds good to me." Izach drops my hand so he can walk with his arm wrapped around Elaine's shoulders.

Izach

When we get back to the house, Sara helps Gran-ma get settled and I get ready to make an early dinner. Not what I had originally planned, but Gran-ma insisted she was hungry and didn't want to wait for dinner. I pull out three steaks and shake seasoning on them as I see Sara and Gran-ma coming out from the back bedroom.

"Sara's going to give me the grand tour. You don't mind, do you?"

"No, that's fine. Sara can show you around. Just take it easy on the stairs."

She blows out a huff. "God, it's been over three years now since I broke my hip. Stop being so damn overprotective."

Sara throws me a smirk with her brows raised. I watch as they disappear up the stairs. Once they're out of sight, I pick up the plate of meat and head out to the grill. After I get the steaks and a few potatoes cooking, I run back in the house and grab the caddy of the plates and utensils from the counter, then I go back outside to pull the table out of the garage. Neither Sara nor I would think about putting a deck on the back of the house because we didn't want a reason not to sit on the front porch. So when we grill, we sit at a table in the driveway. It's better than holding our plates on our laps in the rockers, but doesn't take our need for the porch away.

Gran-ma's voice hits my ears just as I'm pulling the last steak from the grill. "Izach," she calls as she walks down the steps, "God, the house looks great. You really did a good job."

"Why would you have doubts?"

"I didn't say I did. I'm just saying it turned out more beautiful than I ever expected." She reaches the table and sits.

"Where's Sara?" I ask, setting down the plate of meat.

"She's heating up some vegetables or something. Said she'd be right out."

"Oh good, then I don't have to go in and do it." Just as the words leave my mouth, Sara comes outside and heads toward us, holding a bowl in her potholder-covered hand. "Thanks, babe, I was just going to go back in and get them."

"No problem." She comes to me and lifts on her toes to give me a quick kiss.

"Oh my god, you two better knock it off before I lose my appetite," Gran-ma whines.

"Didn't you at one point think we were cute?" Sara asks, moving to her seat.

"That was then, and this is now. You two live together—I know what goes on between you."

"Relax, Gran-ma, it's not 1950. Couples live together all over the world."

"I know, but I thought by now you two would be a little more than a couple."

"Well, since you brought that up…" I look across the table at Gran-ma and Sara, gauging their reaction. "I've been waiting for the time to be right, and I'm thinking that time is now. What do you think, Gran-ma?"

303

"I think now is a pretty good time." She winks at me.

"Then now it is." I slide from my chair, go down on one knee, and move in front of Sara, whose hands have gone up to cover her mouth. I grab her left hand and pull it down to her lap. "Sara Collins, from the minute I met you, you've given me a run for my money. This past year has been a little crazy. We've had some ups and downs—the ups outweighing the downs tenfold—but I wouldn't have it any other way. I'm actually looking forward to seeing what life plans on throwing our way in the future. So, Sara, my love and my life, would you do me the greatest honor in the world and marry me?"

I'm shaking by the time the last word leaves my mouth. I hear Gran-ma bite back a sob, but I can't take my eyes off Sara while I wait for her response.

"Yes," she says in almost a whisper.

"What was that? I couldn't really hear you?" I give her a smirk with one brow raised.

"I said yes!" she yells as she throws herself into my arms.

After kissing—inappropriately for in front of Gran-ma—Sara and I pull apart.

Reaching into my pocket I grab the little velvet box, then flip it open. I slip the princess-cut solitaire ring from the cushion and take Sara's left hand again. Sliding the ring up her finger, I look her in the eyes and say, "I love you."

"I love you more." She dives back into my arms for make-out session number two.

The End.

Research, Education, Advocacy & Support: Self Injury Foundation:
http://www.selfinjuryfoundation.org
The Butterfly Project: http://butterfly-project.tumblr.com
RAINN: Rape, Abuse, and Incest National Network: 1-800-656-HOPE
https://rainn.org/

ACKNOWLEDGEMENTS

This book, although it's so personal to me, has been touched by many people. In an effort not to leave anyone out, I want to say thank you to everyone who played a role in helping it come together. Whether it was to push me or just talk out a scene, I'm so grateful for all the support.

I need to give a giant thank you to my friend Joanne Schwehm. You've been there for me, not only since I typed the first words of FBT, but since before I typed the first book in The Reunion Series. I can't thank you enough for all of the time, encouragement, and support you give me. I always say "I'm going to bother you!" but you always assure me that it's no bother at all, which means the world to me. I couldn't ask for a more amazing friend, and I'll be forever grateful we got thrown together at the NYC13 author event. Love you, doll!

If I remember correctly, Steph Schiefer, you, my dear friend, threatened to kick my ass if I didn't write this book. Well, it's done, and I hope you love it! You gave me the push I needed, and after a couple months of writer's block, you were there to take on sprints and writing binges right along with me. Thanks for always being there, letting me crash on your couch, and snuggle with Olaf!

My beta readers: Amanda Wilson, Karen Isopi, and Joanne Schwehm, thank you so much for taking time out of your busy schedules to beta read for me. Hearing that you all enjoyed FBT made my heart swell! Your feedback, comments, and suggestions were so very appreciated! I can't thank you enough.

Cassie Cox, my editing guru! Thank you so much for helping me make this book come to life. You are always honest and encouraging. Every time you return a manuscript I look forward to opening it and reading your comments, I especially love when something makes you laugh! I greatly appreciate that you make yourself available to me even after your part is done. I so look forward to working with you again!

Sommer Stein, I asked you to work your magic and you certainly did! I can't thank you enough for making my cover more than I had ever imagined. I absolutely love it (I might be a little obsessed with it!) Thank you so much, working with you was such a pleasure and I cannot wait to do it again.

Shannon Marie McLellan, you have been my best friend, my sister, for nearly thirty years, so when I called on you to be on the cover of FBT, I knew you'd jump at the chance, and I can't thank you enough (Shane too!). You, my friend, are beautiful on both the inside and outside, and I couldn't imagine what my life would be like without you. Through thick and thin, until we're old and gray!

To my closest friends, thank you for always understanding and supporting me. Whether I need to talk out a character or a sex scene, I know I can count on one of you to be there. Your love and encouragement means so much that I don't have enough words to express what you mean to me. I love you all from the bottom of my heart.

My family—what can I say? Without you, I wouldn't be me! I love all of you, not only because you support me and love me— despite my disappearing acts—but because at the end of the day, you're always proud of me no matter what. Thank you for pushing me to make my dreams come true.

Last but never least... to the readers, thank you so much for reading Sara and Izach's story. I hope they wiggled their way into your heart like they did to me. I appreciate all of you so much. Your messages and comments mean the world to me. You encourage me without even knowing it. Thank you, thank you, thank you! <3

ABOUT THE AUTHOR

Susan Cairns was born and raised in a small town in western New York, on the shore of Lake Ontario. She currently lives with her three fur-babies: Lucy, Leela, and Bella. They run the househousea small town in weste

Susan loves to travel and is always looking for her next adventure! She has been lucky to keep in touch with many friends who live all across the US and open their homes to her whenever she feels the pull to visit someplace new.

Susan is an avid reader and can usually be found with her Kindle or a book. She also has an eye for photography. All year round, she has her camera in hand, taking pictures of anything and everything, especially her nephews and niece, who are the light of her life.

Stop by and say hello to Susan at:

Website: susancairnsbooks.com

E-mail: susancairnsbooks@aol.com

Facebook: https://m.facebook.com/susancairnsauthor

Twitter: https://www.twitter.com/suzecairns

Goodreads: https://www.goodreads.com/author/show/8145878.Susan_Cairns

Other Titles by Susan Cairns:

The Reunion Series:

The Reunion
The Rebound
The Reason